TOP SHELF

A SEACROFT NOVEL

ALLISON TEMPLE

TOP SHELF

Martin is a ghost. Well, not really, but he might as well be. Job gone, home gone, self-respect gone, and no one even seems to notice. The only person who really sees him is Seb, the artist who lives above the used bookstore.

Seb haunts the edges of Seacroft in search of beauty. He knows how to excavate the hidden value in abandoned things—whether it's in the pages of forgotten books or in Martin's stuttering attempts to rebuild his life—and transform them into works of art.

Two lost souls, Seb and Martin discover the strength they need to face eccentric townies and their dysfunctional families together. But as friendship sparks toward something more, neither man wants to risk what they've only just found. It takes two to fall in love, but it will take the whole community to bring their beauty to life.

This is a work of fiction. Names, characters, places, and incidents are a product
of the author's imagination or are used fictitiously. Any resemblance to actual
events, places, or persons, living or dead, is entirely coincidental.

Cover Design: Cate Ashwood Designs
Editing and Proofreading: LesCourt Author Services

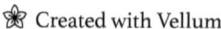 Created with Vellum

For Nana

ACKNOWLEDGMENTS

This book baby took a long time in coming. I feel like I was pregnant for two years, and then the labour and delivery all happened in a rush. If I have forgotten anyone, I blame the mommy brain.

Ana. You read Seb and Martin before anyone else and told me it was good even when it wasn't.

Russ. You always ask me how the book is going.

Jill. You told me this book is more compelling than Toto's Africa, and I am clinging to that.

Elle. You let me pick your brain from halfway around the world.

Dorothy, Sophia, and Blanche. The list is too long. You know why.

You. You're reading this, and that is the most amazing thing.

For news on future releases, join the A-List, my monthly newsletter at allisontemplebooks.com/newsletter.

*T*he exterior of Martin's new workplace did not inspire confidence. Dog Ears Book Shop was a two-story brick building on Seacroft's main street. The sign out front was painted in large black and white spots that were probably meant to look like a Dalmatian, but actually looked more like a cow. The 'Help Wanted' sign was still in the window. If that was an indication of his new employer's faith in his abilities, Martin's career in bookselling would be short.

He'd been told to be here by eight-thirty, and he was early. There was a diner next door, and he'd popped in to grab a tea to go. That had been ten minutes ago, and now the bookshop's locked storefront staring back at him made him worry. What if he'd made the job offer up? What if this was just another punch line on the cruel practical joke that was his life lately? Not being able to hold down an obscure academic position was one thing. Not being good enough to work at a lonely used bookstore in a sleepy seaside community was another issue completely. His thesis supervisor had always said life was not a pony farm, but Martin didn't even want the whole farm anymore. A seat at the trough would do.

A dark sedan pulled up to the curb. Martin hunched into his

tea, avoiding eye contact with the driver. They didn't need to see him like this.

"Thanks, Mom!" A teenage girl with hair like coiled springs got out of the passenger side. She leaned in and spoke to the driver for a minute, before slamming the door and waving as the car pulled away. She smiled when she spotted Martin.

"Are you the new guy?" She hiked her backpack up on her shoulders. Martin nodded, and her smile spread. "Doctor Lindsey, I presume!" She stuck out her hand for him to shake. He juggled his tea and his bike helmet before reaching for her.

"It's just Martin," he said.

"I'm Cassidy. Mrs. Green said you'd be starting today. I'm supposed to show you the ropes." She pulled a ring of keys out of her backpack and stepped around him to the door. She appeared to be younger than any of his former students had been. It said a lot that someone who didn't even have a high school diploma would be training him.

"Have you worked here long?" he asked as she fumbled with the lock. She jammed her hip against the doorframe, and then rattled the doorknob before twisting the key. The heavy old door swung open on groaning hinges that shattered the quiet Saturday morning. A jogger running by turned as he passed. Martin ducked his head while Cassidy waved.

"Since I was in tenth grade. I started working after school, and then Mrs. Green let me work full time over the summers. Now that I'm back at school, I'll mostly be here in the afternoons and on Saturdays." She walked in and flicked a switch by the door. Ancient strings of incandescent lights flared to life. Martin's next question caught in his throat as the bookstore loomed in front of him.

He'd been in once before, when he dropped off his resume, but he hadn't bothered to stay. It might have even been Cassidy he'd handed his CV to for all he knew. It had taken him two tries to walk through the front door, and then he'd finally run in, thrust the paper at the person behind the cash, and fled. It had been embarrassing, but getting this far was an improvement from the trajectory his life had taken in recent months. His doctor had said he should be proud.

Oddly enough, despite that frantic and hasty attempt at applying for a job, he still remembered the smell of the store as he walked in. It was something damp and forgotten, and the space held an incredible sense of age and weight.

Heavy dark shelves of every height and width lined the walls from floor to ceiling. Books were stacked up and down, lengthways and sideways. Martin had read a lot in his life, and he had never seen so many books all in one place.

"Welcome!" Cassidy held her arms out, as if she spoke for every title and every writer represented in the giant space. She glanced over her shoulder. "It's kind of like the TARDIS, isn't it?"

"Bigger on the inside than the outside?"

Cassidy's smile grew. "You watch Doctor Who?"

Martin shrugged, ignoring the little thrill in his chest at the normalcy of this conversation.

"I missed the last few seasons," he said. "It stopped being good after David Tennant left."

"I guess we're not going to be friends after all." Cassidy's green eyes narrowed, but her smile didn't fade.

Feeling a little braver, Martin stepped around a low table stacked with picture books and a sign that read 'For When They Won't F*ing Sleep.' Beyond that, a bookshelf was labeled with '100 Ways to Cheat on Your Diet.' Most of the titles below the sign were pastry cookbooks and European travelogues.

"I made that one," Cassidy said, as Martin examined the sign. It was done in chalk, the lettering alternating orange and green, with what looked like a steaming plate of spaghetti and a glass of wine nestled underneath it.

"It's very nice."

"Let me give you the tour. We won't be open for another half hour."

The TARDIS reference turned out to be fairly apt. Every time they came to the end of a teetering row of bookshelves, Cassidy would turn and take him in a new direction. Somehow though, they never wound up at the front of the store again. Sometimes the shelves were broken up with ancient and over-stuffed armchairs before the books continued. There didn't seem to be any logic to the way they were organized. Instead of standard headings—fiction, non-fiction, travel, mystery—each section was labeled in the same cheeky blackboards as Martin had seen up front. 'Pets.They're Better Than Kids' and 'Old Dead Guys Say Famous Things.'

"Wouldn't it just be easier to organize them by genre?" he asked as they wound their way down another aisle.

"Why? It's more fun this way." Cassidy seemed to know exactly where they were, despite the fact that Martin was hopelessly turned around. They passed a shelf labeled 'Books To Read On Dark Nights.'

"But how do people find what they're looking for?"

She glanced over her shoulder at him, and for all there had to be over ten years between them, Martin suddenly felt like a kid asking stupid questions of a weary parent.

"Have you ever worked in a bookstore before? Mrs. Green said you had."

"In college." It had been humiliating to have to put that little nugget of experience back on his resume.

"When you go to buy a book, if you want a recommendation, do you ask for a contemporary mystery, written in the last two years, by an American writer?"

"Yes?"

Cassidy snorted. "Well, that's not how most people work. Most people come in here, and they say they want something a little funny, a little sad. Something about families, but not some-

4

thing where someone dies. It's easier if we organize them this way."

"But it doesn't make any sense!"

They passed a shelf called 'We Didn't Know Where Else To Put These.'

"It will." She turned another corner, and suddenly, they were back where they started. A cyclist went by, followed by a woman with a stroller. They didn't so much as glance through the window. Martin felt like he'd been on a kind of quest that had lasted a thousand years, only to return home and find that no time had passed at all.

"So the first thing to do is tidy up the kid's section." She pointed to the picture book table. "The Mommy and Me group will be here at nine-thirty."

"Mommy and me?"

"Yes, and then the knitting circle will be here at noon."

"Knitting circle?" Martin checked around again. "Like people? Here? Knitting?"

"Sure! Didn't Mrs. Green tell you?"

"Tell me about what?" Here it was. He'd expected a quiet day of recommending classics and wheezing on the layer of dust that coated everything. It had all seemed too easy, and now he would find out why.

"Oh. Well. A used bookstore is only so popular. Most people just get their stuff online these days. So Mrs. Green figured out that if we get people to come for other things, they might stick around and buy a book or two. It's Mommy and Me at nine-thirty, knitting circle at noon, and the feminist poetry circle at three on Saturdays."

That didn't sound too bad.

"Do I have to learn to knit?" He was pleased he could find humor over the increasing rattle of his heart.

Cassidy laughed, curly hair bouncing on her shoulders. "It couldn't hurt."

No, it was bad.

———

It turned out to be only moderately awful. The Mommy and Me group was the loudest. Eight moms and their little kids invaded just after the store opened. The chaos of a dozen small people flinging books about as they tried to find the perfect story must have been reflected on Martin's face, because Cassidy sent him to the back with instructions on how to run the coffee maker.

It took him a few attempts to find his way out of the stacks of books, and he tried to let himself into a locked closet, but eventually he found a little kitchen area.

The coffee maker there might have been as old as the bookstore itself, and after he'd filled it with water and coffee grounds, nothing happened. He pressed the Start button a few times, but the coffee maker just sat there. He finally unplugged it, counted to twenty, and plugged it in again. It had always worked for the history department's photocopier, and it appeared coffee makers operated on similar principles. A red light on the front flashed, and there was a faint smell like something burning, but then the machine finally gurgled to life.

"I think your coffee maker is dying," he said as he returned to the front of the store.

Cassidy rolled her eyes. "Whatever you do, don't mention the coffee maker to Mrs. Green."

"Why not?"

"It's a touchy subject. Just don't."

The knitting circle was the nosiest group; they gossiped more than they knit. They were also notable because their membership included Mrs. Green, Martin's new employer. Like she had at his interview, the first impression she made upon arrival was one of vibrant color. Bright clothes and brighter scarves fluttered from her body. A sparkling pink and blue butterfly clip accented her fine white hair.

"Oh! Dr. Lindsey!" She clapped her hands, drawing his attention to the bright blue nail polish on her fingertips. "How are you doing this morning?"

The three ladies who had already arrived with their bags of knitting perked up as she addressed him. The attention made him itchy.

"Fine, thank you." He glanced around for Cassidy. He'd been there three hours and already he knew she would be critical to him surviving this day.

"Come and meet everyone." Mrs. Green linked her arm through his and drew him forward. She introduced him as 'Dr. Lindsey' to each of the women who had gathered, and each shook his hand like they were meeting a foreign dignitary. Every handshake made Martin's palm sweat a little more.

"Are you a real doctor?" a woman asked.

As opposed to an imaginary one?

"I have a PhD in German history."

The knitting circle tittered and nodded. Nervous perspiration formed along Martin's hairline, and he was grateful when Cassidy appeared through one of the stacks. She swooped in with a question for Mrs. Green about plans for an upcoming Halloween display, effectively diverting the spotlight off of him.

"She likes the status of having you around," Cassidy said, after the knitting circle had left.

"Who?"

"Mrs. Green."

"I told her she didn't need to call me Doctor at my interview."

"She'll never call you Martin, trust me. It's not glamorous enough."

He wasn't glamorous. He was just Martin. Even when he'd finished his PhD, it had been uncomfortable when people had addressed him as 'Doctor.' The title had always felt borrowed, like sooner or later someone would remember that he shouldn't be in the room and send him away.

He'd been right about that, in the end.

At four o'clock, after the poetry group left, the shop got quiet.

"Did we actually sell any books today?" Martin asked.

Cassidy nodded. "The mommies always buy a few. And I sold a couple more while you were eating your lunch. And these came in." She thumped a palm on a banker's box that sat on the counter. Martin lifted the lid. Inside was a selection of ancient cowboy novels. The covers were worn around the edges and the pages were yellowed.

"Will these sell?" He flipped the first one open. The copyright said 1962.

"Probably not. But Mrs. Green has a policy that we don't turn books down."

"But if you can't sell them, what do you do?"

"Well, some of them—" She was drowned out by the groan of hinges. A man in a blue polo shirt and wire-framed glasses came through the shop's front door.

"Hey Dad!" Cassidy hopped down from the stool she had been sitting on.

"Ready to go?"

"Let me get my bag."

She was leaving? Martin's throat went tight. The shop was quiet, but she couldn't be leaving, could she? It was his first day. Who left someone alone on their first day?

Cassidy dropped her heavy ring of keys on the counter next to the cash.

"You'll be fine. The little key locks the register, and the big one locks the front door. Make sure you turn off the coffee maker and that's pretty well all you have to do."

"Aren't there—aren't there—" He thought back to the years

he had worked in the campus bookshop. "Don't we need to cash out or something?"

Cassidy waved her hand as she headed toward the door. It had seemed so ridiculous that he had been left in the charge of this girl, but now she was leaving him! He dug his fingernails into the old wood of the counter to keep from running after her.

"Mrs. Green does all the accounting on Sundays. Just put all the receipts in the drawer and lock it up when you're done!"

The hinges shrieked once more as Cassidy's father followed her out to the street, and Martin was left alone. The store, with its towering shelves, loomed over him. Despite his earlier anxiety at dealing with more than one person at a time, Cassidy and the various groups of locals had kept the place feeling busy all day. Now he was very aware of the empty silence.

There were thousands of books and not a soul to talk to. The old building had a whole selection of creaks and pops that sounded intermittently. Each one made Martin flinch. He stared as people passed by on the street. Not one of them so much as paused to look through the window, and he was left with a strange sense of invisibility.

Needing a distraction, he made his way to the kitchen and only got turned around once near a shelf labeled 'The Dog Doesn't Die.' He washed the single coffee pot and the mismatched mugs the mothers, knitters, and poets had left behind over the course of the day. It didn't take nearly as long as he wanted it to, and soon he was making his uncertain way back toward the front of the store.

His phone vibrated in his pocket, and the sensation was so unexpected he yelped and reached out blindly to steady himself. Two books tumbled to the floor under his hand. He cursed and bent to pick them up. The first was called *Nothing Lasts Forever*. He slid it back into place, on a shelf labeled with 'The Movie Has a Different Title.' He scanned the rest of the books beneath it. There were a few he recognized, but most were a mystery which, he supposed, was the point.

The second book that had fallen was a beaten-up copy of *Heart of Darkness*. Martin hung on to it and made his way back up to the counter. The phone vibrated in his pocket again. There was a text from his brother Brian.

If Jess calls, don't answer it.

Martin sighed. He wasn't going to play this game. He typed back a pointed reply, but as it hit its fifth sentence, he reconsidered. Brian had done a lot for him, bringing him to Seacroft and giving him a place to live. Berating him via text message wasn't appropriate.

The sense of invisibility pressed in on him again. There were less than two hours left in his first shift. He could do this, despite the tight feeling that rippled over his lungs. He had to do this. He flipped open *Heart of Darkness*. He had read it before during a second-year English class that had cemented for him that he could not be an English major. He'd always liked reading, but he found the rigid format of analysis and critique to be too confining. He'd enjoyed *Heart of Darkness* though.

Martin was deep up the Congo River when a loud thump brought him out of his reading with a jolt. It was after six, past closing time. He waited, but there were no more sounds. Just another quirk of an old building then. The heating system where his office had been in the Humanities building had made louder noises in the dead of winter. It had clanged and groaned as it struggled to bring anything like heat to the upper floors of the history department. Martin had eventually learned to ignore it, after the faculty dean had patiently explained that it wasn't some structural concern and the building wasn't on the verge of collapse.

He slipped around the edge of the counter, slid the deadbolt shut on the front door, and then flipped the sign in the window to Closed. The 'Help Wanted' sign was still propped up on the sill. His hand faltered as he reached for it, and instead he turned back to gather up his stuff and get ready to go.

The next bang was louder, reverberating through the shop's wooden floors.

"Hello?" The word barely made it out of Martin's throat.

From somewhere in the back of the store, another book fell.

His heart pounded in his chest, and he grabbed his phone with trembling hands.

It was probably nothing. Too many books stacked up in a precarious pile on a shelf that was finally giving way. A small avalanche because Cassidy couldn't be bothered to sort books like a normal person. He was an adult, and he was being ridiculous. He steeled himself and went to investigate.

The distinct sound of footsteps had him freezing in place again. Martin's breath went shallow, and he clutched at the phone. Was it inappropriate to call the police on his first day of work? There was someone in the store, and Martin was very sure he had not seen anyone come in since Cassidy had left.

He moved in between the shelves as his mind raced. What if someone had snuck in? Broken in?

Why would someone sneak in to steal used books?

Martin grabbed a cookbook off a shelf labeled 'Everything is Better With Salt' and hefted it, testing the weight. If someone was back there, and that someone was up to no good, Martin could use the book as a weapon.

There was a soft sound of someone humming, and it made the hairs on Martin's neck prickle. He tripped at the edge of the next shelf.

"Cass, is that you?"

Martin froze with the cookbook half-raised to his shoulder. Every part of him went on alert at the sound of a man's voice, much closer than he'd expected.

Another book dropped to the ground.

He peeked around a shelf. The first thing his brain registered was white, and it was almost enough to convince him that he was seeing a ghost. His fingers tightened around the cookbook.

A long pale arm reached up and lifted a book off the very top shelf.

It was a man.

He wore faded jeans and a gray T-shirt. His hair was bleached blond. If he was a thief, he was a terrible one, because he flipped through the book, then let it drop to the floor next to what must have been the other ones Martin had already heard fall.

He was a man though, whoever he was. Tall and solid. Not a ghost. Martin lowered the cookbook. Assaulting a customer on his first day would be a bad career move.

"Excuse me," he said, but it was drowned out as the next book thumped to the floor. Martin hopped back a step, but gathered himself and tried again. "Excuse me. I'm closing up."

"Sure thing," the man said as he stretched up on his toes again, reaching for another book. His shirt lifted from the waist of his jeans, and the skin underneath was so pale it enhanced his ghostly appearance.

When Martin didn't leave, the man glanced over his shoulder, and his face made Martin's heart stop. He wasn't a ghost or a thief, but whoever he was, he was handsome. Blue eyes flicked up and down once, like he was trying to decide the kind of threat Martin might pose.

As Martin inhaled to assert himself again, the man turned back to the shelf.

"You—" Martin swallowed hard, willing himself to stand firm. "You'll have to go."

Those blue eyes darted toward Martin again, like a wrist flicking at a fly. The man grinned, a slow sly grin that made Martin's insides twist.

"You're new, aren't you?" the man said.

Martin's ears burned. He knew a dismissal when he heard one.

"If—If there's something you'd like to buy, I can help you cash out. Otherwise, we'll be open again on Monday at—" What time did they open? It had been nine o'clock on Saturday. Was it the same time on weekdays?

The blond man frowned, and Martin's heart lurched under the stranger's scrutiny. He couldn't remember the last time someone had really looked at him. For all his rising panic at the feeling of being alone in the store earlier, he very much wanted to return to that solitude right now. It was so much better than being the center of this man's attention.

"How long have you worked here?" The strange man's voice was soft and low, rippling through the space between them.

Martin shivered and had to focus to keep his feet planted. "We're closing and—"

"Where's Cass?" The man glanced over Martin's shoulder, giving him a moment to breathe.

"Cassidy? She went home."

"What's your name?" Those eyes were on Martin again in an instant, making him light-headed.

"Martin." Too late, he wondered if he shouldn't have introduced himself, particularly when the other man made no effort to return the favor.

"Well then, Martin." The man took a step forward. "It appears no one bothered to inform you—"

"I'll call the owner." Martin was losing ground and needed to fix this quickly. Calling Mrs. Green to resolve a grumpy customer was absolutely a bad idea, but he was on the verge of being run out of his own bookstore, so there weren't many options left.

To illustrate that point, the blond man's eyes widened and his lips formed into an 'O'.

"No no. Please." He held his hands wide, as his mouth pulled into another grin. Everything about it made Martin want to shrink into himself until he was nothing but a speck of dust on a bookshelf.

"I'm sorry," he said, giving it one last go. "But we close at six and—"

The man didn't appear to hear him. He toed through the pile of books at his feet.

Martin winced as pages bent under his shoes. "Please don't—"

Thin fingers pinched the crumpled pages together and lifted them in the air, the book's heavy covers flopping to the sides. There was the soft sound of paper tearing.

The man tucked the book under one arm. "Don't worry, sweetheart. I'll pay for it." He put a hand in one of his pockets, then actually swaggered toward Martin, whose vision wavered as the man's fingers brushed against his own. Martin gasped at the hard weight of something metal in his palm. The silence of the bookshop was broken by the sound of coins tumbling out of Martin's frozen hand and onto the floor.

"That should cover it." The man whispered it low. The feeling of his breath on Martin's skin made him turn into a Martin-shaped statue, frozen in place as the other man slid past him.

"Nice to meet you," the man said. "I'm sure we'll see each other again."

It felt like hours, but it probably was only a matter of seconds before he trembled and broke out of his daze. The floorboards creaked as the man walked away. Martin knelt and collected the coins he'd dropped. They were all nickels and dimes, and they totaled up to just under two dollars.

A door closed and the shop fell quiet.

Martin wound his way back the way he'd come. Nerves boiled inside him, and he hesitated around every blind corner between shelves, half expecting the blond stranger to leap out at him like some deranged Jack in the Box. He stumbled into the open space at the front.

He was alone.

Martin went to the door. It surprised him that the hinges hadn't made their booming wail as the man left.

His hand stopped as he reached for the deadbolt. It was still in position. The door was locked.

Where had the man come from? And where had he gone?

2

Seb laughed as he went up the stairs to his apartment. That had been a bit mean, but also sort of fun. Seb considered it his sacred duty to test out the new employees, and he'd seen his fair share at Dog Ears over the years. He was surprised Cassidy hadn't mentioned him.

Martin was kind of cute though, if you got past his trembling scarecrow persona. His plaid shirt had been at least a size too big, and his belt had been pulled to the last hole. Even then, his pants had hung off his frame, but his face had been nice to look at, with high cheekbones and soft brown hair that had fallen unironically into his eyes.

You had to admire his fumbling attempts at courage. The cowardly lion daring Seb to put his dukes up was adorable. The urge to flirt had been impossible to ignore, and watching Martin stammer his way through the role of tough guy had been fun.

That last bit, with the change, had possibly been a step too far, even for Seb, but then again, he never had been able to resist the opportunity to make a dramatic exit.

The new guy really was cute.

Seb set the book on his working table. The book was useless. The weight of the paper was wrong, and the gloss wouldn't fit with anything else he was using at the moment. He'd pulled it out of the pile at random, but when the pages tore, he knew he'd have to keep it.

His newest acquisition appeared to be a compendium of European mid-1960s fashion, and not in a good retro kind of way. Men in orange crocheted vests and too-tight plaid pants smoldered at him from behind sideburns and pencil-thin moustaches.

Seb turned the page. Girls rode scooters down quaint cobblestone streets, but the clothes didn't get any better.

Maybe he could laminate them into placemats and sell them online. Hipsters loved that kind of thing.

The next page showed a woman in a flowing bathing suit and a hat that looked like a traffic cone, and he pushed the book away in disgust. No wonder it had been top-shelved. And now it was his. All this so he could make a dramatic exit.

Behind him, the laptop on the coffee table squawked, and the screen flashed.

Incoming call from
Oliver.Stevenson85
Oliver?

Seb swallowed hard. He'd expected it to be Kenneth, his agent, doing one of his pop check-ins to make sure Seb was actually working. He'd been excited to chat and pleased to report he was running ahead of schedule.

But Oliver?

Why on earth would he be calling? Seb hadn't talked to his older brother in months, and always on the phone.

Still feeling the adrenaline from his unexpected run-in, Seb took a deep breath and accepted the call.

The screen blinked, and the speakers crackled. For a second, everything was pixelated, and Seb had the idea that maybe this was a wrong number, someone with his brother's name but not, in fact, his Oliver. But then the image righted itself, and his older brother smiled at him from another room in another city.

"Hey Seb. I wasn't sure if you'd be there."

It was Oliver's voice. Oliver's face. Something behind Seb's right eye flickered, a split second of panic that, if he let it, would have him running from the apartment and probably out of town.

"Well, here I am!" He forced himself to smile and sit up straighter. The top of his head disappeared from the frame, but he didn't bother to adjust the laptop. Whatever Ollie wanted wouldn't take long.

"I—I don't think I have the right phone number for you anymore."

He did. Seb had seen Oliver's number in his list of missed calls from time to time, but he almost never left a voicemail and, when he did, it was never specific enough to prompt Seb to call back.

"Dunno," he said. "What number do you have?"

Oliver frowned, and in that moment, he looked so much like their father it made Seb's blood go cold.

"I—" Oliver looked around him, like he was trying to find something. "My phone is in the other room. I'd have to go get it so . . . "

The connection went quiet. Seb waited.

"How have you been?" Oliver asked finally. He smiled, but whether it was lack of sincerity or something lost in translation over an internet connection, it didn't reach his eyes.

"Awesome!" Seb grinned, refusing to let his brother see him sweat. "Really good. I've got a big show coming up."

"Really?" Ollie's question sounded genuine this time. "That's great, Seb! When is it? Maybe I can come down."

Seb's grin faltered.

The show was a big deal, as Kenneth reminded him every

time he called. A big step in his career. He pictured being toasted, celebrated by adoring patrons.

He had never pictured anyone from his family among the crowd.

"It's, um, not for a bit yet. And anyway, don't you think the partners would object to you sneaking away, even if it's to bask in your screw-up artist brother's glory?"

"You're not a screw up." Oliver's face turned sad. The blue eyes they shared squinted at the screen, like he was trying to see if Seb was all right.

More like prying into his life.

"Yeah, yeah," he said. "The comment about the partners still stands. How long a leash are they really going to give you?"

Oliver's gaze shifted somewhere offscreen. Seb couldn't be sure, but he thought his brother might be blushing.

"I—" Oliver cleared his throat, tugging at the collar of his shirt. A dark tie sat snug around his neck. The tie meant he'd been to work today, even though it was Saturday. "Don't worry about that."

The conversation died into silence again. Seb leaned back against the couch and stretched, making something in his shoulder pop.

"I ran into Greg Ellis the other day," Oliver said.

Seb snorted. "That asshole? How is he?" He hadn't thought of Greg Ellis in probably close to fifteen years, not since the last time Seb had blown him in their college dorm shower and told him he was done messing around with straight boys.

"Married. Fat. Working in the finance office on campus."

"Perfect." Seb laughed at the thought of poor, handsome, conflicted Greg, growing into a sedentary heterosexual life with a mortgage and the obligatory two-point-five kids.

"He says hi." Oliver's eyebrow arched.

"I'm sure he does."

"Are you seeing anyone these days?"

"No." Not like Oliver meant it. His brother had always been big on monogamy, whereas Seb preferred no-commitment hookups when he made time to visit Kenneth in the city. This had become especially true since he'd come to Seacroft, where dating opportunities were limited at best. The queer community in town was so small as to be nonexistent, or else so deep in the closet Seb would need a map of Narnia to find them.

"How's Cooper?" Not that Seb cared. Cooper's family had known Seb and Oliver's since the dawn of history, but as a boyfriend for his older brother, Seb had never liked the guy. His name made him sound like he should be driving his Jag out to the coast on weekends to wine and dine Oliver on a yacht called the *Lady Clipper* or something equally douchey.

Oliver cleared his throat. "Cooper and I broke up."

"Small miracles, I guess. He was an ass." No sense in sugarcoating it. Not that Seb had ever kept his thoughts on Cooper and his porcelain veneer smile to himself when Oliver had still been infatuated with him.

Oliver laughed. "Yeah, he was. Just took me a while to figure it out."

Another lapse into silence. Seb's finger hovered over the button that would end the call.

"Have you talked to Nana lately?"

Oliver's question caught Seb by surprise. This was a departure from their usual pattern. Every few months, Oliver would call on a day when Seb was too busy to check the phone's screen before he answered, or when he was feeling sorry for himself. The conversation was always brief and pointless, small talk between two people who shouldn't have treated each other like strangers. Then Oliver would say he would come visit one of these days, and Seb would say he looked forward to it. The promise would hang there until their next stilted phone call.

The unspoken rule was that they never talked about the rest

of the family. No matter what news Oliver might be calling to relay, they did not talk about their relatives. Ever.

"No, I haven't talked to Nana in a bit." He squashed a fluttery feeling in his chest.

"You should. She'd like to hear from you."

Seb bit his lip but forced himself to keep looking at his brother. Whatever Oliver was playing at, Seb wouldn't let him win.

"I don't think I have her number here." Another lie. He'd had it memorized since he was a kid and called it more than once when he needed to get away from the endless tension at home.

"I'll email it to you." On Oliver's side of the computer, there was a tapping of keys on a keyboard. Seb bit his lip. There was no way to protest without being the bad guy.

"Is she—" The question caught in his throat. "Is she okay?" The idea that their Nana, who had been such a solid constant figure in his childhood, might not be was impossible. Seb remembered her strong hands, showing him how to grip a paintbrush to get the texture he wanted on the canvas. Her lilac and sugar smell as she listened to Seb try to explain the image he had in his mind.

"Oh! No!" Oliver seemed to realize he'd said something wrong. He shook his head so hard his image blurred on the screen for a second before it settled back into place. "She's fine. Fine."

Guilt rumbled under Seb's collarbones. As infrequently as he spoke to Oliver, he talked to his grandmother less. She was his biggest supporter, yes, but she was still his father's mother, and there was a Philip Stevenson-sized gap in their relationship. Seb had no interest in filling it, never mind how hard it must be for her.

"Well, I've got to get some work done tonight," he said, patience waning. "If you're ever in town, let's—"

"It's her birthday." Oliver's voice was pained.

Seb's eyes narrowed. "I know that." He sent her flowers every year.

"There's—" Now Oliver looked uncomfortable. He leaned back in his chair and loosened his tie. "There's a party, alright?"

"What party?"

"A swingers party. What kind of party do you think, asshole? A birthday party."

Oh. Oh no. That was bad. Seb would much rather hang out with a bunch of horny suburbanites than do what he was pretty sure Oliver was proposing.

"Where?"

"At the house, okay? Mom and Parker, they're organizing a family dinner and then—"

"No." If their sister, Parker, had any involvement in planning this, it would have all the pomp and circumstance of a military pageant, and Seb was not putting himself on parade.

"Seb." Oliver leaned toward the screen.

"No!" Seb stood up so fast he knocked the laptop off the edge of the coffee table. He swore as it crashed to the floor.

"Come on," Oliver was saying, even though he was tilted sideways.

"No. Absolutely not."

"But Nana—"

"I don't care. I'm not going to the house. You know that."

"I told Parker you wouldn't come to the dinner, but if you could—"

"No."

"I promised Nana you'd be there."

Angry words and years of hurt clogged Seb's throat. Shaking his head, he picked up the laptop. Oliver's face on the screen was miserable, but Seb could see it all. The spontaneous call. The way Oliver had tracked Seb down online, so they'd have this conversation face-to-face and turning his brother down would be harder. It was such a scummy lawyer thing to do, and Seb had fallen for it.

"No."

This was why they never talked about family. Oliver should have stuck to the rules.

"Please."

Seb shut the laptop.

———

As he left the store, Martin was still rattled by his ghostly visitor. He'd checked all the doors twice. Everything had been locked, but there was no sign of the man in the store either. Martin had checked every aisle and every corner. Finally, with no other option but camping out in the empty store, waiting for what? The man to return? For him to slide through the walls and throw around more books like a *Ghostbusters* extra? Martin let himself out, locked up the store again, and headed home.

The bike ride back to Brian's took less than ten minutes, and the wet salt smell of a town so close to the ocean made his head spin. When Martin previously came to visit his brother in Seacroft, he always assumed the town felt small because he only knew a few places in it. Now that he lived here, it turned out there wasn't much to see, especially once the tourists went home after Labor Day. The beachfront souvenir shops pulled down their shutters for the season, and the whole town got sleepy.

He pedaled home, trying to relax. He'd always preferred cycling to driving. Too many things could go horribly wrong inside a giant metal box hurtling down the road. The bike was safer. The physical activity was good for him too, and he was calmer by the time he got home.

"Hey, Smarts!" As Martin came in the front door, Brian was sprawled out on the couch. Martin cringed at the use of the childhood nickname. It had been funny when he'd won the city spelling bee in fourth grade. It wasn't funny now.

"Hi." He let his backpack drop to the floor. His collared shirt stuck to his back where he'd sweat through it from the last of the late summer heat.

"How did it go?" Brian turned the sound down on the TV and pulled himself up to sitting. He smiled up at Martin, but its wary edge flared the buzzing feeling under Martin's skin. How had it come to this? His brother was worried that Martin couldn't handle a part-time job in a used bookstore.

He shrugged, slumping onto the couch next to Brian. He considered telling his brother about his encounter with the blond poltergeist, but ghost stories were more likely to worry Brian than anything.

"Good, I guess."

"Did you smile?"

Martin grimaced, which was as close to a smile as he got these days.

"C'mon, Smarts! You gotta smile more! Women like men who smile." To demonstrate, Brian grinned, showing the tooth knocked out during a high school football mishap. Something green was wedged in between two of his lower teeth too.

"Charming."

Brian snorted. "Smarty! You gotta try!"

"Don't call me that!"

"But you've been doing so good lately!"

He'd been fine at home with Brian, where things were simple and predictable. Outside, in a public place where anyone could come in, was a different story. It shouldn't have been, but *should* wasn't worth much these days. Martin should also still have been at Mount Garner, assigning readings and figuring out what he was going to do when his funding ended after Christmas.

Martin squirmed, putting as much space as he could

between him and his brother, which wasn't much. Since Brian's ex-wife had literally taken half of everything they owned when she moved out, the old pull-out couch that doubled as Martin's bed was also the only piece of furniture in the room.

"I'll be fine." It was his mantra, meager though it was. He had to be fine. He'd lost too much already. Too much time, too much credibility. His academic career had gone up in flames, and now his older brother was hovering like a mother hen.

They watched some reality show where middle-aged dads brought in their minivans and their rusting sedans, and a crew of guys with a lot of tattoos and even more piercings sent them home in the same car but with a bigger engine and a paint job that almost always involved flames or barbed wire. It made no sense to Martin. Brian heckled them the whole time.

"What's for dinner?" Martin asked as the credits rolled.

"Hmm?" Brian's expression was blank, flipping through channels.

Martin mashed the heels of his hands against his eyes and groaned. "It's your night to cook!"

"No it's not! I just cooked ... "

Martin waited for realization to dawn. It was Brian's turn to cook and—"Shit. I forgot." Brian at least had the good grace to look ashamed.

"Did you remember to go shopping?"

Brian shifted and glanced away, like a guilty golden retriever. Martin sighed and stalked off to the kitchen.

"I'm sorry!" Brian called after him. "I'll order a pizza."

They'd eaten more pizza since Martin had moved in than his first year in undergrad. Back then, his Freshman Fifteen had been more like Freshman Eighty. Undoing the damage had taken years, and Brian seemed intent on luring him back to the dark side.

The old landline phone rang on the wall.

"If that's Nick, do you want to come to The Dugout to watch the game tonight?" Brian asked from the other room.

Martin didn't follow baseball, and he would need a tetanus shot before entering Brian's favorite bar, and anyway, his brother didn't want him to come. It was an excuse to keep an eye on him. Since Martin had come here, Brian was nervous leaving him alone at home. The first few weeks, it was reasonable; Martin had barely been able to dress or feed himself. Now, though, Brian's attention was getting oppressive.

"I'll pass." He picked up the phone's handset. "Hello?"

"Hey, Marty!" The woman's voice was cheery, but the sound made Martin's heart skip.

"Hi, Jess."

There was a loud thump, like a body crashing to the floor. Martin stuck his head out into the hall and found Brian on the ground, groaning where he'd fallen off the couch. He flailed his arms like he was warding off a swarm of bees, his eyes turning desperate as they met Martin's.

"How's the job hunt going?" Jess asked.

"Pretty good. I'm working a few days a week at Dog Ears downtown."

"That's great!"

It wasn't, but he appreciated her saying so.

There was a pause, and Martin waited for what he knew would come next.

"Is Brian there?"

Martin glanced to where Brian was still crouched on the floor. His older brother shook his head so violently it bounced off the side of the coffee table. He slapped a hand over his mouth to muffle his shout.

"No. He's at work." Martin went back to the kitchen. Lying to his brother's ex-wife had not been part of the agreement when he'd moved in.

"Oh." Jess sounded disappointed. "Doesn't he usually have the day off on Saturdays?"

And that right there was why lying was a bad idea. Lies had very short legs.

"Yes! Usually. But not today. Um. He got called in to cover for someone. He might be done, though, so don't call the firehall, but then I think he said something about going to get some pizza for dinner." On cue, his stomach growled.

"I called his cell too. He's not picking up."

"Maybe he's driving? Shouldn't talk and drive, you know?" Shouldn't lie for the older brother who couldn't even remember to buy the necessities of life, but Martin had always been loyal to a fault.

"I guess so." Jess didn't sound convinced.

"I'll tell him you called?"

"Do you know if he got the letter from the lawyer?"

Martin gritted his teeth. Brian owed him more than a pizza over this.

"I'm not sure. I'll get him to call you when he comes back, okay?"

"Yeah. Sure."

"Jeez, Smarts." Brian wrapped an arm around Martin's head as he hung up and ground his knuckles into Martin's scalp. "All those years of university and no one ever taught you how to be a better liar?"

"Get off!" Martin shoved at him.

"Oh come on! Lighten up!"

"Stop!" Martin stumbled back as Brian released him. Brian laughed, and Martin glared as he smoothed his hair back into place.

"You never did like it when I did that to you when we were growing up either."

"Maybe you should take the hint."

Brian laughed. "So you coming to The Dugout tonight or not?"

"You can't keep hiding from her."

Brian's grin went tight around the edges. "I'm not!"

"You are! It's not fair to make me cover for you like you're still the high school football star trying to date two girls at once."

Brian's smile fell completely. Guilt twisted in Martin's throat, and his cheeks heated. He shouldn't have said that.

"I'm not hiding." Brian pulled a beer from the fridge. "I'm right here. She's the one who left." He stomped out of the kitchen.

Martin sighed. It wasn't fair to judge. No matter how many letters hung off the end of his name, he wasn't exactly the poster child for successful adulthood. He didn't know what had gone wrong with Brian and Jess. Maybe implying Brian had cheated was too close to home.

"She wanted to know if you got a letter from a lawyer?"

"If she has something she wants to say to me, she can say it herself!"

The back door slammed, and Martin was left alone in his brother's half-empty house.

he bookstore on Monday turned out to be less of a hotspot. Fewer customers and no supernatural visitors. Martin turned the "Open" sign over at ten, but the first customer didn't come in for hours.

The poor hotspot metaphor extended into the literal when Martin discovered the store had no reliable Wi-Fi signal. He'd been so busy on Saturday he hadn't even noticed. There was one network called *Get Your Own*, but it was password protected.

At noon, an elderly man arrived with a box of books. Martin, who had been hunched over *Heart of Darkness*, got through initial greetings and chitchat without too much stammering. He'd always been better in one-on-one situations, but even those had been difficult in his last months at Mount Garner. Another small victory for him now.

The man's box held a variety of old hardcover mysteries and political thrillers set in countries that didn't exist anymore. Cassidy had shown Martin the cheat sheet, kept beneath the cash register, laying out pricing for books brought in. It was organized by decade published and whether the book was hardcover or paperback, but that was as scientific as it got.

Martin kept a running tally as he sorted through them. When he came to the end, the total felt disappointingly low.

"I can give you fifteen dollars and twenty-five cents." He couldn't even look the man in the eye as he said it.

"That's fine. I have to buy a few books for my wife anyway."

Martin's head shot up. "You're okay with that? You could make a lot more if you sold them online." He ran his hands over the spines of some of the books in the box. They weren't exactly literary masterpieces, but there was a market online for everything, and these books were nearly perfect. Uncracked. Even the dust jackets were pristine.

The old man shrugged. "What do I know about that? Just need these off the shelf. Our new place doesn't have as much space as the old one did, and these hardcovers take a lot of room. I'm glad someone else will have a chance to read them."

Martin went to hand the man his money but was waved off.

"I told you, I need some books for my wife."

"Doesn't that defeat the purpose of making space by selling these?"

The old man chuckled and raised a white eyebrow. "Are you married?"

"No." Martin's skin heated around his shirt collar. He hadn't expected for the conversation to turn its attention on him.

"Girlfriend?"

Martin shook his head. What would his customer think if he knew he was being served by a real live homosexual?

"Well, someday you will, son. And then someday after that you'll learn that things don't take up as much space if they're hers." The man's eyes twinkled like a Christmas card Santa.

Despite his discomfort, Martin couldn't help the soft laugh that bubbled out of his throat. "I'll keep that in mind."

The old man patted cold fingertips over the back of Martin's hand.

"You do that. Now help me find something for my missus.

She likes those chick flick novels where the girl always gets the billionaire in the end."

It took some work because of course no one would file the kind of book they were looking for under a heading as simple as 'Romance.' Martin led them on a slow weaving tour of the rows of shelves. The whole way, the man kept up a pleasant stream of conversation without requiring Martin to do much of the talking. He reminded Martin a bit of a friend. Doug was a more-than-mature student who had gone back to school for a history degree after retiring from thirty-five years as a manager at a shipping company. He'd been fond of popping by Martin's office to chat during office hours. Martin had never been particularly in demand, so knowing Doug would show up at one point or another was nice, and Martin enjoyed his company. They hadn't kept in touch as much as they could have once Doug had finished his degree, though.

Eventually, they found a book that seemed to appeal under a chalk board marked 'You Go, Girl!' and they made their way back to the front of the shop.

The blond man from the other night had materialized.

He was leaning against the counter like he was waiting for them, running a hand through his platinum hair. Martin's breath caught as the man smiled at them. It was a bright, confident smile, the kind that drew attention as the wearer walked into a room.

"Hey, Earl." The voice curled around the smile, and Martin would have melted on the spot if there hadn't been a convenient bookshelf to lean against. He tried to stay casual, but the voice brought back the remembered heat of a body close to his and the whisper of breath on Martin's skin as the man had slid past him in the stacks. The sensation wrapped around his stomach might almost have been desire, except Martin hadn't felt anything like that in a long time.

His shopping companion seemed to be completely unaffected by the new arrival, though. The old man waved, his new paperback tucked under one arm.

"Seb. Nice to see you."

"You too. Barb got you spring cleaning again?"

Martin had a flash of irritation over their familiar conversation, as if Sebastian had taken something that belonged to Martin, but then the irritation turned inwards as he realized he hadn't even bothered to ask Earl's name.

Earl collected the now-empty box and threw his new purchases in.

"It's October. Barb has me cleaning all year long." He shuffled toward the door. Sebastian reached around him and pulled it open. The door swung open with its usual grinding moan, and Martin twitched. Earl walked outside, and Sebastian turned and waved, throwing another smile out.

"See you later, Martin." The name was practically a purr. Seb stepped out onto the street, and the door shut behind them with one more wailing protest, taking the old man and the ghost with it.

———

The senior citizens' book club arrived for their weekly meeting at four. Martin hadn't even known they were coming, but that didn't seem to be a problem because they arranged chairs on their own, while one of the members dragged a podium out from nowhere. Another must have gone to the back to make coffee, because she reappeared a few minutes later with a tray of mugs and an insulated carafe Martin also hadn't seen before.

Mrs. Green was the last to arrive. She swanned in, a flurry of green skirts and pink scarves, and the ladies who had gathered greeted her with much fanfare. They went through the same performance they had before, where Mrs. Green introduced him as "Dr. Lindsey," and he tried to remember how to be gracious.

Meeting new people had never been his strong suit. His colleagues had worked the room, schmoozed, and chatted with donors and other faculty members. But Martin should have at least been able to be manage with this small group of Seacroft's literary septuagenarians. Even after everything, he should still be able to do that.

It was a relief when Mrs. Green called the meeting to order and he could disappear back behind the cash register.

As the book club was wrapping up, the door howled open, and Seb stepped back into the store.

Despite the now nearly reflexive thundering of Martin's heart at Sebastian's arrival, he almost giggled. At least Seb had now confirmed he used simple human means to enter the building.

Why he kept showing up at the store was still a mystery, though.

Unlike the book club's polite interest in Martin, there was palpable excitement as Seb unzipped his leather jacket. He was only a few feet away from Martin, but it was like he came with his own spotlight while Martin continued to fade into the shadows.

"Oh it's our artist in residence! Seb, I'm so glad you came to see everyone." Mrs. Green floated toward him. She turned her back to Martin and drew Seb toward the rest of the group. The late afternoon sun poured through the store's windows, giving him a golden halo around his pale skin and hair. He was gorgeous, and in that moment, Martin hated him. Just a little.

He didn't realize he was staring until Seb's indulgent gaze landed on his face.

"How's it going?" His grin was friendly, like he was inviting Martin to share an inside joke.

Of course, all Martin could do was blink and stammer. Only Mrs. Green whisking Seb off to meet his public kept Martin from diving under the counter to hide from wherever that grin was about to lead.

"We're so fortunate to have Seb in Seacroft," Mrs. Green said after everyone had gone.

Martin was stacking up the last of the chairs. "He's certainly very popular."

"Oh yes. Well. If you'd seen his work, you'd understand why. He has art in galleries all over the east."

He was an artist? That explained his flair for the dramatic.

"He likes coming to the bookstore." Martin tried to stay casual as he said it. No sense letting Mrs. Green know he'd nearly clubbed her favorite artist with a cookbook.

"Well, he has a key for the back, but the lock sticks, so he uses the front when we're open."

Martin paused as he pulled the podium back where it had come from. "He has a key?"

Mrs. Green's eyebrows climbed up toward her fluffy white hair. "Why, Dr. Lindsey, didn't I tell you? Seb lives upstairs."

———

"I found one!" Cassidy appeared in the door with a heavy-looking book tucked under one arm. The way her lips twitched around her smile, like she was trying to hold back a gush of words, made Seb pause with the knife alarmingly close to his thumb. He set it down and turned, giving her his undivided attention.

"What did you get?" He nearly choked on cold coffee as Cassidy held the book open to a black-and-white photo. It featured a woman in a nearly transparent dress, with another woman's hands strategically placed to keep the photo just this side of a parental advisory. Cassidy cackled as she slammed it shut and clutched it to her chest.

"Isn't it perfect?" She rushed toward him. He leaned away instinctively, like the book might be contagious.

"That was downstairs?"

"Top shelf, just like you said!" She did a happy dance while the old floorboards of his apartment creaked underneath.

Maybe like he'd said, but not quite what he'd meant. He'd expected fairy tales. Something easy with big recognizable illustrations. Instead, his protégé had brought him porn? Straight porn at that. Seb shuddered and reached for the book. The cover was unremarkable: plain gray with a single word, *Expression*, written on the cover in blue lettering. He lifted the edge gingerly with his knife and peered at the first page. Maybe not porn, but it definitely toed the very edge of the line. On a different page, a woman wearing what might have been a fishnet was wrapped around a man wearing what could only be described as nothing. Once again, her hands were cleverly placed to ward off the morality police.

Seb let the book fall shut again. "How old are you?"

Cassidy's eyes narrowed. "Eighteen?"

"Cass."

"I turned seventeen in August. Come on! Please! It would be so amazing for my application!"

Seb ran a finger over the book's corner, letting the pages ripple under his thumb. Cassidy yanked it from his grasp. Paper bit into his skin as the book slid away, but years of calluses and tiny scars kept him from feeling any real pain. Seeing her submit it as part of her art school applications would be pretty funny. He could picture an admissions review panel coughing discretely as they opened up her submission and tried to ask their carefully prepared questions about influences and artistic vision. He snorted at their imagined discomfort and passed her the knife.

"Fine." This was a new medium for her, so odds were good she'd screw it up before it was ready anyway. If it turned out okay, though, he planned to be a fly on the wall with every faculty.

Later, as Seb rose to get a glass of water, she said, "I was thinking maybe I could talk to Dr. Lindsey about my application."

"Who?" Had her parents signed her up for another psychologist? Seb supported Cassidy as much as he could. She was an amazing artist, one of the best he'd seen for her age. Sometimes he wanted to shake her uptight parents and scream at them that there was nothing wrong with their daughter.

"Martin? The new guy downstairs?"

Seb couldn't suppress the laugh that came out. "He's a doctor?"

"Not *that* kind of doctor." Cass gave him her very best eye roll, loaded with all of her seventeen years of wisdom. "Mrs. Green says he's a famous professor."

"Oh yeah? What does he teach?" He'd known his fair share of awkward academics over the years, the kind who buried themselves in knowledge to hide their social shortcomings. It would explain Martin's perpetual frightened, fish-out-of-water expression.

"I don't know." She flipped through pages, then paused to run her fingers down the spine of a naked man who stood with his arms spread.

"He didn't say?" Seb tried not to sound too interested. He couldn't say why exactly, but he'd enjoyed his run-ins with the bookshop's newest employee. Something about the way Martin seemed to squirm under his own skin made Seb feel devilishly giddy. It would be disappointing if he turned out to be a visiting professor slumming it among the regular folk for "research purposes."

"He doesn't talk much. Mrs. Green made him sound like a pretty big deal, though."

Seb bet she did. His landlady had a propensity for collecting local personalities, and he was happy to play the role of reclusive artistic genius for her to parade around to her friends and admirers. It had been the unspoken part of the deal when he'd moved in. If he had to be trotted out and shown off among Seacroft's blue-haired set to add a certain bohemian flair to the bookshop, so be it. The rent on the apartment hadn't gone up in years, and he had easy access to all the books he needed to fill galleries for the rest of his career.

The idea that nervous, twitchy Martin—sorry, Dr. Lindsey—might be in some way trying to usurp Seb's position grated.

"What makes you think he can help you with your application?"

Cass shrugged. The defeated slump of her shoulders made him tense. It always showed up when she talked about school, her parents, and most other aspects of her life that weren't her art.

"I still haven't started my essay."

"Fuck the essay."

"No!" She shook her head. "You keep saying that, but I have to have a good essay!"

"My essay was shit, and they still let me in." In fact, his college application essay had been more than shit. Halfway through his second paragraph, he'd written *"But that doesn't matter because you're not reading this anyway."* He had no idea if anyone had ever seen it. His acceptance at Watersmith College had been a done deal from the moment he'd printed his last name on the top of the form.

"My grades are already shit." She said it so softly he almost didn't hear, but they'd had this fight before, so he knew her plan of attack.

"You don't need them." He pointed at the back corner of the apartment where they'd stacked the finished pieces for her portfolio. "Cass, they can't teach you anything you don't already know. They're going to make you sit in history lectures about classical periods and take a philosophy credit because it will broaden your horizons. You don't need any of that! You're already better than I was at your age."

Her eyes were sad, which only made it clear how very much of a child she was. He liked hanging around with her. She was funny and daring, and she picked up the things he taught her amazingly fast, but then she got her pouty expression going and very firmly cemented her status as a hundred percent a high school senior and not an adult.

"I guess." Her defeated look made him want to pull his hair out. She saw her art as a last resort, the only thing of value she had to offer to the world—she'd more or less told him as much in the time they'd been working together. Her parents, who had forced an army of tutors and psychologists on her for years, had taught her that attitude. There was nothing wrong with her, but her parents didn't see it that way, and she worried they were right.

He hated it because he knew that feeling only too well.

"Besides, who knows what Martin's specialty is? He probably teaches astrophysics or something and wouldn't know a well-crafted sentence if it bit him in his superior ass."

He meant it as a joke, but she stared at him like he'd taken away the last life raft on a sinking ship. He clenched his teeth in frustration. He was doing everything he knew for her. She had real talent, and she didn't need some twitchy professor in over-sized flannel to tell her so. Not that she'd ever believe Seb. It was too ingrained in her from her parents, her school. Breaking away was a huge task.

An image of Oliver's sad face on Seb's laptop screen flashed in his mind.

Exactly.

Oliver had been scared his whole life and had never managed to escape. And now he was some nervous messenger boy in a tie, sent to beg Seb to come back to the fold.

Fuck that.

Cass let the book fall shut.

"I want to Frankenstein it," she said.

"Electrocute it until it comes to life?"

"No! Cut out different parts so you can flip the pages back and forth and make different bodies. Like one of those kid's books with snowmen!"

Seb considered the book's innocuous gray cover.

"That's kind of dehumanizing."

"That's kind of the point." Her green eyes flashed, and he had to smile. His partner in crime was back.

4

---

*M*artin wasn't a swooning school girl with a crush, but realizing Seb lived *upstairs* set him on edge. The bookstore was big, but the knowledge that there was another person in the building made Martin feel exposed.

Now that Martin had all the information, the idea that Seb was some kind of ghost seemed silly. He'd figured out pretty quickly that the locked door in the back of the store led upstairs to Seb's apartment and not to an off-limits storage closet. Over the course of the past week, he'd heard noises he couldn't believe he'd missed. The steady pace of feet on the floorboards overhead. Sometimes the quiet thump of a musical bass line. Martin was not alone.

The shop's front door squealed open, and he nearly dropped his book. He'd finished *Heart of Darkness* over the weekend and moved on to a travelogue called *The Road to Little Dribbling*, found on a shelf labeled 'It Sounds Dirty, but It's Not.'

"Oh, sorry!" The woman who came through the door smiled at him broadly as he fumbled to catch his book. "Didn't mean to scare you."

Martin set the book down and rubbed his palms over his thighs. "Good morning. Can I help you?"

"I hope so." The woman flashed a smile again. "We're meeting Mrs. Green this morning to talk about the blues night."

At the mention of "we," Martin realized there was another woman standing behind her. He blinked, because for a second, it was like he was seeing double. The two women were nearly identical. Brown hair, blue eyes, same excited smile. One was a little shorter, the other one a little older, but they were definitely related, if not sisters.

"Mrs. Green isn't in this morning," Martin said.

"Really?" The first woman's smile tightened. "But we had an appointment."

"Mom," the woman behind her said. "We can go to the florist's next and ask about donations for the raffle. Then we can come back to see if she's here."

"You're new, aren't you?"

The woman's question made Martin's heart speed up. How small was this town that everyone knew a newcomer immediately? He didn't want their attention. He wanted to sell a few books and go home to sleep on his brother's lumpy couch.

"Yes."

The older woman eyed him up like she might be fitting him for a new suit—or maybe trying to decide if he'd make enough of a meal to be satisfying.

"Okay!" The second woman was still grinning, but now she put a hand on the first woman's shoulder and tugged her gently back. "Don't mind her. She gets excited when her master plans start to fall into place. I'm Penny, and this is my mother, Carol Anne." She stuck out her hand, and Martin shook it.

"Martin. Nice to meet you."

"Likewise." Penny looked around the shop. "Well, this place certainly has character."

"I told you." Carol Anne pointed to the two cracking leather couches by the window. "The ensemble will go over there, and our Master of Ceremonies will stand in front of them." She winked at Martin, and his blood went cold.

"Did Bruce file the paperwork for liquor licenses?" Penny asked.

"Last week. This place is smaller than I thought though. How many tickets did we say we'd sell?"

Penny opened a blue folder and flipped through pages. "Seventy to seventy-five."

Carol Anne surveyed the front of the bookstore. "Better take that down to sixty. The fire marshal won't be happy if we overfill it."

"Overfill it with what?" Martin struggled to keep up.

"Slow down, Mom. You're scaring him." Penny patted Carol Anne's shoulder. "She's excited. Let us know when we get to be too much."

Carol Anne waved her off and continued to circle the room. "Penny and I are heading the committee for Seacroft's annual blues festival." She reached into a file folder and pulled out a sheet of brightly printed paper decorated with seashells and musical notes.

"Next month," Penny pointed at the list on the poster, "we're holding concerts sponsored and hosted by local businesses, all culminating in a charity dinner at the Big Smoke Diner next door. Dog Ears," her fingers slid down the page until Martin saw the name of the bookshop, "is hosting a trio from Seacroft High's senior jazz band."

"How do you feel about public speaking?" Carol Anne tilted her head.

"Not great?" That was an understatement. Didn't most people fear public speaking more than death? Even on his best days, Martin would have chosen a few hours in a closed casket over addressing a room of people.

Actually, a closed casket sounded peaceful.

Carol Anne didn't appear to hear him. "We need an MC for

the event. It's usually been Hank Peterson, who used to be the DJ on the local radio, but he got scooped up by some news show in Raleigh, and he and his wife, Leslie, well, they just up and left. I told him we'd still love to have him, but I suppose Seacroft is too small for him. You know, some people—"

"Mom." Penny's eyes widened. "He doesn't need all of that information in order to be our MC."

Martin had no idea what was happening, but he was sure of one thing. "I'm not very good at public speaking."

"Don't be silly." Carol Anne wriggled her fingers at him. "Look at that face, Penny. Isn't he perfect?"

"Wouldn't Mrs. Green be a better choice to MC anyway?" Martin scrambled for a way out of this. "It's her store after all."

Carol Anne's eyes narrowed, and she grabbed up the papers spread over the counter. "I think we've been stood up. Penny, let's go over to the florist's. Martin," she smiled, "it's been a pleasure. Here's Penny's business card. Email her your measurements, and she'll get you squared away for a tux rental, okay?" Without waiting for his agreement, Carol Anne exited the store.

"Tux rental?"

"Don't worry." Penny shook Martin's hand. "I'll get you through it. A suit will be fine."

Martin's head spun like he'd just been run through a laundry machine spin cycle. Now Penny and Carol Anne were leaving under the impression that he'd volunteered to MC a concert?

Penny must have seen the growing panic on his face, because she set down her folders and leaned across the counter.

"How long have you been in town?"

"A few months."

"You have family here?"

"My brother, Brian Lindsey. Do you know him? He's a firefighter."

She shook her head. "That's okay, though! My husband and I

43

own the diner next door. Why don't you come by sometime? Bring your brother!"

Some of Martin's tension leached out. When Brian had tried to get Martin to hang out with Nick and the rest of the guys, Martin balked. He wasn't the most sociable person at the best of times, but Penny's kind smile and the warm light in her eyes made him believe he could trust her.

"That would be nice. Thank you."

Penny grinned. "Give me a call and let me know when you're coming. My husband, Tim, makes the best baked beans in the state. You've got my number." She waved one last time and left the store.

As the shop fell quiet, Martin grinned. He might have just made his first friend in Seacroft. Being so excited seemed stupid. His first friend? What was this, kindergarten?

Brian would be pleased to hear about it at least. Especially if it meant a decent meal. Maybe he'd give Martin more breathing room.

And then Martin's happy little mood burst because had he also just agreed to MC a public event? That sounded an awful lot like talking to a crowd of people, possibly even trying to be funny, or smart or—

He sank back down onto his stool and buried his face in his hands.

He'd made a friend, and now he was doomed.

———

Cassidy came into the bookstore late on Thursday afternoon.

"Hey!" She pulled down the blue hood of her rain coat, shaking water droplets onto the counter.

Martin put down *Little Dribbling*. "Hey. I thought you weren't working again until the weekend."

"I'm not. I just need to get something upstairs."

Martin stiffened as the weight of Seb's silent presence pressed down on him. He hadn't seen Seacroft's artistic genius in a few days.

"Upstairs?"

"I left my charcoals in Seb's apartment. I need them for class tomorrow."

A tiny ping of worry shivered down the back of Martin's neck.

"I don't think he's home." Despite the silent certainty that Seb, with his sly winks and his dominant stride through the stacks, might appear at any time, Martin hadn't heard him at all that day. No muffled music. No creaking footsteps.

"It's okay." Cassidy fished around in the pockets of her coat. "I have a key."

Now the worry ratcheted up another notch. Remembered voices hurled accusations at him. They said he should have done more, said more. Instead, he'd done nothing until it was too late. Panic was a vice that tightened at the bottom of his skull and forced him to think over what he really knew about Cassidy. She was seventeen, he was pretty sure, and she had the key to Seb's apartment.

He followed helplessly as she made her way toward the back of the store.

"Maybe you should wait until he's back?"

"It's fine! I can't stay long. I borrowed the car, but I have to pick my mom up from work at six." Cassidy put the key in the lock and gave the door a push with her hip, like she knew exactly where it would stick, before she turned the key and the door popped open. Martin's breath went shallow as he looked up the narrow, dimly lit staircase.

"Come see my work!" Cassidy set her foot on the bottom step, which popped as something shifted under her weight. She didn't look back. Martin was left to watch as she turned at the narrow landing and disappeared. He hesitated. She was prob-

45

ably telling the truth. He was catastrophizing for no good reason. But the idea that she was there alone propelled him forward, up the enclosed space of the staircase.

As he reached the top, new scents replaced the bookshop's overwhelming smell of dust and old wood. There was coffee and something faintly chemical. Dusty windows facing out over Seacroft's main street let in thin rainy light.

A flash of color caught his eye. A hardcover book sat on a table below one window. The spine said *Songbirds of North America*, but the cover had been carved away, revealing the menagerie underneath. Layer upon layer of birds took flight from the pages. Someone had painstakingly cut out the space around bird after bird, going down and down, page by page, so tiny beaks and bright feathers peeked out at him, one beneath the other. An entire flock, contained in a book that couldn't be more than a few inches thick.

He was about to trail his finger over the bright crest of a cardinal, partially obscured by a dull brown bird, when Cassidy's voice broke into his silent awe.

"Do you want to see?" She was at the far end of the room, holding a large tube of heavy paper. Her smile went a little shy, and his throat tightened at the reminder of how young she was.

Cassidy knelt to roll the paper out. It was long, and stiff and tried to curl up on itself.

"Can you pass me one of those?" She gestured to the floor-to-ceiling bookshelf against the wall, and Martin obligingly pulled out a couple books. Like the book on the table, these were old and hardcover. He dropped them as he pulled them off the shelf, because they were significantly lighter than he'd expected.

"Cass?" a voice called, and Martin's mouth went dry.

"Hi Seb! We're upstairs!" Cassidy answered without any hesitation. Footsteps sounded on the stairs, like listening to Jack's giant climb the beanstalk.

One of the books had flopped open when Martin dropped it, and he was momentarily distracted as the words on the page shifted. But the words weren't moving; he was seeing several pages at once. He bent to lift the book, and the pages rolled as the spine shifted in his hands. Once again, he was struck by the sense that the book was lighter than it should be. The pages had been cut, but unlike the bird book on the table, this one had no images. Instead, small rectangular-shaped perforations dotted the lines of text so words on subsequent pages were visible. He turned the page, delicate as lace.

He flipped the cover shut. The title had been carved away, but the author's name was left. Calvin Forrester. Martin turned through the first few pages again. The original book's topic was nearly unintelligible with so few of the words remaining. How would Mr. Forrester feel?

"What are you doing?" Seb was standing surprisingly close.

"I was just—"

"How did you get in?"

"I was showing him my project." Cassidy was still crouched on the floor.

"That's not your project." Seb's cool eyes were on the book in Martin's hand.

"She asked for something to weigh it down."

"It's not a paperweight."

"No, I can see that," Martin said as he bounced his hand up and down with the open book in it. The spiderwebbing of pages fluttered in the breeze. Seb's eyes widened, and his nostrils flared.

"Stop that!" He pulled the book out of Martin's hands. "It's not a toy."

Martin's face flushed, and his insides squeezed. He hated how he couldn't control the reaction. Who was Seb to make him feel like this?

"It's art." Cassidy interjected from her spot on the floor.

"Cass."

"You cut up a book?" Martin's frustration tried to boil over. He shouldn't be the only one upset here. He wanted to hold the book again, really heft it. If the rest of the pages were like the ones he'd seen, only a third of the words remained.

"And what if I did?" Seb's voice was flat.

Didn't he understand? "Those are someone's words."

"Words no one was going to read. It was about agricultural best practices in New England, printed in 1977."

"That's not the point. It was someone's work. You can't deface a book like that." Despite everything, Martin's spine straightened. Whatever awkwardness he normally felt in Seb's presence gave way to anger on behalf of the unknown writer's lost words.

"What do you know about it?" Seb brushed past him, his shoulder pushing against Martin's.

The casual dismissal made Martin's face heat. He never seemed worthy of Seb's time, but he was suddenly unsure Seb's interest was something to aspire to. "What gives you the right to ruin someone's work like that?" He thrust his chin out. This was one place where he could hold his ground. He'd made a career out of unearthing the words of lost writers.

Seb slid the book back onto the shelf where it had been. "What gives you the right to judge me for it?"

"I wrote my dissertation on—"

"Your dissertation?" Seb's laugh was low and mean as he turned back to face Martin. One blond eyebrow arched.

"I told you he was a doctor," Cassidy said.

"A doctor. Is that right? Doctor Martin?" He stepped forward. Despite Martin's conviction, the accusation in Seb's eyes forced him to take a step back.

"That's right."

"Like a real doctor? Or one of those fake doctors? The ones with all that useless knowledge that only qualifies them to judge the rest of us poor slobs who actually had to go out and face the real world?"

"Real" doctors. Because, those who couldn't do taught. He'd heard all the things PhD stood for: Post hole digger, pathetic hopeless dreamer.

"I worked hard for my degree." Years of hard work. He'd loved those years before he'd finished his doctorate, when his direction had seemed so clear. And now he was defending them to someone who didn't even see what was wrong with cutting up a book. How had he gotten himself into this? He'd only been trying to save Cassidy from giants.

"What are you doing in my house?" Seb asked again.

"I wanted to show him my portfolio," Cassidy said.

"Well, he's seen it." Seb gestured behind them without looking away from Martin. "Now you can go."

5

Seb was being a dick, but he couldn't shut his mouth off. First blood. All confrontations went that way. When Martin started to argue, Seb's default was to go on the offensive. Hurt, anger, and then defiance crossed over Martin's face, and Seb was momentarily impressed. Maybe he was more than a cowardly lion after all.

Martin's posturing about his fucking doctorate sealed his fate, though. As if all the useless information gave him credibility to be anything but a world-class snob. Seb couldn't help his reaction, and it didn't take much to glare down the nervous professor.

"I'm sorry for intruding," Martin said, then walked wordlessly out of the apartment.

"That wasn't very nice," Cassidy said when he was gone.

Seb had to bite back a dozen angry words before he replied. "Please don't bring people into my apartment when I'm not here."

"He wasn't hurting anything."

"It's my home, Cass. You can't bring people up here and let them touch my things." He'd nearly gone nuclear at the sight of the book in Martin's hand, delicate pages flapping. He hadn't seen any tears in the paper, but that didn't mean everything was still intact.

"You sound like my sister." Cassidy rolled up her drawing and secured it with a cord. "Don't touch my things, Cassidy. It's too complicated for you to understand, Cassidy. I'm not stupid, you know?"

Seb sighed. He was still irritated, but upsetting Cass wouldn't solve anything.

"You're not stupid. I'm sorry if I overreacted."

"You should apologize to him." Cass picked up her charcoal tin and slid it into her backpack.

Seb groaned.

Fuck.

She was right. He needed to apologize.

Cass rolled her eyes as she hefted her backpack onto her shoulder.

"I have to go pick up my mom." She stalked to the door and thumped down the stairs, taking extra care to bang her bag against the wall with every step.

Seb collapsed on the couch, flinging his arm over his eyes. That had been a disaster, and Martin never stood a chance. Seb had more than three decades of practice winning even the most vicious of arguments. Someone should have told Martin there was no withstanding the Stevenson men when they got pissed off about something.

Even if the something they were pissed off about wasn't the oblivious and well-meaning professor standing in front of them.

As Seb had come around the last corner on his way back to the apartment, Oliver called again. Seb had been dodging pretty successfully since their ambush Skype session, but Oliver seemed to take the silence as a challenge. He called more frequently, and finally, in a fit of annoyance, Seb had picked up.

"For god's sake, Seb," Oliver had said, apparently going for the direct approach since the bush beating had failed so completely last time. "I'm not asking you to move back in or get on your knees and grovel as soon as you arrive. But I need you to fucking be there."

Seb hadn't responded in words longer than four letters before he'd told Oliver he had to go. If he'd stayed on the phone any longer, he would have started yelling right there on the street, cursing a stream so foul one of Seacroft's kind citizens would have called 911 on him for creating a public disturbance. Anger and frustration had vibrated through his bones as he'd pushed into the bookstore.

Martin's misfortune was being in the wrong place at the wrong time, holding the first piece Seb succeeded in getting placed at a juried show. He had unleashed all of the feelings he hadn't been able to set free, and Martin, and even Cass a little, had been collateral damage.

The vibration of his phone in his pocket made him jump. As he prepared mentally for another yelling match, his jaw clenched. He was relieved when the caller ID said it was Kenneth instead.

"Hello, darling," Kenneth said as soon as Seb answered the call.

"Hello, Kenny." He grinned as he pictured Kenneth's silent pout at the nickname.

"How's everything in the salt mine?"

"Fine."

"Fine? Fine as in you're ahead of schedule and you've come up with something even my genius wouldn't expect? Or fine as in you've been frozen in indecision since my last call and nothing has been moved ahead, but you don't want me to find out because you know I'll be pounding on the front door of that hovel you call a studio by tomorrow morning?"

"You're not usually the one to do the pounding." Seb couldn't help the evil grin that spread across his face, which grew when Kenneth let out a cry of mock outrage.

"Don't distract me with your ham-fisted innuendo. You know I can give it out as well as I take it."

"Ugh. I don't need those mental images. We've kept the whole thing professional this long. Let's not break the streak, okay?"

"I have no idea what you're talking about. We've never been professional. Do I have to remind you about that New Year's Eve after the exhibit in Charleston?"

Seb had tried hard to forget that particular party. "I was drunk. I can't be held responsible for what comes out of my mouth when there's champagne."

"Or what goes in your mouth apparently."

Normally, their banter would have had Seb digging for the filthiest joke he could think of, but his earlier bad mood still clung to the edges of his laughter. He didn't feel up to seeing who could make the other one crack first.

"What are you calling for? It's not really to check on my progress. I'm ahead of schedule, like I was when you called last month and the month before that."

Seb had known Kenneth since their freshman year at college, when they were the only two out gay boys in their dorm. Kenneth was the sole reason Seb had survived their full year business mathematics course. When Kenneth graduated with his shiny commerce degree and Seb started selling pieces more widely, he hesitated to add business to their friendship. But letting Kenneth act as his agent to the various galleries along the East Coast had been one of the smartest choices he'd made in the last ten years.

"Of course you are, darling. I wouldn't expect anything less from you. I'm actually calling because I have news. Good and bad. Which would you like first?"

Seb rubbed a hand over his eyes. "Just tell me the bad news and get it over with."

"I was hoping you were going to say that!"

"Kenny . . . " He toed off his shoes and lay back down on the couch with a sigh. He'd apologize to Martin later.

"Schiller pulled out of the exhibition."

"What?" Exhaustion evaporated as Seb sat upright again.

"Naomi was vague about it. I don't know much. Personal reasons. It sounded serious."

Seb's hand tightened around the phone as he tried to stay calm. This wasn't bad news—this was a nightmare. He'd literally had this dream, where he showed up at a gallery to find out that the whole thing had been cancelled and no one had thought to tell him.

"Okay." What else was he supposed to say? Arlene Schiller was an icon. It would have been her first time exhibiting new work in over a decade, and Seb had been invited to contribute pieces on behalf of the artists influenced by her. Just being asked was a gift, and he'd spent the last six months getting ready. Without it, though, he could have completed and sold several pieces to collectors to generate a little cash flow. On his work table, the book of European fashion sat quietly. It turned out to not be a bad choice. The paper held together under his knife better than he'd expected. He could have it ready to sell fairly quickly.

"I've got a few things I could ship down to the Diving Bell Gallery, if you think they'll take them?" The Diving Bell had done well for him over the years. They had at least a few buyers who kept an eye out for his work.

"Well, I could call Ina at the Bell," Kenneth said, sounding like he hadn't thought of it until now, "but sweetheart, I don't think Naomi would be very happy with that idea."

"What?"

"Because they weren't able to find someone else to take over the gallery on short notice, so they're going to continue with the exhibition and broaden the scope. They want three more pieces from you! She says she'd always wanted to include more of your

54

work, but with the restrictions on the space, there wasn't room. You can do it though, right? Three pieces? You've only got a few months to go."

Seb hurried over to the work table and flipped through the fashion book again. The woman in the traffic cone hat who'd caught his eye. A man farther back in a set of crocheted swim trunks. They'd make a cute couple.

"I can do that." He could, if he slept six nights a week instead of seven.

"That's my boy. I already told Naomi you would. We should celebrate. I'll bring the champagne?" The last question was a verbal leer, but Seb was already running his fingers through the pages of the book, planning where to take it next.

"Sure," he said. This unlikely book, forgotten on the bookstore's top shelf, was about to send his career into light speed.

6

On Sunday, Martin woke up with a mattress spring poking him in the back and a fight roaring in his ears.

"I'll call the lawyer!" a woman's voice said.

"You and your lawyers." This was Brian. Martin shifted just enough to get off the spring and then lay still, burying his head under a pillow.

"I wouldn't have to use the lawyers if you would answer the goddamn phone." Jess. The screen door banged open and shut. Loud footsteps came up the hall.

"Why would I answer my phone? So you can nag me some more?"

"I'm just asking you to be fair!" Jess and Brian were in the house, coming up the front hall. Martin's pillow wasn't doing much of anything besides making it hard to breathe.

"I'm being fair!" They were right outside the living room now. "You wanted half, you got half."

"That's not what I'm saying."

Martin lay frozen on the pullout while his brother and former sister-in-law argued in front of him.

"Look at this, Jess! I don't even have a goddamn bed for my brother to sleep in!"

Martin's eyes widened, and he tried to pull himself up to sitting. The blankets slipped down to his waist. He'd slept in one of his old Mount Garner History T-shirts and briefs, which seemed like totally acceptable attire when he and Brian were alone in the house. With Jess here, he didn't feel like he could get out of bed.

"Um, good morning?" he said, hoping one of them would take the hint.

"Hey, Marty. Sorry about all this." Jess smiled at him, the same kind smile she'd always given him.

"Don't be nice to him!" Brian took a step forward, planting himself between Jess and Martin. His big frame cast Martin in shadow. "He's not part of this. Say whatever you came here to say, take whatever thing you think is the rest of your fair share, and then get the hell out."

Jess's eyes went teary. Martin's chest twisted, and the line of tension in Brian's shoulders softened a bit too.

"You're a real jerk, aren't you?"

"I don't know what you want from me!" Brian's voice was strangled.

Martin searched desperately for a way to escape. Unfortunately, there weren't many options short of dumping himself onto the floor and crawling under the mattress.

"I can't keep living like this!" The words cracked in Jess's throat. "This in between where we're not together but still not finished with each other. I don't know who I am!"

Adrenaline burst through his body at the distress in Jess's voice. Martin really shouldn't have been here. Never mind they were technically in his room, as much as the living room could be considered his. He needed an escape.

"Can I go make some coffee? Maybe we can sit down, sort out—"

"Shut up, Smarts, This isn't about you." Brian didn't even bother to turn around, and Martin nearly bit his own tongue as his cheeks flushed. Their invasion this early on a Sunday morning had left him with no choice. Silently, he slunk out of the room.

As hurt and panic washed over his scalp and down his throat, he found clean clothes in the dryer. It was time to leave. He'd grabbed his phone as he'd snuck out of bed, but his coat and scarf were by the front door, where Brian and Jess had moved their argument. Instead, he grabbed an old hoodie of Brian's, then took off into the backyard at a near run.

His bicycle was in the garage. Neither Brian nor Jess, who were now yelling on the front porch, said anything as he made his way out onto street.

"You're the one who said you couldn't do it!" Jess said.

"You're the one who left!"

Across the street, a man walking a small dog had stopped to watch the show. He didn't so much as glance at Martin as he pedaled away.

It was cool for October, and still early in the day. The ride kept his core warm, but his fingers, nose and ears were red and burning by the time he stopped. He was at the beach, and the cold stretch of ocean was deserted. Struggling, he wheeled his bike out onto the sand. He let it fall against an old log before collapsing right next to it.

It was windy, and the waves were up, rolling and crashing to shore. The sound was soothing, blocking out the roar in his head. He sniffed and pulled his limbs closer. A lone seagull padded up the sand on knobby legs and webbed feet, stopping a few feet away to stare at him with belligerent eyes. No doubt it was looking for a snack: old bread or discarded French fries.

"I've got nothing." He *had* nothing. No things. No career, no home. He couldn't stay. He'd needed Seacroft to be a reprieve, a sanctuary. When Brian came to get him, he'd thought his brother's concern was real. It had been such a relief. But that concern had been temporary, and now Martin had no one to turn to and no place to go.

A figure appeared down the beach, moving confidently where the sand was wet and firm as the tide went out. As he got closer, the white-blond hair under his knit cap became visible.

A small flock of sandpipers scurried ahead of Seb—because of course it was him—and took off when he neared, flying in tight formation over the surf. The guy had to have an entire production company that followed him around to ensure he always made an entrance.

Martin had no desire to deal with Seacroft's favorite son. He shifted, ready to take his bike and pedal onwards, even though he had no destination in mind.

"Dr. Lindsey, I presume!" Seb's voice cut through the roll of the waves.

Martin scowled at him. "Don't call me that."

"What, do you expect your students to just call you Professor?" Seb smirked at him.

He didn't have students. One more thing to add to his Nothing List.

"Or maybe sir?" Seb's blue eyes danced.

"What do you care?"

Seb laughed, apparently oblivious to Martin's turmoil. "I bet the girls loved you. They'd swoon whenever you walked across the quad in your sweater vest, wouldn't they? Tweed Tuesday? Wooly Wednesdays?"

Martin glared, but it only seemed to encourage him.

"Let's see. Threadbare Thursdays. There's always that one sweater that you can't throw out because you wore it the night you finished your dissertation. And Fleecy Fridays because let's not forget that height of fashion."

"Would you shut up?" Martin leapt to his feet, wobbling in the soft sand. He was so tired of this man, this town, all of it.

"No wait! I forgot. It's Turtleneck Thursdays! Although,

sometimes you mix and match and wear those on Tuesdays. Sometimes with tweed!" He clapped his hands together in delight. The sound ricocheted inside Martin's head.

"What do you want?"

"Just being sociable. I know it's not a skill set they promote in your usual circles, but trust me, if you're going to succeed in the cutthroat world of previously-owned literature, it's something you might want to work on."

Succeed. That wasn't really even an option, was it? Not anymore.

"I'll take my chances as an anti-social failure then."

Seb shrugged, the leather of his jacket creaking. "That's the spirit! Join the outcasts and losers club like me!"

"You and I have nothing in common." Martin fought a shiver. He'd been still for too long, and the cold was seeping from his fingers up his arms and into his chest.

Seb bit his lip as he eyed Martin, and whatever he saw made him laugh softly. "Rough night? Got a little carried away with Seacroft's vibrant club scene?"

Martin glared at him for another second, but then he blew out a long breath. "Rough morning. I'm too old to be sleeping on a couch."

"I get that." Seb scratched at his head through his hat. "Got plans for today? We could go grab a coffee or something."

"The last time we spoke, you told me to get the hell out of your apartment."

Seb grinned sheepishly. "Yeah, I owe you an apology. You got caught in the crossfire of a family disagreement. I was a dick to you, and that wasn't fair. The least I can do is buy you a coffee."

"You don't have to do that."

"Yeah I do. My grandmother would kill me if she knew how rude I had been." Seb slung an arm over Martin's shoulders. Martin couldn't remember the last time someone had touched him. He wanted to recoil and press farther into it at the same time. So, despite his misgivings, he allowed himself to be led back to the street.

They stopped at a small coffee shop, where they each ordered. Then Seb also asked for a medium coffee in a large cup.

"Who's that for?" Martin asked as the server passed them three paper cups.

"Cassidy. She's probably already at my place by now."

"Your place?"

"Yeah. You coming?"

Martin hesitated. Seb must have seen his discomfort, because he offered a kinder smile than he normally did. There was less superior amusement, more sympathy.

"Come on," he said. "This is still part of the apology. Cass is coming over to work on her portfolio. You didn't get to see it last time. Come for a minute and check it out. What's the worst that could happen?"

Martin had a long list starting with his own experience and ending with the limitless worst-case scenarios his brain could conjure up, but he followed Seb to the bookstore and up the creaking staircase to the apartment.

"I let myself in," Cassidy said as they came through the door. She took the third coffee from Seb. "You're out of soy milk again."

"I only keep it around for you," Seb said. "Tell me again exactly how one milks soy? Last I checked, it's not a mammal."

Cassidy laughed. Her smile grew as she spotted Martin. "Hi! Seb didn't tell me you were coming over!"

"We ran into each other." Seb set the tray of drinks down on a little table. Martin hesitated by the door until Seb lifted one of the paper cups and held it out to him.

Stalking back out into the cold was still an option. He could go home. Jess had probably left, but Brian would still be there. Martin didn't feel like talking to him.

"You okay?" Seb's question snapped Martin out of his brooding.

"Fine. Thanks for the coffee." He held the cool blue of Seb's gaze and shivered. Seb looked away for a change.

"Martin wants to see your portfolio," Seb said as he passed Cassidy.

She straightened again and grinned. "It's pretty awesome. Come see!"

It *was* pretty awesome. She pulled out the long tube of heavy paper and unrolled it across the living room floor. The papers were thick and longer than he was tall. The ends kept trying to roll back, but Martin let her choose books from the shelf to hold them down.

"What do you think?"

What did he think? He could barely take in what he was seeing. Each page featured a monochromatic landscape, long shadows stretching from spindly trees, and roads that extended into a horizon that looked miles away.

The depth was staggering. A pale moon seemed to shimmer in one, as a figure in a field danced in the moonlight. Martin wanted to get down on his hands and knees, press his face to the floor, and see if anything else was on the page, some addition that created the third dimension. "You did this?"

"Girl's got skills," Seb said behind them. He sat at the desk beneath the window, hunched over a book with a small utility knife in his hands.

"Is it chalk?" Martin asked.

"Charcoal," Cassidy said.

"It's amazing." He didn't know how to tell her what it made him feel, especially the one lonely figure, its back to them as it trudged up the long endless road in the middle of the page.

"She has an eye for shadows," Seb said.

"Do you really like it?" Cassidy asked, her arms crossed over her chest.

Martin could barely tear his eyes away from it as he nodded vigorously. "I don't know a lot about these kinds of things, but this is really good."

"I hope so."

"Cass is going to art school next year. New York or Rhode Island. The big time!" Seb didn't look up as he spoke.

"If they take me." Cassidy didn't sound confident.

"They'll take you."

"But—"

"Professor, tell her they'll take her."

"Oh." Martin stuffed his hands into the front pocket of his stolen hoodie. "My background's in history. I don't know much about—" He broke off when Cassidy's expression clouded. She chewed on her lower lip and scuffed her shoes on the floor. Seb arched an eyebrow at Martin, a silent command not to screw this up. "But these are really amazing. If it were up to me, I'd accept you for sure."

Cassidy's smile said she could tell he was improvising. "Thanks."

Martin glanced over her head at Seb again, who considered them both for a moment before he nodded and went back to his book.

Cassidy bent to roll up her drawings. As she returned the books to the shelf, Martin wandered over to the table, watching Seb slice through the cover with a steady hand.

"Do you ever make drawings like Cassidy's?" Martin asked.

"No one's drawings are like Cass's."

"That's not what I—"

Seb set his knife down again. "I can draw, if that's what you're asking. But I started working in repurposed books after art school, and it's where I focus all my time now."

"And people are okay with you cutting up their books?"

"I'll say," Cassidy said from the other side of the room. "You should see how much some of his pieces sell for!"

Seb shrugged off her compliment. "It's just a book. I agree that the writer's work has value. But a book is a mass-produced consumer product. If I worked with old VHS tapes or CDs, no one would give me a hard time."

"But if they—"

Seb waved him off. "People get so hung up on preserving books, but the books I use are at the end of their lives. They're on the top shelf of a used bookstore in a town that most of the world doesn't even know exists. If I don't turn them into something new, what do you think happens to them?"

"Someone would buy them eventually."

"Downstairs, we shelve from the middle," Cassidy said from across the room.

"So?" Martin's brow furrowed.

"The newest books go in the middle of the middle shelf. The books that don't sell get pushed to the outside and then eventually up or down a shelf. The ones on the top and bottom shelves are the oldest books in the store. No one is going to buy them. Some of them have been here for years."

Martin's frown deepened, his lips pressing together. He'd always believed books had to be taken care of. Shared maybe, but never disposed of. What Seb and Cassidy were saying made sense, though. There was a separation between the words written and the paper they were printed on.

He tilted his head, trying to understand what Seb was doing from this new perspective. "So you carve out the words you don't want and keep the ones you do?"

"Found poetry. It's where I started, like the book you had the other day. I mostly work in images now, though."

"The birds?" The book of songbirds sat on the far corner of the table, feathered inhabitants watching him carefully.

"That's not one of my better pieces, but yes."

Not one of his better pieces? Martin hadn't had a chance to really look at it the last time, but it was cut so intricately, so many small layers revealed. The work and patience it must have taken was incredible.

"Seb shows his stuff in galleries all over the place. I saw one on a field trip to Wilmington last year!" Cassidy came and sat at the table, pulling out a heavy gray book from her backpack.

Seb smiled at her. "I've been lucky enough to develop a bit of a following."

"More than a little! Your Shakespeare project sold for more than six thousand dollars!"

"Shakespeare project?" Martin tried not to sound judgmental. Apparently, nothing was sacred under Seb's knife.

Seb laughed. "It's not about the money. And Shakespeare's overrated. I was doing him a favor. I cut out anything that wasn't a dick joke or some other kind of innuendo. It was still surprisingly intact when I was done."

Cassidy giggled. As the apartment lapsed into silence, Martin hovered where he was. The two artists hunched in front of him, intent on their work.

"Well, I should get going." Better to head off the inevitable awkwardness. They clearly had a plan for the day, and he was intruding. "Thanks for the coffee."

"You can stay for a bit, if you want," Seb said without looking up. "I don't have TV, but there's all the books you can handle downstairs, and the Wi-Fi password is ThisIsMine27, no spaces, with the first letter of each word capitalized."

Martin paused, thinking of the one password protected Wi-Fi network he could access from the bookshop.

"Are you *Get Your Own*?"

"Well, I'm not sharing with all those busybodies downstairs." Seb glanced up at Martin from under his lashes. His pale pink lips stretched into a smile that held something other than his usual sarcasm. Martin swallowed hard as attraction stirred in his chest, a dusty feeling he hadn't encountered in quite some time. He shouldn't have been surprised Seb, with his charm and good looks, rattled it loose. Martin trembled as he tried it out for a second, then dismissed it as quickly as it came on.

Seb didn't appear to notice, or feel the same thing, so Martin excused himself, promising to return. He went downstairs and pulled a few books off a shelf labeled 'Why Can't We Be Friends?'

When he returned, he settled on Seb's sagging green couch. It was surprisingly comfortable, not broken down so much as well-worn. Loved. Martin relaxed deeper, waiting for a spring to pop out of nowhere and remind him that this wasn't his place, but the cushions let him sink in.

Lulled into a tentative comfort by the quiet industry of the apartment, he sprawled along the couch and worked his way through half of the first book. It was a western saga about feuding families, the kind who made Brian and Jess's earlier scene look positively functional. Martin slipped into the story, losing track of time until Cassidy shook his shoulder.

"Sorry." She giggled as he startled. "I'm making grilled cheese for lunch. Do you want one?"

"Oh. No." He checked his watch. After one o'clock. He'd been there for hours. "That's fine. I don't want you to—"

"If you say you don't want her to go to the trouble, I'll throw this book at you. She's offering. Take her up on it." Seb's voice was low, and Martin's eyes darted to him. Seb glanced up from the book he was cutting into, smirk and eyebrows back in their permanent expression of sly teasing. Martin pressed himself a little more deeply into the couch.

"A sandwich would be great. Thanks."

"Ketchup or no ketchup?"

Martin wrinkled his nose. "No ketchup."

Cassidy sighed and glanced across the room. "He was doing so well, too."

Seb gave a one-shouldered shrug as he cut a long line through the book under his hand. "He'll learn."

They ate on their knees, hunched around the coffee table. Martin couldn't remember the last time he'd had a grilled cheese sandwich. The sandwich was delicious, simple and comforting, reminding him of cool fall days at home when he and Brian had been kids.

Martin didn't have much to say, but Seb and Cassidy kept up an easy conversation. Seb laughed openly at Cassidy's jokes, unrestrained in a way that Martin hadn't seen before. When he laughed, Seb's eyes and forehead crinkled, showing real humor. It was a contrast to the wry smirks he gave in public, where he always seemed ready with the punch line Martin couldn't see coming. His kindness toward Cassidy was a side that might be worth getting to know instead of simply admiring from a distance.

"Can I ask you something?" Cassidy said.

"You're not really giving him a choice, are you?" Seb's reply made Martin realize the original question had been directed at him.

"Oh." He set down his plate and brushed crumbs off his knees. "Sure."

"You were a professor, right?"

Her use of the past tense made him flinch. "That's right."

"So you taught a lot of classes?"

"Yes."

"So you must have graded a lot of assignments? Read a lot of essays?" She twisted a strand of her curly hair around one finger.

"Just spit it out, Cass." Seb chewed on his grilled cheese.

"Would you help me write my application essay?" Cassidy said it so fast Martin nearly missed it, and then her eyes went wide.

"Oh. Um. I'm not really—that wasn't . . . " He tried to think how to explain. "An admission essay is more of a personal state-ment. My students wrote academic essays. Research and—"

"But it's an essay." Cassidy was twisting her curls into small braids now, her fingers working quickly. "I know it's not the same. I want to know if mine's any good, and maybe, you know, you can check for spelling and things like that? My spelling sucks."

Here, Martin's colleagues would roll their eyes and mutter about the artificial security blanket of computer spell checkers or the abysmal literacy rates in high school graduates.

The more he rolled the idea around in his head, though, the more he thought there might be some value. Before he'd had to devote all his time to research and teaching classes, he'd done some private tutoring in the last year of his undergrad and again in the first year of his master's program. He'd always been more comfortable in those one-on-one settings than in a lecture hall. He wasn't sure he'd ever be able to hold his own in front of a class again, but surely he could manage this.

Cassidy's eyes were full of hope, and he had to stamp down the fear that her trust in him might be misplaced.

"Sure. I can read your essay."

The change on Cassidy's face was like the sun coming out. She hopped to her feet and ran around the coffee table, flinging her arms around him without any hesitation. It surprised him, and he blushed furiously when he caught Seb watching them, but eventually he found all the muscles he needed to hug her back.

"Thanks," she said. "Thanks a lot."

He tried to sound confident as he said, "No problem."

———

It had been an odd day. After working on the fashion book most of the night, Seb went out for an early walk to clear his head before Cass arrived. He hadn't expected to find Martin talking to seagulls and staring at the ocean like he was contemplating an autumn swim. Since the scene in his apartment days earlier, Seb truly had been trying to find a moment to apologize. He led with what he now considered their usual repartee, where he teased and Martin stammered, but everything about Martin had been askew, from his moody scowl to his even more rumpled than usual appearance. With his messy hair and baggy hoodie, he might be coming off a three-day bender.

As Martin growled they had nothing in common, Seb pushed down the urge to poke at him to see what would happen. He still didn't know what made Martin tick, but starting a new argument before apologizing for the last one was bad form. So he'd offered a coffee and a place for Martin to hang out for a few hours.

As the afternoon wore on, though, Martin turned out to be pretty good company once he stopped hovering on the edges. He mostly lay on the couch reading, but eventually he wandered over to look at Cassidy's project, turning a little pink when he saw the book she was working on.

"What about the drawings?" he asked as he took in the two naked men, legs wrapped around each other for the purposes of symmetry and barely enough modesty.

"Seb said I needed to diversify my portfolio."

Martin stared across the table with wide eyes, but Seb held up his hands.

"I mentor. I don't censor. She'll get enough of that on her own." He waited for Martin to protest, either with a return to the sanctity of books or by pointing out Seb was corrupting Cassidy's young mind. Instead, Martin simply watched them for a while longer without any obvious judgement before he returned to the couch and his book.

A little after five, Cass's phone vibrated out a cheerful samba rhythm and nearly danced off the table. Seb's hand twitched at the sound, and he almost cut off the arm of the man in the polyester suit he was painstakingly carving around.

Cass heaved her book shut with a dramatic sigh and went to

pack up her things. "My mom's here. Thanks, Seb. I'll see you this week. I don't work on Wednesday or Thursday. Martin, could you help me with my essay then?"

"Sure." Martin still didn't look excited at the prospect, and Seb maintained the whole thing was stupid and pointless. But she was insisting, and the kind professor had agreed to help, so who was Seb to get in their way?

Cass's footsteps thumped dully on the stairs as she made her way out. Seconds later, the bookstore's door groaned, and the building fell into silence.

Martin glanced at Seb out of the corner of one eye. "I should probably get—"

"Takeout?" Seb forced a smile and pushed up from his chair. "I think that's a great idea."

Martin shook his head. "No. I should go. I appreciate you letting me hang out with you guys today, but I wasn't looking for a babysitter."

"Of course not." Seb studied him again. Illuminated from behind by the living room lamp, Martin seemed especially defined, a comic book character with an extra thick line to make him stand out from his background. It was like he'd been dropped into the space, somewhere he didn't belong.

He might not need a babysitter, but he definitely needed a friend.

"Got plans for tonight? Hot date?" Improbable, but since it was still unclear what Martin had been doing at the beach so early that morning, Seb was keeping an open mind. Who knew? The professor might like getting a little freaky at night.

"No." Martin heaved a sigh that would have made Cassidy proud. "But Brian will wonder where I got to. I left in a hurry this morning."

"Brian? Is he your boyfriend or something?" No way Martin was with someone. Everything about him felt so abandoned.

Whoever this Brian guy was, he was doing a lousy job looking after him.

Martin's crooked smile flashed with dry humor that Seb hadn't seen before. "If he were my boyfriend, I could break up with him. But he's my brother, and you can't pick your family, right?"

A couple thoughts pinged through Seb's brain all at once. First, not picking your family was one of life's true tragedies.

Second, Martin hadn't balked at the mention of a boyfriend.

What an interesting development.

"You can call him? Seriously, there's no rush to leave. The light's bad for me to keep working anyway. I'm going cross-eyed." Apparently, Martin's sad face and the sudden prospect that he might be gay were enough motivation to lie. Seb had hours of potential working time left, but not letting Martin wander off was suddenly more important.

"I can't call him. My phone died," Martin said.

"Use mine. Please. You're doing me a favor. I'm too pretty to go blind before I hit my thirtieth birthday." More lies. He had hit thirty, knocked it out of the ballpark, and already run the bases.

Martin's eyes slid over his face. Seb preened before waggling the phone in his direction, but Martin shook his head. "I don't even know his number. It's programmed into my phone, but I have no idea what it is."

"His loss. So what do you want? Chinese? Pizza? There's a Thai place down the street that has amazing garlic pork. I'd offer to cook, but I'd probably kill us both and burn this place down in the process. In the interest of self-preservation, I'll buy us dinner."

Martin sat down heavily on the couch and leaned back, hands over his eyes. "This town is determined to make me fat again."

As he stretched, the hem of his hoodie rode up, stopping just at the waistband of his jeans. Another quarter inch would reveal

71

skin, and Seb found he wanted to see it. Whatever Martin was, he was not fat. Lean, possibly even wiry. But not fat. Seb watched intently as the shirt pulled up a bit farther, exposing just the thinnest line of skin and a swirl of dark hair. Then Martin exhaled, and his clothes settled into place again. His gray eyes blinked open in time to catch Seb staring.

"I don't think you have to worry too much about your weight."

Martin's cheeks went pink, like he knew what Seb had been doing. "I didn't mean to say that out loud."

Seb laughed as he flipped through his phone to find the take out menu he wanted, trying to ignore the way his pulse had picked up. "Were you a fat kid growing up?"

"I wasn't a skinny kid. Not fat, just soft. But then I went to college. That's when I got fat."

Seb looked him over once more. The individual parts of him —long arms, crooked nose, sad eyes—weren't specifically attractive, but put together, something about him was compelling.

"Clearly, you got not fat again."

Martin's palm trailed over his hoodie, across his stomach. Seb was suddenly intrigued by what the body underneath all those clothes might look like, but then Martin's hand dropped, and he glanced away again. He was holding something back, and Seb couldn't put his finger on what it might be. He left it alone and ordered dinner.

The nice thing about living in a small town where ribs and beans were considered the height of gourmet: Thai takeout was fast. Fifteen minutes later, boxes of garlic pork and pad thai covered the space Seb cleared off from the working table. He couldn't remember the last time he'd actually sat down to have a real meal in his apartment. Making a fuss over dinner when he lived alone was a lot of work, and his table was usually full of materials. Better that way. Eating formally at the table brought back too many unpleasant family memories.

"How are things downstairs?" he asked as they poked at their food with chopsticks.

"Fine. It's busier than I thought it would be. For a bookstore."

"I think Mrs. Green makes as much money renting the space as she does selling books."

Martin nodded, looking glum. "There are a lot of groups. I'm not so good with people, especially when it's a lot of them."

"That must have made teaching challenging."

Martin stabbed at his plate, the chopsticks moving up and down without picking anything up. Seb pieced together the little bits he knew. Dr. Lindsey, illustrious professor, living with a brother and hiding away in a used bookstore. At no point during the day had Martin brought up his research or his credentials, and that was usually the first thing fussy academics like him wanted to talk about.

Witness protection, maybe?

"Can I ask you a question?" he said. Martin squinted up from his meal. Seb laughed, remembering his earlier joke to Cass, and held up his hands. "Fair enough. But can I?"

"I guess."

"What are you doing here?"

Martin froze mid-chew as his cheeks went pale. Seb didn't mean to make him uncomfortable, but too many little things didn't add up.

"You invited me?" Martin said once he'd swallowed.

"What? No. Not here. I mean—" He waved his arms around him. "*Here.* Seacroft. The bookstore."

"Oh." Martin's shoulders slumped.

"I mean, I can't imagine we're a step up from wherever you were before."

"Mount Garner College."

Seb paused. "Mount Garner? That's a good school."

"Pretty good."

"But you left?"

Martin studied him, and Seb stared right back, taking a second to really examine him. Brown hair, gray eyes, a nose that didn't quite sit straight. Or maybe his jaw was a little askew, making everything else appear crooked. There was a scar on his chin, an old one by the looks of it. If he weren't so nervous all the time, he would probably have been handsome, with full lips and a sharp edge to his jaw.

Martin plucked at the zipper of his hoodie. "There were mitigating factors."

"What? Were you deflowering underclassmen during office hours?" He laughed at the idea of Martin playing Naughty Professor with some twinky student.

Or maybe it was Martin on his knees while a more senior colleague...

There was a choking sound across the table. Martin's face had turned bright red, and his eyes were wide. His cheeks ballooned as he struggled to swallow whatever was in his mouth. In the end, he discreetly turned his head and spat it into a paper napkin.

"No." His voice was hoarse. "It wasn't about me. I was unlucky." He picked at his food some more but wouldn't meet Seb's eyes. Whatever had happened was clearly a sensitive topic, so Seb backed up.

"What's your PhD in?"

Instead of launching into the minutia of whatever his specialty was, though, Martin hesitated, like he was trying to decide if the answer could be used against him. What made him so allergic to disclosing any kind of personal information?

"German history."

Seb stomped on the instinct to bristle. With someone else —*with his dad*—the two word answer would have been an implication that Seb wasn't sophisticated or important enough to understand. But Martin didn't seem to be like that. Seb did his best to keep his voice light as he said, "All of it? It goes on for a while."

"It's really specific." Martin pushed the plate away. "Most people aren't all that interested."

"Trust me. My dad was a professor." That was the kindest thing Seb had said about Philip Stevenson in years. "I know the drill."

"Your dad's a professor?" Martin perked up. Of course he did. They knew how to sniff out their kind. "Where does he teach?"

"He's retired. What was your thesis about?"

"The persecution of gay Germans in the lead up to World War II. I wrote my thesis on the life and work of Werner Bergmann."

"That must have been fun."

Martin's jaw tightened—a small reaction, but an important one. Seb knew how to spot the little signs when he'd stepped on a nerve and had learned how to take advantage of them a long time ago. It was a matter of survival with his family. The twitch in Martin's jaw was the same kind of gesture as the tip of his chin while he'd defended his position about Seb's work the last time. Whatever he was keeping to himself, Martin was willing to stand up for this.

"It was important work," he said, his voice dropping. "Bergmann was a poet and a political activist. They didn't even know he existed until the late nineties when someone found a box of his drafts in a secondhand store."

Seb grinned as Martin appeared to come to life. "How is that possible?"

"He died in a concentration camp, and most of his work was burned."

Wow. Seb blew out a breath. What would being so completely erased from the record that you disappeared for more than forty years mean?

"Is that why you freaked out about my work?" he asked.

"I didn't freak out." Martin's eyes narrowed, and Seb's heart beat faster. Finding something Martin would push back on was sending little sparks up and down his veins.

"You practically accused me of censorship!" He laughed. "Over an agricultural manual."

Martin's cheeks flushed. For all he so obviously tried not to draw attention to himself, every thought and feeling he had were plain to see for anyone who bothered to look. Seb would have to show him how to lock that down.

"What you do isn't censorship. We could argue about it being disrespectful, though."

"Disrespectful?" Seb had heard that word a lot in his life. Almost every time he spoke to his dad, he was reminded how little respect he had for his father's achievements. But Philip had never cared for anything Seb had ever accomplished either, so they were basically even.

"Books are important." Martin's determination pushed itself a little further forward.

"You're such an academic." Seb couldn't help it. He'd heard it all before. The respect the written word required, the sanctity of the knowledge contained between covers. The same old bullshit.

It was the wrong thing to say now, though. The light in Martin's eyes faded, and he scraped his chair back to stand.

"Not anymore," he said. "Thanks for letting me hang out today. I should get going."

Seb went to protest. He hadn't meant anything by his remark. It was a reflex to old hurts more than anything Martin had said, but Martin slunk to the door and disappeared down the stairs without another word.

Too late for apologies.

Again.

7

*M*artin was waving goodbye to the mystery writers group when Penny bustled into the store, a broad smile on her face. Dread filled Martin. He'd managed to forget about his impending death-by-MC over the last few days.

"Good afternoon." Penny bubbled as she dropped a stack of papers on the counter. She fished around in a large satchel, digging for something buried deep inside. "I need some help. Mom wants me to take some measurements. She's worried about seating. Can you give me a hand?" She snapped the end of a tape measure just beneath his nose.

They moved around the space, holding opposite ends of the tape measure, and pausing while Penny made notes.

"So how are you doing? Enjoying Seacroft?" she asked.

"It's different. I'm used to the small community of the college where I used to work."

Penny's laugh shook dust from the closest shelves. "There's somewhere smaller than Seacroft?" Her smile dimmed as Martin tried to stammer an explanation. "Sorry. I've lived here my whole life. It always seemed so tiny when I was growing up. Nosey neighbors and everyone all up in everyone else's business.
"

"Everyone I've met so far is pretty nice." A few didn't even make his heart feel like it might leap out of his chest when they came into the store.

"Oh, they're nice. But I thought I'd move away when I grew up, start somewhere new and exciting. Then I met my husband, and the diner was always his dream. So I trusted that this was the right place for us, warts and all." She sighed happily, staring out the big front window, and Martin envied her.

Warts and all. Martin had nearly choked on his dinner when Seb made the joke about sleeping with students. Up until then, he'd been having a nice time, and Seb probably hadn't meant anything by it, but it was several heartbeats too close to the truth.

What would Seb have said if Martin trusted him enough to tell him the whole story, even the warts?

"That's a lot of faith to put in one person."

Penny give him a knowing look and tugged at one of her pink seashell earrings. "I'm not a religious person. But I do believe things happen for a reason. When Tim said he wanted to stay in Seacroft, I cried for a week straight. He was miserable too, so I don't want to make it sound like he forced me into anything. But I took a chance. He asked me to trust him, and I did. Not every day was a good one, but now, five years later, the diner is always busy, we've got two little boys, and I think it's going to be all right."

Martin gave her a smile. Letting someone have that much control felt impossible. "What would you have done if you'd realized you had to leave? Or if the diner hadn't worked out?"

She shrugged and gave his arm a pat. Penny couldn't be any older than he was, but the gesture was so maternal. No one had looked after Martin like that in years.

"Tim says we can't worry about what might happen, only what's in front of us, and he's right. If we'd worried about the future when we were starting out, we wouldn't have opened for business that first day. And if we make a mistake—and trust me, we've made lots—then the next day, we try again."

Something in his chest uncoiled. Try again. He felt like he had tried every option available to him in the last few months, but what had he actually done? He'd taken the job at Dog Ears because it was easiest and safest. He still hadn't talked to Brian about the scene with Jess. Things at the house were tense. Brian spent a lot of nights out, and Martin mostly avoided him when they were both home, instead choosing to eat by himself and go to bed early. He had nowhere else to go, but he wasn't doing much to make himself at home in Seacroft either. There were too many things he wasn't talking about.

The afternoon in the bookshop got quiet again. Martin used Seb's Wi-Fi to wander the internet and check the Mount Garner website. It was the same as always, with smiling students and promises of academic excellence. Nothing had changed. Martin was gone, and there was no outward sign that it made any difference.

"Goddammit!"

Seb's shout broke the silence, followed by heavy footsteps on the stairs. More crashes sounded as books fell from a shelf somewhere deep in the store.

Martin hurried to inspect. Just like the first time they'd met, Seb had his back to him, flinging books from the shelves like an angry blond apparition.

"Can I help you?" Martin asked.

Seb glared at him over his shoulder. "You could find me something that isn't going to break my heart."

Seb's heart seemed pretty well defended.

"Tough day?"

Seb bent, shuffling through the books at his feet until he found one toward the bottom and flung it at Martin. The pages fluttered. This time, Martin was prepared for the lightness when he caught it. He opened it to find a black-and-white photo of a man in a very small pair of swim trunks, carved out from the pages around him.

"Not your type?" Martin asked, which begged the obvious question of who Seb's type might be. Martin flushed. Whatever the answer, Seb's type was definitely not failed professors who could barely keep themselves on an even keel.

"Look farther back." Seb resumed pulling books off the top shelf and flipping through them before tossing them to the floor in disgust.

Martin did as he was told. Behind the man was a woman in what looked like a knitted cape and a pointy hat. Then after that a couple on a moped. "This is really cool."

Seb snorted. "Keep going."

One more flip, and Martin came to a woman wearing a ball gown. Her head was missing, and a slash through the paper made the edges flap as he turned the page.

"Oh."

"Fucking right, oh. I knew the paper was crap, but I thought it would be fun, and now look!" Seb tossed another book over his shoulder.

"Can't you just cut her out and keep going?"

"No. The narrative is ruined now." Seb kept pulling books out.

"Can I—Can I help you find what you're looking for?" Martin asked. After a few weeks, the bookstore's bizarre shelving system was actually starting to make sense.

"It's fine." Seb moved on from the shelf, leaving a trail of rejected books on the floor. His eyebrows were creased together in a frown, the lines around his mouth deep and tight. Clearly, he didn't want Martin's help.

But Martin had to start making a space for himself some-where, and he might as well begin by soothing his most idio-syncratic customer. He left Seb and turned the ancient coffee maker on. A few minutes later, he brought two mugs out, stepping carefully around the small mountain of books on the floor.

"Want some coffee?"

"Not now."

Martin hesitated for a second, then squared his shoulders. He extended a mug. "I made you some coffee."

Seb took it distractedly. Then his eyes narrowed as he saw the chaos behind them, and his shoulders sagged. "Shit. I'm being a dick again, aren't I?"

Martin shrugged. "You'll clean up the books later, right?"

Seb grinned at him. This close, the smile made Martin shiver. His grip tightened on the mug, but he held Seb's gaze. Trust. He had to trust someone, and Seb kept showing up, so why not him?

"How big a problem is it?" he asked. "The lady with the missing head?"

Seb sighed as he glanced at the discarded book on the floor. "It was coming together. There was a whole story there. A day on the Adriatic. A glamorous evening dancing."

"Sounds romantic."

Seb's eyes sparked with humor. "That was the idea. But then my hand slipped, and her head was gone and . . . " He sighed.

Martin struggled to think of the next thing to say. He needed to share some of his secrets, but it was terrifying, even in the quiet bookstore. So he stuck to small talk. "Were you working on it for something specific?"

"The Schiller exhibit. It's a show I have coming up. I need three more pieces. And I don't have time for mistakes." He took another sip of coffee, then lifted the mug gently toward Martin. "Thanks for this."

They stood in silence. Seb scanned the shelves. Occasionally, he'd pull one down and flip through it quickly, then put it back and move on to another one. Martin twitched, working up the nerve to speak again.

"I didn't sleep with my students. That's not why I lost my position."

Seb's shoulders tensed, and he gave Martin a guilty look.

"I'm not sure if you know this, but I'm not always a jerk. But I do seem to say the wrong thing around you a lot."

Martin wasn't sure how to respond, so he barreled on.

"The department chair was, though." His stomach rolled. He hadn't spoken about this with anyone. But it was eating him alive, and all the other not-talking at Brian's house compounded it.

"And?" Seb's blue eyes assessed him.

Martin's pulse pounded in response to old panic. He could say he didn't want to talk about it, that he'd only wanted Seb to know he hadn't behaved inappropriately, and leave it at that.

But Penny said if he screwed this up, he'd be able to try again tomorrow, so what was the worst possible outcome? He'd find himself alone in the bookstore, still sleeping on his brother's pull-out couch.

"I'd known about it for a while. Not for sure, but enough to have suspicions. Lots of 'office hours' at weird times. I didn't want to know, but—"

"Did he catch on and get you fired?"

"No. Nothing so Hollywood as that. He was sleeping with this student in his undergraduate lecture. She was nineteen, so there wasn't anything illegal, but it turned out she was just one in a long line of affairs. He'd been discreet in the past, but this time word got out. The administration tried to keep it quiet, but the student involved wasn't having it. The campus newspaper printed the story, and the whole school lost its mind." Cold sweat trickled down his spine as memories started to play like a highlight reel in his head. "The students demanded that the chair be reprimanded, but the school decided to go with the 'consenting adults' argument instead."

Seb shook his head and snarled. "Fucking old boys' club."

"Everything they did to resolve it made it worse. And then it turned out he wasn't the only one." The second week, when the school paper ran a story about a retired professor who had several relationships with students over the course of his career, saw the beginning of demonstrations on campus. First, they were small, but as the university continued to try to protect its reputation and handle the situation quietly, the dissatisfaction grew. The longer it went on, the bigger the crowds got. "The protestors started coming to classes. Any time someone from the history department had a lecture, they would be there." Martin took a sip of his coffee to calm his shaking hands.

"They protested at your classes? That doesn't seem fair. You didn't do anything wrong."

He hadn't, but, "At night, all cats are gray."

"What?"

"It's a saying. In German, it goes—"

Seb waved him off. "And the school didn't fire him? Any of them? That wouldn't have stopped it?"

"He was the chair. He brought in a lot of funding." Months later, more removed from the chaos, that reasoning was clearly backwards. But at the time, surrounded by angry voices, nothing was clear. "He even told the school paper that relationships like his happened at campuses all over the country. They probably do, but—"

"That's no excuse."

"Of course not." Getting to class had been like running a gauntlet. The students shouted accusations and insults, while the university kept asking for cooler heads to prevail and talking about decades of sterling academic excellence. "The administration dealt with it badly. They were more interested in protecting the staff and their reputation than they were in admitting anyone had been wrong." He shook his head. His knees were trembling. They were back where he had started this story.

"But they fired you and not the others?" Seb's eyes flashed.

"The chair was encouraged to take a long sabbatical." He was probably on a beach somewhere, working on his next book and flirting with the cabana attendants. "I—" Had Martin resigned? It still wasn't clear. "It got pretty bad. I'm sure you've noticed that I can be a bit—"

"Skittish?" Seb raised an eyebrow and Martin laughed. His laughter warmed over some of the tension that had formed in his neck and shoulders. He could tell this story to its end.

"I'm not a horse. I was going to say shy. Asserting myself has never been my strong suit." He'd tried. Mount Garner had been his home. When the university continued to sweep everything under the rug, Martin attempted to reason with his students. "They didn't like it when I explained the university's position. Not that I thought what happened was okay, but there was a lot of funding at stake." He'd been wrong, but at the time, his world was going to pieces, and no one seemed to be able to fix it.

"What happened?"

Martin shivered. "One of the students followed me home, and they started organizing protests outside my apartment building."

"But that's harassment!" Seb's declaration was so welcome. Martin had been waiting months to hear someone say it.

"Free speech. At least, according to the police. They were on public property and not posing a safety risk, so—"

"So what did you do?"

Shame clawed at the small spark of confidence that had flared to life. "At first, I tried to pretend like it was all normal, but I'd lie awake at night, picturing them outside my house and on campus while I tried to get to class. It felt like they were everywhere. Like their only purpose was to shine a giant spotlight on me and point out all my failings. I wasn't brave enough to bring forward my concerns about the chair. Wasn't strong enough to confront him myself. And then the voices in the dark pointed out the other things I wasn't. I wasn't prolific. I had a few

84

publications, and that was it. I wasn't a very good teacher. Too shy to really hold my students' interest." The list could go on for hours. He'd never been cut out for academia, not really, but he'd found his niche and stayed there because the idea of packing up and moving on to something new was even more terrifying than a lifetime of lectures to students only there for the credit hours.

"And then?" Seb's sad eyes said he got the point.

"And then one day I didn't get out of bed. Because why bother? No one wanted me on campus. Not the protesters. Not my students. No one from my department even noticed when I didn't show up. The administration still had its hands full." It was like he'd become invisible. Or like he'd never existed at all. He'd worked hard for his PhD and his place on the faculty, but in the end, his presence had signified nothing.

"How long were you like that?" Seb's voice was soft.

"Three weeks, give or take a few days." It was a bit vague. He hadn't exactly marked it into his calendar. *Stop interacting with the outside world, Monday, 8 a.m.*

Seb whistled. "That's a long time."

It was and it wasn't. Time hadn't meant the same thing then.

"Brian finally came when he hadn't heard from me." As they talked, they'd moved away from the pile of books out toward the open front area of the store. Martin sank onto one of the old leather couches by the window. Talking about this was good, but the telling was exhausting.

"Are you and your brother close?" Seb settled on the couch opposite him.

That was a complicated question. "He was the only one who was worried about me." In the time since he'd come to Seacroft, the time he'd spent recovering, talking to doctors and finding a way back to himself again, Martin hadn't heard from a single one of his colleagues at Mount Garner.

"And this—" Seb motioned at the store around them. "Working here is, what? Penance? Therapy?"

"Baby steps. The doctors and Brian and I, we agreed that I should take things slow. Stay somewhere familiar with a support system. Find jobs that were in my comfort zone. And Seacroft isn't exactly an employment hub so here I am." Also, if he stayed in academia, the stain of what happened would follow him everywhere. The scandal hadn't reached the public, but it was known in his small professional circles. Anyone who saw Mount Garner on his CV would ask questions, and Martin didn't want to face them.

"It's my fault," he sighed. "I should have told someone years ago, but I was afraid what it would—"

"Why should you do them any favors? I don't see that they've done anything for you."

"But maybe if I'd—"

"Shh." Seb leaned across the space to clasp Martin's shoulders. He squeezed him gently, and Martin blinked, shaking off the guilt starting to swallow him. "It wasn't your fault. They closed ranks, and you got left on the outside. You weren't the first, and you won't be the last. It's how the system works."

They gazed at each other. Seb's eyes were dark, his mouth set in a determined line. He looked ready for battle, but this time, he would be fighting on Martin's side.

Penny knew what she was talking about.

Martin took one of Seb's hands in his, feeling the strong warmth against his skin.

"Thanks," he said.

"Fuck 'em. They don't know what they lost. You can join the land of misfit toys with me and Cassidy. You'll like it here."

Cling together, swing together. It was the best offer Martin had heard in a while.

8

A week later, Martin was shelving a box of new books when he found something amazing. On the top shelf, above where he was working, was an old copy of *Alice in Wonderland*. The pages were yellowed, but between the chapters were fly pages: heavy paper with black-and-white illustrations.

Could Seb use this? Cutting it up still seemed like a shame, but Cassidy said nothing on the top shelves ever sold. Martin tucked it aside to take it up to Seb's once he was done shelving. Maybe they could have dinner. Martin had gotten paid so he could offer to treat Seb, in return for the Thai food the weekend before.

The front door groaned open.

"We're closing!" he called.

"Oh, that's okay," a man's voice replied. "I'm just passing through."

Martin popped his head out from behind the stacks. A tall African American man in horn-rimmed glasses and a bright plaid scarf smiled at him.

"Well, hello there." He carried an umbrella and pointed it in Martin's direction. "I don't remember you being here last time I came. And trust me, honey, I'd remember a sweet face like yours."

Martin fought a blush. "I don't think we've met."

"No, we have not."

If Seb's usual stride was a swagger, this man sashayed. It was like he'd walked right off the set of *Queer Eye* and into the bookstore.

"Kenneth P. Morgenstern. And you are?"

"Martin." He shook Kenneth's hand. His skin was smooth and warm. "Martin Lindsey."

"Pleasure. Where have you been hiding?"

Martin didn't understand the question. "I was in the stacks?"

"Kenny?" Seb stood at the end of the aisle, pale skin glowing in the shadows. His face was bright with a wide smile, aimed at the new arrival.

"Sebastian." Kenneth put an arm over Martin's shoulder and walked them both toward Seb. "You didn't tell me I had a new reason to visit you out here in the backwater. I was just meeting Martin, and he is delightful."

"You're scaring him, Kenny." Seb's voice was serious, but his smile was growing. "Let him go."

Kenneth's lips pressed into a pout. "I'm not scary. Am I, Martin?"

"Well, I'm not—"

Kenneth released him and clasped Seb in a big hug.

"Asshole." Seb laughed.

"Back at you." They clapped each other on the back. "Introduce me properly to your friend."

Both men turned. Seb beamed at Martin, while Kenneth cocked his head to one side.

"Martin, this is Kenny," Seb said.

"Kenneth," Kenneth corrected.

"Kenny," Seb said firmly.

Martin grimaced as old feelings of invisibility tried to swallow him. "Nice to meet you."

Seb patted Kenneth's chest. "Kenny and I met in college, and now he's my agent. He's also a flirt and a manwhore, so don't believe a word he says."

"Except the part about your sweet face." Kenneth winked. "You can believe that."

"I should get back to work." Martin ignored the flash of hurt along his sternum as Seb led Kenneth away, their laughter trailing behind them, leaving Martin alone in the store.

———

"What are you doing here?" Seb asked. Kenneth threw a small overnight bag on the couch.

"Happy to see me?"

"That depends on why you've appeared in my town with no warning."

Kenneth almost never came to Seacroft, preferring to have their meetings over the phone or Skype, or coercing Seb to come up to Raleigh to talk about something really important. Everything about Kenneth was urban and stylish, so nothing about Seacroft fit him.

Kenneth flipped through a book on Seb's table, one of the ones he'd found the week before with Martin. It was another pictorial history, a chronicle of the parties and extravagances of the last century's Hollywood golden age.

"Oh, I like this," Kenneth said as he turned the pages.

"Thanks. But, Kenny, what are you doing here?"

"Tell me more about that little darling downstairs. He's cute. A bit twitchy, but I can help him with that."

"He's not on the market."

"Honey, you've been in White Bread Land too long if you think that boy is straight."

"He's not straight."

"Perfect!"

"Kenny." Seb clenched his jaw to force the words out slowly. "What. Are. You. Doing. Here?"

Kenneth flopped down on the couch and sighed. "Anton left."

"Who?"

"I told you about him."

"No, you didn't." Not that he could recall, but it didn't matter, Seb had his answer. Kenneth's latest boy toy had split, and he was bored.

"Sure I did. Greek. Tattoos. Super flexible?"

"You should have called first. You know I'm working. And I botched a piece last week so I had to start over. Now's really not a good time." Seb moved a stack of books off one of the chairs around his work table so he could sit down.

"Are you behind?" Kenneth lifted his head off the back of the couch. "How far?" Leave it to Kenneth to switch from personal angst to business in an instant at the first indication of something going off track. With him, business came first. Flexible, tattooed man candy was second.

"It's fine. If I work through the weekend," he leaned on the last word, trying to get Kenneth to take the hint, "and put in a couple more late nights next week, I'll be mostly back on schedule."

"Fine. You always say fine. That's the other reason I'm here. I'm not sure you know what fine is. Let me see what you've got."

Seb pulled the pieces for the Schiller exhibit off the shelf, laying them out on the table for Kenneth's inspection.

"I'm going to try to get you a reading at the opening," Kenneth said.

"What? Why?"

No one had paid much attention to his earlier found poetry works in a while. The pictorial pieces were more accessible and gave Seb a greater variety of material to work from. Despite what Martin might say about a writer's words being sacred, Seb had always seen it as making something of his own. Drawing inspiration from what was around him. No different than painting sunsets or drawing the faces of the people who came into the bookstore. Martin seemed to be coming around to the idea though. Maybe if Seb read one of the carved works to him he'd understand. He might like poetry. His thesis had been about a poet, so that had to be a good sign, right?

"Hello?" Kenneth's hand waved across Seb's vision, making him blink.

"Sorry. You were saying?"

"I was saying it's time to up your profile. Stop letting people observe your work passively and start having you actively show its depth."

He'd created the poems so early in his career. He'd liked the challenge of making the words fit together. Back then, on the rare occasion there had even been a formal opening for a show, he'd only ever been asked to say a few words over a glass of wine before patrons went back to mingling.

Standing in a gallery, reading from one of the carved poems to an audience, would be a different experience. Kenneth would stand at the front of the group, looking smug. Martin would be there too, and Seb would have to protect him when Kenneth—

"Hey!" Kenneth's voice snapped him back to reality again. "Where the hell do you keep going?"

"Sorry. Sure. Reading. Set it up. What's the worst that can happen?"

"You'll crash and burn and become the laughing stock of the North Carolina art community?"

Sebastian snorted. Kenneth was his biggest cheerleader, but also kept him firmly tethered to reality at all times.

"So tell me more about the shy boy downstairs." Kenneth tucked one leg underneath him where he sat.

"Nope. We're not going there. You're like a dog with a bone."

"You said he's single. Why wouldn't I? Unless you're already—"

"No." A few days had passed since Martin confided his whole story to Seb, and it had stuck with him. He regretted even more giving Martin a hard time about his career, when Martin was doing everything he could to claw back to some semblance of functionality.

"So you're not interested in him?" Kenneth grinned.

Was Seb interested? It was complicated. Martin, with his soft eyes and crooked smile, was cutely uneven. But beyond any attraction was a different kind of desire. Seb was in no position to be anyone's lifeline, but he wanted to help Martin get back to himself.

"It's not like that. He's just—He's had a hard time of it lately. He doesn't need you screwing around with him."

"Sounds like it might be exactly what he needs." Kenneth's grin turned lascivious.

"I said no, all right?" Seb's jaw tightened. Kenneth could never be what Martin needed. He was too selfish. Too flighty. "This is my town and my people, including Martin. You can't waltz in here unannounced for a weekend and start looking for fuck buddies just because the pool in the city is getting shallow. You're the one who drained it."

Kenneth turned to stare up the ceiling with a weary sigh. "You used to be more fun than this. You need to get out of here more often."

Seb ran a hand through his hair. He didn't mean to lecture, but the idea of Kenneth flirting with and possibly fooling around with Martin made him feel unexpectedly protective. "Sorry. I'm tired. I haven't been sleeping much."

Kenneth rose to his feet and pressed his hands to Seb's cheeks, squeezing them until his lips puckered out. "I understand. You just leave it all to Uncle Kenneth. Now take me out for dinner. Is there anywhere in this town with a menu that isn't eighty percent deep fried?"

———

Martin liked Saturdays best. The groups kept the store busy, and Cassidy worked the whole day with him.

She'd brought him her application packages for art school, though, which was proving challenging. Most of the schools had a general personal statement requirement, and many of the art programs wanted a separate artist's statement about the vision she had for her work.

"I don't know what to say." She stared down at the blinking cursor on her laptop. "I can't just tell them I want to go to art school because it's the only thing I'm good at."

"Not the only thing," Martin said.

"Just about." She sounded defeated, and they'd barely started.

"That's not true. You're a big help around here, and I know the Mommy and Me group really appreciates the books you pick out for them every week." While the chaos of so many preschoolers still made Martin flinch, Cassidy seemed to revel in it.

"Yeah, but that's not a skill. I'm only good at drawing and picking out kids' books. I can't say that in an essay."

"People of Seacroft! Good morning!"

Seb and Kenneth emerged from the shelves. Kenneth's scarf and umbrella were gone. Instead, he wore a houndstooth sweater and slim fitting pants. Seb walked half a step behind him in his usual jeans and leather jacket, eyes twinkling with amusement as his friend strode through the store.

"Dr. Lindsey!" Kenneth said as he approached the cash register. "It's nice to see you again today."

Despite his earlier good mood, tension clenched at Martin's insides. The use of his formal title meant Seb had told Kenneth more about him, and the knowledge that he'd been the topic of conversation twisted in his guts.

"Hi," he mumbled, shooting a glance at Seb, whose face was bland.

"And who are you?" Kenneth's attention was already on Cassidy. "Your skin, your hair, my dear, you look like a doll. It's a shame Sebastian isn't a painter, because you should be someone's muse."

Cassidy twisted one curl around her finger and blushed down at her keyboard. Martin wanted to put an arm around her shoulder, but worried the gesture would draw Kenneth's attention back to him.

It didn't seem to matter, though, because Kenneth beamed at both of them as he did up the buttons of his wool coat.

"Sebastian and I are going off in search of brunch. We had a late night and need some sustenance. He is a gifted artist and a terrible cook. Would you like to join us?"

Surprisingly, the part Martin's brain latched onto was the mention of a late night. Doing what? Was Kenneth Seb's boyfriend? Seb had never mentioned anything about being with someone, but maybe he kept personal things to himself.

"They're working." Seb's voice was patient amusement, like he was explaining foreign concepts to a small child.

Kenneth pouted. "Surely the illustrious Dr. Lindsey could join us? You don't mind if we borrow him, do you?" This last question was directed toward Cassidy.

"Oh. No. I couldn't—" Martin started, but Cassidy shook her head.

"Why don't you go? It'll be quiet here until the knitters are done, and I can try to come up with some ideas for my essay."

"See?" Kenneth spread his hands and smiled. "No problem. I don't get down here often. It's good to acquaint myself with the people in Seb's life."

Martin frowned over Kenneth's shoulder again, but Seb

didn't return the look. Martin was in Seb's life? He was still smarting over the "illustrious" comment, and now he found he really did want to know what Seb said about him. Kenneth's smug face grated on Martin in every way, but he didn't like the idea of leaving the two of them alone knowing he was a topic of conversation.

"Sure." He forced a smile. "I'll go with you. Just let me get my coat."

———

The brunch options in Seacroft were limited. Martin suggested Penny's diner, but Seb led them down the street to a small pub. Kenneth looked dubious, which made Martin push ahead of him while Seb assured them the food would be good.

"They do a real English breakfast. The mushrooms are amazing," Seb said as they sat in a booth toward the back. He looked at once sophisticated and shabby in his torn jeans and worn jacket, while his hair seemed to have an extra shine. Kenneth sat next to Seb, leaving them to face Martin, who had to look like a wreck. It was laundry day at home, which of course meant he'd gone to get clean clothes out of the dryer only to find them still in a wet ball at the bottom of the washer while Brian gave him a sheepish apology. Martin had been forced to pull out an ancient henley from a box of stuff he'd brought back from Mount Garner. The shirt was faded at the seams, and he'd only noticed the small hole under one armpit once he'd gotten to work. Compared to Kenneth and Seb's style, Martin felt like the poor cousin they'd just picked up from the bus station.

Seb and Kenneth struck up a lively conversation, something about a brunch they had been to.

"Do you remember the waiter there?" Kenneth asked.

Seb groaned as he took a sip of his coffee. "So pretty. The one with the tattoos! What was his name?"

"Lewis?" Kenneth waggled his eyebrows.

"No, not Lewis. Lucas maybe?" They both frowned, and then Seb's expression cleared. He snapped his fingers, and Kenneth's face lit with a smile.

"Levi!" They both said, then dissolved into laughter.

Martin sat across from them, hands folded in his lap, unease turning in his stomach as their conversation continued without him.

They ordered quickly: the full breakfast for Seb, an omelet for Kenneth, and yogurt and granola for Martin.

"Watching your weight?" Kenneth asked from under his eyebrows as the server left.

Martin bristled. Who was this guy to judge? They didn't even know each other. "It never hurts to be health conscious." Truthfully, the current of nervousness thrumming in Martin's veins was killing his appetite.

"Keep it up." Kenneth grinned. "It's obviously working well for you."

Martin frowned, but the comment made Seb laugh.

"Kenny's mostly harmless. He tends to go for quantity over quality in his conversations."

Martin gave them both a tight smile, trying to get his footing. This man was Seb's friend, and Seb was, he hoped, Martin's friend, so he should at least try.

"Seb says you're his agent?"

"Among other things. Sebastian's endeavors only keep me so busy. I represent a few other creative individuals in the region, and dabble in real estate on the side."

"Kenny flips houses."

"Not me, personally." Kenneth put a hand to his throat. "I've never been handy. But I know a good investment when I see one, and a crew of strong men with tools is always fun to have around, don't you think?"

Seb laughed. The history between them was obvious. The

extent of their togetherness wasn't clear, but their schtick was born of years of familiarity. Martin tried to ignore the growing feeling of being the third wheel.

"How long have you known each other?" he asked.

Kenneth smirked again and glanced at Seb. "Too long. We were in college together until Seb dropped out. He was the best wingman a guy could ask for, though, so I felt I should return the favor and keep his artistic ass out of debt and obscurity once I graduated."

"You dropped out of college?" Martin asked.

Seb squinted at him, then at Kenneth, but he shrugged. "They weren't teaching me anything I didn't already know."

"A man of the people, our Sebastian." Kenneth smiled. "Who needs a diploma from the elitist college system when you can scrape together a living using a utility knife and glue?"

"I don't hear you complaining when your commission check rolls in."

Kenneth inclined his head. "And what about yourself?" he asked Martin. "Sebastian says you're illuminating the world on the works of lost poets and gay icons."

Martin gripped his mug a little tighter. They *had* talked about him. Seb had told Kenneth about his research. Fear pinged in his chest over what else Seb might have said.

"I wouldn't go that far," Martin said. "Bergmann was a man who stood up for what he believed in while facing incredible evil. He wasn't trying to be an icon."

"Real icons never are." Kenneth quirked an eyebrow.

"You said he was an activist, though?" Seb sounded interested, whereas Kenneth sounded like he was looking for an opportunity to make a joke. Martin focused his attention on Seb and was rewarded with a smile that made his heart skip.

"Bergmann was part of a group of poets and artists who met regularly and produced work with queer themes. Most people don't know that Germany was pretty socially liberal in the years between the wars. Bergmann lived with another man, Oscar Strauss, and it's thought that they were lovers."

Kenneth opened his mouth to speak, but Seb jumped in first. "You said they only found out about Bergmann's works in the last thirty years or so?"

Martin nodded. He admired Bergmann's story and enjoyed telling it, despite the tragedy of its ending.

"There were a few poems known beforehand that have been attributed to him in the last decade, but until they found the box of his drafts, there just wasn't enough evidence to prove that they had all been written by one poet. Strauss fled to Belgium as the political climate changed, but Bergmann stayed. In his letters to Strauss, he talks about how the Nazis were looking for collaborators, members of their inner circle who would turn on the others in return for protection. As far as we can tell, Bergmann refused, and they shipped him to a concentration camp."

"Tragic," Kenneth said. "So, Dr. Lindsey. What brings you from the ivory towers to this charming little backwater? Sebastian says it must be witness protection, but I think it has to be something more nefarious."

Martin's next breath got caught in his throat. Even Seb's smile tightened in the corners.

"Kenny, come on." Seb nudged him gently in the ribs. "That's not what I said."

"What *did* you say?" The happy little buzz under Martin's skin at the chance to talk about his work died.

Seb was looking downright uncomfortable now. "Nothing. I told him a bit about your research, and that you worked at Mount Garner. That's all."

The server appeared with their food, announcing each dish cheerily, while Martin glared across the table.

"Sebastian's father has a long association with the academic world, did he tell you that?" Kenneth asked as he cut into his omelet.

Martin poked at his yogurt. "He said he used to teach."

"Used to teach? You make it sound like he led story time and gym class." Kenneth laughed. "Philip Stevenson was a giant in his field, wasn't he?"

Seb grunted.

"Your father is Philip Stevenson?" Cold rushed through Martin. If Seb told Kenneth about Mount Garner, had he told other people? His family?

Seb glanced up from his breakfast with flat eyes. "You've heard of him, I suppose."

"He was the AHI Chair on European Literature. Of course I know who he is."

"I'm surprised you've never crossed paths," Kenneth said.

They had. Sort of. Martin had gone to enough conferences in his career to have seen Philip Stevenson a few times. To say their paths crossed was generous. It was more like playing six degrees of Kevin Bacon, the university edition. Martin stuck close to his supervisors and immediate colleagues, while Philip Stevenson glided through the room on a cloud of impressive dignity and publication credits.

"You didn't tell me." Martin said again. He picked at his yogurt, but the flavor was sour.

"I know!" Kenneth's eyes went wide. "You can't stay locked away in witness protection forever. Sebastian, you should introduce Dr. Lindsey here to your father!"

9

Kenneth was the worst kind of shit disturber, and Seb was going to kill him as soon as he came up with somewhere convenient to hide the body. He'd been caught up in the banter that he and Kenneth had developed over years and had stumbled blindly right into trouble as Kenneth led the conversation to Seb's father.

Kenneth leered at him, like he was still waiting for the "Who's there?" to a terrible knock-knock joke. Martin's face was clouded with a mix of hurt and anger that Seb didn't understand.

"What time are you heading back to the city?" he asked Kenneth.

Kenneth frowned. "It's only Saturday. I thought I might—"

"I have to get some work done. Big show coming up, remember? Can't tell the Schiller people that I'm late on the delivery because my agent distracted me, can I?"

Kenneth's lips thinned. "Of course not."

The rest of their meal was awkward. Martin spoke when spoken to, and Kenneth's teasing turned half-hearted, which left Seb with the task of trying to keep conversation going. Mostly, they ate in silence. Seb snuck glances at Martin and tried to understand what part had upset him so much. Was he angry that Seb hadn't told him who his father was?

Back at the bookstore, Seb hustled Kenneth up to the apartment before he had the chance to say anything else to Martin.

"I don't know what game you came up here to play, but you can be a real asshole sometimes, you know that, right?"

"Of course!" Kenneth's smile was unrepentant. "Although in fairness, I didn't come up here with a game plan. I wanted to check in on you. But then I saw that beautiful man downstairs, and—"

"You can't fuck with him like that! There was no reason for you to be such an ass!"

"I beg to differ." Kenneth collected his overnight bag and stuffed his scarf into it. "Watching the way you lurched to protect him at every opportunity has been all the payoff I need."

"What?" Confusion blended with Seb's irritation.

"You're such a sucker for outcasts and lost causes. How could you not be attracted to him?"

"I'm not!" He sounded petulant, even to his own ears.

"Of course you aren't, honey." Kenneth rested a palm on his cheek. "It's understandable. Those hangdog eyes follow you everywhere. It has to be good for your already considerable ego. And he has an amazing ass. You've noticed, right? Good thing he's so calorie conscious."

Seb ground his teeth and tried not picture Martin's ass. "Please call the next time you want to make the trip out here, okay? I'll make sure to be out of town."

Kenneth snorted as he zipped his bag shut.

"I think twenty-four hours in this tourist trap will last me for at least a decade." He reached out and pulled Seb into a quick hug. Seb held himself stiff for a second before he relaxed enough to pat Kenneth's shoulder. Seb knew exactly who his friend was. Kenneth would always have his back, even if it was to stick the occasional knife into it.

———

Seb waited until just before six o'clock to go back down to the shop. Martin and Cass were huddled around her laptop.

"It's still stupid." She slumped back in her seat.

Martin glanced over the top of the laptop screen to meet Seb's eyes, but as Seb went to wave a silent greeting, Martin quickly looked away again. He squinted and chewed on his lower lip.

"What's the first piece of art you remember making that you were really proud of?" he asked. Cass shrugged, and Martin's face went pinched. "Okay, go home and ask your parents what they remember."

Cass snorted. "They're going to say something stupid like the time I thought I'd fingerprinted a whole galaxy on craft paper."

Seb smiled. He'd had some of those. He'd shown them proudly to his grandmother, so enthralled with the way the colors swirled and splattered together. The whole universe on a piece of smooth white paper.

"Ask them." Martin put his hands on his hips and snuck another look at Seb. "Make a list. I have an idea, but you need the list first."

"Okay." Cass shrugged into her coat and slipped the backpack over her shoulders. "I'll see you later." She let herself out. Martin followed her and locked the door with a click. When he turned, his gaze was on his shoes, and he made as if to walk past Seb, so Seb reached out and caught him by the wrist.

"Kenneth went back to the city."

"I saw that. He blew me a kiss as he walked out."

Seb smothered a laugh. Even after he'd told Kenneth not to be an ass, he couldn't help himself.

"I'm sorry if he—He was a jerk at lunch. I'm sorry about that."

"You're sorry?" Martin pushed his chin forward. "I didn't tell you everything that happened before I left my job so you could turn around and tell your friends. I'd hoped I could trust you more than that."

"I didn't—I mean you can—" Seb floundered, while Martin's eyes flashed with anger.

"He knew an awful lot about me." His voice was low. "Where I worked, what I studied. I guess he got all that from you."

Seb pursed his lips. "I only gave him the basics."

"Witness protection?"

Okay. Maybe a little more than the basics.

"Did you tell him why I lost my job, or did you let him assume I was sleeping with my students like you did?"

Seb's pulse picked up at the hurt on Martin's face. The witness protection joke seemed harmless enough in his apartment, but Martin was clearly upset. "I just said you'd left. But I'm sorry." He meant it. "I wasn't thinking."

Martin crossed his arms over his chest. Instead of his usual plaid shirts, today he wore a dark henley. It stretched tight over his shoulders, proving once and for all there was some muscle on his lean frame. The worst part was Kenneth might be right. Seb seemed incapable of ever saying the correct thing around Martin, but, mixed up in his desire to take care of him, Seb also felt more than a passing attraction to the nervous professor.

"Is your father really Philip Stevenson?" Martin asked, and Seb's musings cut off abruptly.

"Unfortunately."

"Unfortunately? He must be—"

"A pompous jerk who is only interested in spending time with the people he deems worthy of his interest and presence? Basically, yes. I haven't made the cut for years."

Martin frowned, probably as he tried to reconcile the

legendary Dr. Stevenson and his entourage of tweedy admirers with Seb's words.

"It's fine." He clapped Martin's shoulder, relieved when Martin didn't move away or brush him off. Maybe he'd earn some forgiveness after all. "He'd like you. He just doesn't like me."

"I saw him speak at a conference. He talked about representations of nature in post-World War II Italian literature. I thought it was interesting."

"No doubt. How long ago was that?"

"About three years ago?"

"Then you've seen him more recently than I have. I haven't spoken to or seen my parents in over four years."

"Why not?"

Seb sighed, brushing his hand down Martin's shoulder. "We had a difference of opinion. About everything."

"That must have been hard." Martin's eyes, dark with his anger a minute earlier, went soft, and Seb had to focus to keep himself from bristling. He didn't want Martin's pity, but he would take Martin's forgiveness.

"I'm sorry. About Kenneth."

"It's fine." Martin shrugged and went back to the cash register. Seb followed after him, because it wasn't fine.

And also, now he was thinking about it—*thanks again, Kenny*—with Martin walking in front of him, the professor really might have a nice ass. His baggy khakis made it hard to be sure, but there was just enough shape to catch Seb's attention. His pulse fluttered as Martin bent behind the counter—and, yes, most definitely, definition appeared under the fabric as the pants shifted and stretched tight with his movement.

Martin stood up again, and Seb had to clear his throat and tug at the collar of his T-shirt to collect himself. Now was not the time to be propositioning the professor, as much fun as it sounded.

"I found something." Martin held out a cream-colored book.

"*Alice in Wonderland*?" Seb's eyes went wide. He'd had the same edition as a kid.

Martin's smile was shy, like always, but now it felt like a temptation.

Martin didn't need that from him.

Seb shook himself and accepted the book.

"I found it on the top shelf," Martin said. "That means it's fair game, right?"

"Fair game?" Seb flipped through the pages.

"For you to do something with?"

"You'd be okay with that?" Seb raised an eyebrow. The single action made Martin flush, which in turn made Seb's mouth go dry. Now that Kenneth had awoken the idea in Seb's brain, it was stuck there.

It got worse when Martin said, "I don't think Lewis Carroll was big on dick jokes. So you'll have to behave yourself."

Seb muttered a hasty thanks and fled before he did anything else requiring another apology in the morning.

———

Cassidy didn't work at the store on Monday, but she appeared at quarter to six with a box. She hefted it onto the counter, and something inside rattled.

"This is your fault." She scowled. "I asked my mom about my old art projects like you told me to, and she took me to the attic and showed me this."

Martin lifted the lid, pulling out the bottom half of an egg carton. Fuzzy green pipe cleaners, bent at odd angles, stuck out from one end.

"Caterpillar?" He held it up to inspect it.

Cassidy moaned and bumped her head off the counter a few times. "No college wants to hear about my preschool crafts."

"Now hang on." Martin pulled a few more things out. A ceramic disk with a tiny hand print pressed into the center had the word "Cassidy" scrawled in messy block letters on the bottom. A construction paper silhouette of a child's head. Little Cassidy's curls had obviously been a challenge for whoever had traced it out because the result was an irregular shaped blob with the tip of a nose on one side. Cassidy moaned again when he held it up. He laughed and dug through more, pulling out a square canvas stretched over a frame. Cassidy's eyes widened when she saw it.

"My mom kept that?" Her finger traced the edge of the canvas. In the center was a painted red rose with a twisted black stem.

"What is it?"

"They sent me to summer camp when I was eleven. I hated it. I suck at sports and the food was so bad. But there was an art class in the afternoons. Everyone else wanted to go swimming, so there were like six of us at the class." She smiled. "I worked every day for two weeks on this. I was so proud when I came home. I wanted my mom to frame it and put it up where everyone could see."

"And did she?"

"No." Cassidy's mouth twisted. "It's okay, though. It sucks. I can see that now."

The painting wasn't a masterpiece, but it was better than anything Martin could do.

"I think it's pretty good."

"No." She ran a finger around the outside curve of the rose. "The shadows are all wrong. See here? The light's coming from a different place than it is on the rest of the flower. I didn't know much then."

"But you were proud of it?"

"Well, yeah." Despite the fact that she was disparaging the

work now, Cassidy rushed to defend her younger self. "I worked hard on it."

"And you wanted other people to see it."

"I guess." She shrugged, but Martin persisted.

"You made something that you wanted other people to see and appreciate. You wanted them to see you and what you could do."

"They taught us about mixing colors. It was really the first time I'd ever heard of color theory. It's a red rose, but there's so much blue here, see?" She pointed at the base of the rose. "And yellow up near the top, where the light is coming from a different angle. It was so cool. I'd never been very good in school, but I got colors. I wanted my mom to hang it up so I could tell other people about it and prove that I didn't suck at everything."

Martin watched her as she gazed at the painting. Compared to the depth and feeling her drawings upstairs conveyed, this was much more rudimentary—a single red rose on a white canvas—but the way Cassidy looked at it, he could feel the whole story.

"We just found a topic for your essay."

"This?"

"I think so." Martin smiled, excitement growing inside him. If he knew about any topic, it was being seen and having your work recognized for its inherent value, even years after the fact. He could help Cassidy with this.

Cassidy frowned at the painting. "But I'm supposed to tell them about how good I am. No one would accept me based on this painting."

Martin shook his head. "You've got the portfolio to show them that. The essay is about who you are, what your work ethic is like, and why you're passionate about what you do. Try to explain how you felt when you were painting this, and why it was so important to you that people see it. Talk about how creating things makes you feel. I bet you they'll like it."

A slow grin spread on her face. "Do you think so?"

"You don't have to pretend to be anything you're not," he said. "They'll see how much your skill has grown. Everyone has to start somewhere. Tell them how you felt when you found something you knew you could be good at."

Cassidy's smile grew the whole time he spoke. She pulled her backpack off her shoulders and rummaged through it until she pulled out a laptop.

"Can I work here a bit? I can start and you can tell if you think it's good?"

Martin checked his watch. His shift would be over in just a few minutes, but it wasn't as if he had any other plans.

"Sure."

Cassidy took the flower painting and the laptop to one of the couches and hunched over, tongue peeking out between her lips as she booted up the screen. Martin watched, feeling a little thrill that she'd liked his suggestion.

He locked up the shop and went to the back to throw out the last of a pot of coffee he'd made earlier. He wasn't sure how late Cassidy would stay, so he wandered the shelves, looking for something new to read.

"Hey." Seb's voice behind him was so unexpected that Martin yipped. He turned to find Seb with his hands in his pockets and a sly grin on his face.

Martin returned the smile. "You're going to have to show me how you pop out of nowhere like that," he said, as his racing heart slowed. "The first time I saw you back here I thought you were a ghost."

Seb's teeth flashed as his smile spread. He ran a hand through his hair, making it stick out at odd angles. The motion exposed the soft skin under his arm, just below the sleeve of his faded T-shirt. There was a freckle halfway to his elbow.

"Are you closing up?" he asked.

"Just locked the door."

"What are you doing tonight?"

Martin paused his contemplation of that freckle. "Tonight?"

"Yeah. Or now, rather? The store's closed. Sun's going down, so it's night, or evening at least. What are you doing now?"

The base of Seb's neck started to go pink. The slow blush made Martin's ears warm and his breath speed up.

"I was going to read a book." He pulled a book at random off the closest shelf. When Seb laughed gently, Martin checked the title. *The PMS Diet*. He fumbled the book and slid it back in its place.

"Want to go out for dinner?"

Martin blinked. "Dinner?"

"Yeah." Seb rubbed the back of his neck, and Martin suppressed a shiver. "Out. Not just takeout. I owe you a better experience than that godawful brunch with Kenneth last weekend and—"

"Oh." Martin's heart sank. "I can't. Not tonight. Cassidy's here. She's working on her essay, and I think we're getting somewhere with it, so I said she could stay."

"Oh." Seb's smile went tight. "That's good. Maybe tomorrow then?"

Something wasn't being said. Asking if Seb's dinner invitation was more than friendly was stupid, and anyway—"I can't tomorrow either. I'm meeting Penny."

"Penny?" Seb's pale brows knitted together.

"She's helping to plan the blues festival?" When Seb's expression didn't clear, Martin explained. "They're hosting an event here. I'm the MC. I still think that's a terrible idea, but they won't let me back out. Penny's coming by to help me practice my speech. I thought you knew about the event, though. You're going to come, right?"

"Wouldn't miss it." Seb laughed, but Martin wasn't sure what was funny. "Don't worry about dinner. I'll catch you some other time." He turned on his heel and walked away, leaving Martin to wonder what had just happened. He'd said the wrong thing somewhere, and he wasn't totally sure how or what.

He was pretty sure, though, that Seb had tried to ask him out on a date.

10

*S*eb stayed up all night the following night working on a new project. The *Alice in Wonderland* Martin found was the perfect final piece—especially the illustrations—for his Schiller submission. He pulled each out carefully and set them aside.

When he was small, his grandmother had taken him to see a stage production of *Alice*. He'd been so enthralled that, afterwards, he'd demanded she read it to him. He'd never been much of a reader, but each of Alice's encounters conjured up images of the play, and so he'd endured the words. The illustrations were a magical reprieve. He'd made his grandmother pause while he'd inspected each one carefully.

The painstaking work of building his new piece provided a distraction from the mortifying memory of stumbling through an attempt to ask Martin on a date, and then getting obliviously shot down because he'd been too scared to actually say what he'd meant. He didn't know how to be around Martin. He didn't want to frighten him when, if he were anyone else, Seb would have pushed him up against a wall and kissed him. So he'd tried a softer approach, which backfired spectacularly. And Martin had shot him down to help Cassidy with the essay she didn't need to write, and then so he could plan do-good community events.

Seb fell into an exhausted sleep a little after the sun came up.

He woke up again after noon, stomach growling. Since Martin hadn't picked up on what he was asking, Seb had forgone dinner in favor of sulking in his apartment, so he hadn't eaten in more than twenty-four hours. He slunk out of bed and took a quick shower before making his way downstairs to forage.

Unfamiliar voices echoed in the bookstore.

"So we're going to put a bar here."

"Won't that create a bottleneck with people coming in?"

Seb came around the corner of the last shelf to find Martin holding crystal. Seb also recognized Penny from the diner next door, and he'd seen the older woman around town. She had an arm over Martin's shoulders. The familiar gesture made unexpected jealousy tighten in Seb's gut.

"So we'll put it over there." Penny's eyes widened as she spotted Seb. "Where did you come from?"

"He does that." Martin gave him a soft smile that made little pins and needles prick along his scalp, and his earlier jealousy blew away like smoke on a breeze. "Seb, this is Penny and her mother, Carol Anne."

"Well, since you're here." Carol Anne came across the room to slip a hand under Seb's elbow and tow him back toward Martin. Not that Seb needed much encouragement on that front. "Help move this table so we can see if putting the bar over there is going to be a problem. Martin, take the other end."

Martin put the vase down on the counter by the door and hurried to obey. It was all a bit silly. There was no reason Seb couldn't lift the table by himself, except that with help, he was able to move it without disturbing the pyramid of books stacked on it. As they set the table down, Martin's gray eyes locked with Seb's.

"Penny, honey. Go pretend you're standing in line."

Penny cleared her throat as she came to stand in front of them. The sound made Martin blink, and Seb shivered as their connection dissolved. Apparently, his awkward prom date routine from the night before was not enough to deter his interest.

"Yes, hello." Did Penny curtsy? Her curly hair bobbed as she did it. "I'm parched. Do either of you know how to make a gin fizz? Or what about a Tom Collins? How about a Moscow Mule?"

The shop's front door swung open, and the doorknob caught Seb at the bottom of his spine. He grunted as he was pushed forward. The table rattled, and the books collapsed in a heap.

"Hello? What's going on?"

Mrs. Green stood in the doorway with her arms crossed. Her pink lips were pressed into an angry line as she eyed Carol Anne.

"Hello, Diana!" Carol Anne didn't look the least bit ruffled by Mrs. Green's death glare. "We're just making the final plans for the blues night."

"Blues night?" Mrs. Green's thinly plucked eyebrows arched, and the sparkling periwinkle butterfly clipped to her hair fluttered ominously. "What blues night?"

"We discussed this. The school's jazz trio is going to play."

"In the bookstore?"

Carol Anne's confident smile faltered. "Yes. It's a ticketed event. We've almost sold out."

"I don't remember anything about it." Mrs. Green waved a hand in dismissal. "All community events in the shop need to be approved by me, and I do not remember approving anything like this."

"Maybe if you ever bothered to read any of the emails I sent—"

"I never saw any emails."

Carol Anne's face flushed. Seb glanced at Martin, who returned his gaze nervously.

"It's been planned for months," Penny said, coming to stand by her mother. "We've been by a few times. Martin has been a huge help."

Mrs. Green's gaze swung around to Martin, and he blanched.

"You agreed to this?" she said.

"I thought—"

"You do not have the authority to make those decisions. You are my employee." Her eyes narrowed further, turning mean. Martin swallowed, and Seb's heart started to pound a warning. He'd seen that look on Martin's face too many times. More often than not, Seb caused it, but here he could help instead.

"Mrs. Green." He stepped in front of her. She blinked, like she hadn't even seen him until that moment.

"Oh. Hello, Sebastian."

He smiled at her, the way he knew she liked. "The idea of a blues night is elegant, don't you think? We were just discussing where to put the bar. It's going to be quite the event."

"That may be." She tapped one well-manicured hand on the back of the other. "But the fact is that I was not consulted when these plans were made. The bookstore is mine, and while I'm happy to let community groups use the space—"

Behind him, Carol Anne made an exasperated noise, and Penny cleared her throat. Seb didn't acknowledge them. His landlady was idiosyncratic. Despite her dusty, cavernous bookstore, she liked shiny things which gave her a certain status. Seb kept his attention on her, feeling like a snake charmer. If he looked away, the spell might be broken, and she'd turn her venom back on Martin.

"But just think about it. It's a ticketed event. Very exclusive.

And Carol Anne said it's nearly sold out, so you know people are looking forward to see what the venue has to offer."

"And a fundraiser," Penny spoke up. "We'll be donating part of the money raised to the Seacroft Food Bank, on behalf of the organizing committee."

Mrs. Green tilted her head, like she was considering this. Seb plowed forward.

"And to increase the bookstore's contribution, I'm donating a piece of my work to a silent auction."

"You are?" Mrs. Green asked.

"You are?" Carol Anne said.

Seb risked a quick glance over his shoulder to wink at her.

"Of course. It's part of the reason the event has been so popular."

"Yeah, sorry, Mom," Penny said. "Seb and I talked about that. Guess I forgot to mention it to you." Penny was quick on her feet. Seb had to admire that.

"So you see, the bookstore is playing a critical part in this campaign. The organizing committee is very grateful for your participation. The donation from the silent auction is sure to be significant." He was winning. Her arms were still crossed, but her long nails had stopped their tapping.

"A donation?" she said.

"A large one."

"Well." Mrs. Green fiddled with the buttons of her soft pink cardigan. "If there's going to be a donation, it would only make sense for me to present the check to the food bank."

Seb had to blink to keep from rolling his eyes. Someone, Penny maybe, coughed to smother a laugh.

"Well actually, Bruce Goodwin, as chair of the festival board, will—" Carol Anne's comment was cut off with a soft squeak, like someone, also probably Penny, had pinched her.

"I'm sure some kind of arrangement can be made." Sebastian's face was frozen into his permanent grin. He took a step back and wrapped an arm around Martin's shoulders. The other man inhaled and stiffened against him, but Seb kept smiling. "And of course, Martin will be donating his time to organize the event, and he'll be the MC. Dr. Lindsey takes the stage!"

The bookstore descended into silence. They were all holding their collective breaths. Seb nearly swallowed his tongue when Martin slid one hand to rest in the space between Seb's shoulder blades. His smile relaxed, and he pulled Martin closer until the professor's surprisingly solid body was pressed along his side. The urge to pull him all the way in was almost painful, but now wasn't the time.

Mrs. Green's eyes narrowed again, and Martin shrank back, but Seb held his ground, keeping them both where they were, shoulder to shoulder.

"I'd like to make a speech," she said finally. "Thanking everyone for coming and for their donations."

Penny stepped forward and shook Mrs. Green's hand.

"Of course! I'm sure everyone would enjoy that, wouldn't they, Mom?"

Seb glanced behind him in time to see Carol Anne give a tight-lipped smile.

"Of course they would," she said.

"Then it's settled. This will be delightful. Sebastian," Mrs. Green held out a hand toward him, "thank you so much for organizing all of this. I'm sure with your involvement, it will be a memorable evening."

Sebastian shook her hand as Carol Anne sighed. "Oh yes. He's been instrumental since the beginning."

When Mrs. Green had left, the four of them all let out a long exhale.

"What just happened?" Martin asked.

"A silent auction?" Carol Anne said.

"That's actually a really good idea." Penny giggled.

Seb beamed at them all. "You're welcome."

"Did you really plan this whole thing without asking her?" Martin was still pressed against Seb's side and showed no inclination to step away. The pressure of his hand on Seb's back was pleasantly distracting.

Carol Anne snorted. "Of course not. It's not my fault she doesn't pay attention at committee meetings. Honestly, I don't know why we still let her come to those things, but we're always short of board members so..." She shrugged. "We passed a list of events around back at the beginning of the summer. She was there. I remember because I expected her to make some kind of demand like today, but she didn't say a thing. She's just being spiteful."

"Spiteful?" Martin asked.

"Didn't Penny tell you?"

"Tell them what?" Penny sounded just as confused as Seb felt.

"Don't you know where she gets her money from? It's not from selling used books, that's for sure."

"She's hoarding her treasure deep inside her cave?" Penny asked. Beside Seb, Martin laughed softly, the sound vibrating through Seb's arm. His toes curled inside his shoes. He needed Carol Anne and Penny to leave so he could pull Martin deep into the shelves and kiss him silly, his earlier plans to take things slow be damned.

"Mrs. Green is the single biggest property owner in Seacroft," Carol Anne said. "She owns every building on this street except the diner. I heard she wanted to buy that too, at the same time you and Tim did. She was going to open up a cute little coffee shop next to her bookstore. It would have made it a real destination."

"That was her?" Penny said. "She drove the sale price on the building through the roof! I thought Tim was going to have a heart attack before we signed the purchase agreement."

"I don't think she ever forgave you two for buying it out from under her." Carol Anne sniffed as she glanced out the window.

"A dragon never forgets," Penny murmured ominously.

"That's an elephant, honey."

When Penny and Carol Anne left, Martin collapsed on the couch, and Seb sank next to him. "Sorry about the 'Dr. Lindsey on stage' thing. I know you're nervous about that part."

"It's okay. I couldn't be any more nervous than I was right before you said that." Martin ran a hand through his hair, making it stick up in fluffy clumps. "I thought for sure she was going to fire me."

"Speaking up for yourself really isn't part of your skill set, is it?" Seb clenched his fists to keep from smoothing the hair down. Martin winced and gave him a sad smile, which made Seb laugh. He slipped his arm over Martin's shoulder again. "I argue with everyone. Stick with me, and I'll show you how it's done."

"Thanks. It's been a while since someone's stood up for me like that."

The admission made Seb's heart twist. That right there was why he couldn't drag Martin into the stacks for a quick grope. He needed more than that. He *deserved* more than that.

"We can look out for each other." Seb made his smile look as innocent and angelic as possible.

Martin laughed, and his head lolled on the back of the couch until it was turned to Seb. "You don't need someone to stand up for you. I've seen you do it."

"No. But my closest friends are a seventeen-year-old and my douchebag agent. You could be good for me." He sighed. Their faces were incredibly close. Martin's eyes were flecked with green. When he licked his lips, Seb's good intentions fled once more. He wanted to kiss him. The distance wasn't far, and he thought Martin wouldn't even mind.

The door screeched open as a new customer walked in. Seb

leapt up as if the couch was on fire. Martin blinked a few times, staring up at him with sleepy eyes.

"Back to work," Seb said, forcing a smile. "If anyone else comes in and gives you a hard time, you know where to find me."

11

—————

*W*hen Martin got home that evening, the house smelled like a campfire.

"Smarts!" Brian said as Martin entered the kitchen. He wore an apron that said *Lick My Fingers*.

Martin hesitated. "What's that smell?"

"I'm making dinner! On the barbecue."

"You know how to use the barbecue?"

"Come see! You're going to love it."

Martin let his brother tow him through the house and out into the small backyard. A plume of black smoke rose from the ancient barbecue, making Brian curse, and a black cloud enveloped him when he lifted the lid. They both coughed as the smoke disappeared, revealing skewers of chicken and mixed vegetables on the grill.

"You made these?" Martin asked in disbelief.

"Well." Brian poked at them with a pair of tongs. "I bought them. Did you know they've got skewers like this all made up at the store?"

Martin eyed them. Despite the smoke, the skewers looked perfectly edible.

"What's wrong?"

"What do you mean?" Brian kept rolling the skewers on the grill, like a street hustler moving his cups around to confuse his audience. Martin wasn't sure his brother knew what he was doing, but he appreciated the effort, unless—

"Are you selling the house?"

"No!"

"Did you break the oven?"

"Of course not."

Martin didn't think Brian actually knew how to work the oven.

"We've been living on takeout since I got here. Is this an apology, or do you need to ask me for something?"

"Can't I make dinner for me and my little brother just because I want to?" Brian continued to shuffle their dinner on the grill. The green peppers were starting to shrivel.

"I think they're ready."

"Oh good." Brian sighed. "I wasn't sure how you were supposed to tell. There's no timer on this thing, did you know that?"

They settled themselves at the big kitchen table. Martin tossed them a salad, which Brian grumbled about, but helped himself to once they were sitting.

"Are you dying?" Martin asked.

"Smarts, sometimes I feel like cooking."

Martin chewed nervously on his surprisingly well-cooked chicken.

"So how's work going?" Brian asked. "You're liking it?"

"It's fine. The store's not really busy, but the people who come in are nice enough."

"Yeah? That's good. That's really good."

"Sure." Martin took another bite of his dinner and wrinkled his nose. The chicken was good, but the onion was a little underdone.

"And you're making friends?"

"Did you kill someone? Are you going to jail?"

"No!" Brian's voice rose, but then he sighed and set down his fork. "But I've been a dick lately, and I felt bad, okay? I told you to come stay with me, and I know it hasn't been great. This thing with Jess, it's—I'm sorry. I haven't been the best brother, and I wanted to apologize. If you're going to be a jerk about it, though . . . " He grabbed up his plate and went to stand.

"Sit down." Martin held up his hand. Brian glared at him for a second, but then slumped back down in his seat.

"I was just trying to do something nice." He poked at his food.

"It is. It is nice. Just surprising that you know how to make anything that won't give us both salmonella by the morning."

Brian scowled at him from under his brows, but a half smile formed on his lips. "You're such a priss. You and your fancy words."

"What? Salmonella? It's a bacteria. Everyone should know what it is because food poisoning is not fancy."

Brian laughed. "You've always used big words. Mom and I didn't know what you were saying half the time once you got to high school."

Martin remembered. His mom would praise him, and Brian would roll his eyes and call him a loser. One happy little family.

"I can't help the words I use." He'd been self-conscious about it when he'd been a teenager, but he'd been self-conscious about everything. His vocabulary, his weight, the way he'd rather read books than play sports with his brother.

"I know that now," Brian said. They'd been so different, growing up. Brian had been the fun one, the athletic one, always with a girlfriend. He'd been an okay student and got a job at the fire department right away. Martin was the first person in their family to get a four-year degree. His family was good, sturdy, blue-collar people, and they'd never been quite sure what to make of him.

"I've been tutoring the girl who works at the bookstore with me," Martin said. "She's applying to art school and needed help with her application essays."

"I bet you'd be good at that." Brian smiled at him without any hint of sarcasm. "You do have all those big words. I bet colleges like that kind of thing."

Martin shrugged, embarrassed by his brother's compliment. "It's just a personal essay. It's not that hard."

"For you, maybe. I could never do something like that."

Martin considered his brother. He'd always admired Brian growing up, and the quiet envy in his voice now was a surprise.

"You're pretty smart too."

"Yeah." Brian picked at a piece of chicken. "So smart I can't even get my wife to move back in."

Martin straightened. "Do you want to get back together?"

"I think it's too late for that." Brian shrugged, looking miserable. It was the first time he'd expressed any clear opinions on the breakdown of his marriage. Mostly, since Martin moved in, Brian dodged Jess's calls, and avoided talking about it with Martin at all costs.

"Brian, I—"

"It's okay, Smarts." Brian gave him a forced smile. "There's something you can learn from your older brother. Don't make the same mistakes I did when you find someone."

It was Martin's turn to look down at his plate.

"I don't see that happening anytime soon."

"Oh come on. You're a smart guy. Good looking too. Bet you ... er ... guys love those Lindsey eyes."

Martin thought of Seb's eyes, blue and laughing. They had been so close on the couch. Seb's skin was lightly freckled, including one on his lip at the highest part below his nose. Martin thought Seb might kiss him, but instead he'd pushed away and left Martin there to gape.

"Wait. Did you meet someone?" Brian's voice cut through his cataloguing of Seb's features.

"No."

"You did, didn't you? You've got the dopey look on your face. Is that—I mean—Did you? I mean, how does that work?"

"How does what work?" Martin wasn't following.

"If I met a girl I liked—when I met Jess—I just knew. You know? I walked right up to her and told her I was buying her a drink. But, if it were a guy . . . what do you do?"

Martin tried not to be annoyed. "We take our shirts off and flap our arms while we turn in a circle squawking like a chicken. It's the secret gay mating dance. They teach it to us in a special after-school health class."

Brian snorted. "Don't be an ass."

"Don't ask asinine questions. We're not a different species. We spend time with each other. Go out on dates."

Seb had tried to ask him out on a date. Martin, predictably, had panicked and turned him down by pretending to not understand. Was it too late to take it back?

"So you're dating someone?" Brian leaned forward expectantly in his chair.

"No. I—we'll see."

"Is he cute?"

Martin couldn't stop the blush that spread over his ears. If he tried to describe Seb, he'd start talking about his freckles and the way his blue eyes were ringed in black on the outsides. "Do you really want to know?"

Brian finished his dinner and leaned back in his chair with a soft belch. "Not really. Dudes don't do it for me. But whatever makes you happy. I'm sure it will be good. You're the smart one in the family."

———

Seb was halfway through the *Alice* project. He was also out of coffee. In fact, he was out of nearly everything. He wasn't sure how long it had been since he'd been shopping, or if he'd slept the night before. The Cheshire Cat grinned at him maniacally from where he'd perched it back in its tree.

He needed sleep or caffeine, and he wanted to get the caterpillar placed on its mushroom before he called it a day. He pulled on his jacket and made his way downstairs. Martin sat by the cash register reading a book.

"Don't you ever go home?" Seb asked.

Martin smiled as he glanced up. Seb really liked it when he smiled. "It's three-thirty. I've still got a few more hours."

Seb checked his watch again. The numbers swam in his vision, but then resolved to show Martin was right. "My mistake. I'm going to Penny's for coffee. Can I get you anything?"

Martin shook his head. "No, I'm fine. But I was thinking, after I close up, if you're not busy, we could—"

The shop's phone rang.

Martin's interrupted question hung between them. He visibly struggled between finishing it and answering the phone like a good employee. Seb's heart sank when Martin sighed and picked up the handset.

"Hello, Dog Ears Book Shop, how can I help you?" He frowned as he listened, before his eyes met Seb's. "Yes, just a second." Martin placed his hand over the receiver and held it in Seb's direction. "It's for you?"

Seb was as baffled as Martin, but he took the phone.

"Hello?"

"Seb, don't hang up!" Oliver's words were a rush. Seb's grip tightened. Twice now his brother had managed to track him down and surprise him.

"Ollie?"

"Please don't hang up!"

"How did you know to call me here?"

"You told me once you lived upstairs from a bookstore. The only other one in town is a chain. I called them too, but they said they were in a box store and didn't have any upstairs tenants."

"What the hell? So now you're stalking me?"

"Who is it?" Martin whispered.

Seb put his hand over the receiver. "It's my brother."

Martin's eyes widened. "You have a brother?"

Seb smirked and rolled his eyes, trying to tell Martin it was a long story. One he'd like to share, if Martin was interested.

"Seb? Are you there?"

Seb growled and put the phone back to his ear. "Why didn't you call my phone?"

"I did. I have been. It always goes straight to voicemail."

Fair enough. As he'd gotten farther into the *Alice* project, Seb had set his phone to Do Not Disturb. He pulled it from his pocket to find over a dozen missed calls from the past few days, mostly from Oliver.

"What do you want?"

"It's Nana. She's sick."

Seb's heart lifted into his throat. He hesitated, glancing at Martin, still watching him with raised eyebrows. If this was serious, Seb shouldn't be having this conversation standing in the public space of the bookstore.

"I'll call you back," he said.

"Seb! No, don't hang up."

"I'll call you right back, I promise." He handed the phone to Martin.

"Everything okay?" he asked.

Seb rubbed his eyes. He didn't want to have this conversation now. He didn't want to have it ever, but especially not right now, when he was running on no sleep. His brain was stretched and fried, but he'd promised Ollie he'd call him right back, and his brother had proven he wouldn't be put off anymore.

"It'll be fine. I'll see you later, okay?" Seb waved as he hurried out of the bookstore.

Seb sat down on a bench on the corner at the end of the next block and pulled his phone out again. His hands shook as he tried to flip to Oliver's most recent missed call, but was saved the trouble of dialing when the phone started to ring.

"Ollie?" The name trembled in his mouth.

"Seb, I'm sorry. I thought you should know."

"Of course I should know!"

"Listen, it's some kind of respiratory infection. She's stable, but—"

"Is she in the hospital?"

"She should be home later today or tomorrow morning."

Seb closed his eyes and exhaled. He didn't want to think about his grandmother, frail and alone, in a hospital bed. She'd always been immaculate, coiffed, and fashionable for every occasion. He didn't want to picture her unmade and sick.

"Will she—Will she be okay?"

"She wants to see you."

This time, Seb didn't hesitate. "I can come." He'd have to rent a car. He couldn't leave now—he needed to sleep—but tomorrow.

"She's pretty tired. She'll need a few more days to recover. Listen, I know you're not going to like this, but I want you to think about it, okay?"

Seb had a pretty good feeling he knew what his brother was going to ask. "I'm listening."

"They still want to throw the birthday party. I think you should be there."

Seb closed his eyes and gritted his teeth. Ollie sounded tired, and Seb being an asshole wasn't going to help the situation.

He sighed. "I just don't think that's a good idea."

"Nana wants you there. She keeps asking about you."

Seb had last been to his parents' home four years ago. That

little get together ended with Seb storming out of the house three hours after arriving for what was supposed to be a weekend visit.

Ollie and their grandmother had been the only ones to speak to him since.

"Okay," he said.

"Okay?"

"I'll come to your party. But you're going to keep Dad away from me as much as possible."

"I can do that." The relief in Ollie's voice was clear.

"And I'm getting a hotel room in town. I'm not staying at the house."

"Mom will want you to come for dinner the night before."

"Then I'm bringing a date." The idea sprang to Seb's mind suddenly, but as soon as he said it, he knew he wasn't backing down.

"Seb. You can't. Not after last time."

"This is different. He's a doctor. Mom and Dad will love him."

Oliver chuckled. "You're dating a doctor? How did you manage that?"

"The elusive artist charm is hard to withstand."

"Fine, don't tell me. I'll send you the details. Don't delete them. I'll drive down there and pick you up myself if I have to."

When they hung up, Seb stayed where he was on the bench. Cars drove by, and men and women passed. Seb stared at it all without seeing. He'd stayed away from his family for *four years*. Oliver called from time to time, and his grandmother less often, but he never considered what it would mean if his family wasn't there anymore. Their relationship was difficult, but they were still his family. If his grandmother—When she was gone, would Oliver be enough of a reason to keep in touch?

More importantly, had Seb just told Oliver that he was bringing Martin for the weekend? It seemed like a good enough

128

idea at the time, one more demand to prove a point, but now he was committed. He'd never said particularly complimentary things about his family to Martin. Hell, Martin didn't even know Seb had a brother until ten minutes ago. How the hell was Seb supposed to convince him to spend a weekend with them?

_a_ week later, Seb still hadn't asked Martin about coming with him to his parents' party. He'd tried, repeatedly. After his conversation with Oliver, he'd come back to the bookstore to find Martin busy with a customer. Seb tried to make it back downstairs, but his lack of sleep caught up with him, and he crashed.

The next day, he went out early to the framer's to pick up the case he'd ordered for the _Alice_ piece. He meant to pick it up and get right back to the store, but the case was not right at all. It wasn't the right size, and the glass panels had a blue-ish tint that would not work with how he'd envisioned the piece.

He'd tried to talk with Martin a couple times since then, but Seacroft's population suddenly developed a fascination with used books. Every time he went downstairs, Martin was always helping someone navigate the shelves.

The blues night was on a Thursday. Seb was upstairs working when the beep of a reversing truck shattered his peace of mind. On the street below his window, a large white van parked in front of the store. Carol Anne stood on the sidewalk, a clipboard in one hand as she pointed and gave orders. Two workmen carried rental furniture down the ramp and into the bookstore.

After that, getting anything done was hard. Usually, the store was silent, and Seb could work in peace. Today, strange thumping sounds echoed as furniture was moved around, and instructions were shouted or relayed over crackling walkie talkies.

Around three o'clock, he gave up. The noises downstairs were too foreign and distracting to allow him to make any kind of progress. Martin was once again occupied with a customer as Seb went through the store, so he waved and let himself out onto the street.

When he returned, it was after six. The shop door was locked, and the inside had been transformed. The usual overhead tube lights had been turned off, and someone from Carol Anne's army of volunteers had hung strings of white lights from the tops of all the bookshelves. The heavy couches had been moved out of the way, replaced with tall tables and groups of low chairs. A cluster of music stands and a microphone stood to one side.

He was fishing for his keys when a slim man in a dark suit appeared from the shelves. Seb did a double take—it was Martin. He had shed his usual oversized wardrobe somewhere between the cookbooks and the biographies. As he unlocked the door, he gave a shy smile that did things to Seb's insides.

"Sorry," he said. "I saw you go out earlier, but it's been so busy today. I thought I must have missed you when you came back."

"You look . . . " Seb couldn't find complementary words that wouldn't sound like he was undressing Martin with his eyes.

Even though that was exactly what he was doing.

Martin grinned crookedly. "Penny lent it to me. It's a good thing it fits, right?"

It sure did fit right.

"You look great," was all he could manage. He pulled his cap off, sure his hair was mashed down underneath it.

"You're still coming tonight?" They hadn't really talked about that, but Seb smiled at him, wishing desperately they had talked about a lot of things sooner so he could be the guy on Martin's arm.

"Yeah. I just have to go get changed." He'd stolen the sweater underneath his jacket from Kenneth in college. The collar had holes, and the cuffs had given up their shape almost a decade ago.

"Good." Martin's smile turned nervous. "I might need someone to carry me off the stage when I hyperventilate."

Seb put a hand on his shoulder. "You'll do fine. It's no scarier than talking to a lecture hall of students."

"Yeah, and I was never very comfortable with that either."

Seb took another step toward him, squeezing his hand. "You'll be great!" He stared into Martin's eyes, willing him to believe what Seb was saying. Martin blinked, lashes fluttering. His breath was shallow, and he licked his lips nervously.

"So listen," Seb said. "I have something I've been meaning to ask you."

"Sure." Seb watched Martin's lips shape the word, and he wanted to kiss him. His jaw carried the barest hint of gold-brown fuzz. Seb wanted to run a finger along it. Maybe press that finger against Martin's bottom lip.

"You had a question?" Martin's voice had gone low and soft.

"Right. Yes." Focusing on words was so hard. He shuffled forward another half step. Martin's lips parted again, and he leaned forward slightly under Seb's hand. The bright lights in the store seemed to dim, and Seb gasped as Martin's fingers brushed against his hip, and Martin's eyes flickered down toward Seb's mouth.

"Gentlemen, you're blocking the door." Carol Anne's voice made Seb jump.

Just like that, the spell under the twinkling lights from the bookshelves was broken. Martin hopped out of reach, a hand going to his mouth. The way his skin flushed made Seb want to haul him back and kiss him until he couldn't breathe. Instead, he pasted on a smile and turned to find Carol Anne and Penny standing in the bookshop's doorway. Their twin smirks said they knew exactly what they had interrupted.

"You know, we really did a great job with this place. It's so cozy and," Penny shot a glance at Seb, "romantic."

Seb contemplated murder while Martin coughed uncomfortably behind him.

Carol Anne blew her daughter a kiss. "Why thank you, honey. And you and Martin did an outstanding job of breaking him out of his secret bookstore identity into the next internet heartthrob. You shine up really good, Martin!" She slung an arm over Seb's shoulders. "Doesn't he?"

Seb gave Martin another once over, unabashedly lingering on all the places the suit hugged his frame.

"He really does." His eyes met Martin's, and he stared for longer than was strictly appropriate in mixed company, warming as Martin stared right back.

"Should we give you two a minute?" Penny asked. Martin flushed and turned away, nervously playing with his tie. Seb held back the sigh that threatened to sail out of him. He smiled at Carol Anne.

"I should go change," he said and slipped away.

13

Martin had been a nervous wreck since Penny showed up mid-afternoon with a suit in a bag and a glint in her eye.

"You're representing the community. We can't have you looking like you're in need of a fundraiser yourself."

He swore his own clothes would work perfectly well, but Penny regarded his dress pants and collared shirt with an arched eyebrow. "Did you raid your big brother's closet?"

He protested, but she produced a full-length mirror out of seemingly nowhere and propped it up against a bookshelf. The reflection shocked Martin. When had he gotten so thin? The shirt that fit him six months earlier hung off his body, and the pants were baggy enough to be mistaken for pajamas.

"I was sick," he said to Penny's reflection over his shoulder. "I didn't realize I'd lost so much weight."

"Nothing to be ashamed of!" Penny held the dark suit up on its hanger. "But trust me when I say this will be a much better look for you." The suit was her husband's, but she'd said years of cooking diner food meant it didn't fit him anymore.

"I'm just glad someone can wear it," she'd said, smoothing down his shoulders.

Later, a nervous-looking music teacher shepherded the jazz trio into the store, clucking and bobbing while they set up. Her worries seemed to be completely unfounded, though. The trio struck up promptly at seven o'clock sharp with a mellow arrangement perfectly suited to the environment.

Carol Anne did some shepherding of her own, leading Martin around the room to introduce him to people, mostly members of the organizing committee and the town council. Everyone seemed suitably impressed when Carol Anne gave them a little information on his background. Martin managed to keep from trembling too much as he shook hands with the apparent who's who of Seacroft.

Most interestingly, Seb seemed unable to take his eyes off Martin. Every time they happened to pass by, Seb gave him a smile, and his blue eyes darkened in an expression Martin hadn't seen before. Seb often looked at him with curiosity, amusement, or sometimes pity, but this was new and intense.

Martin's speech was scheduled for eight o'clock. All he needed to do was thank everyone for coming, announce the amount of money raised so far, and remind everyone to bid on the silent auction. Then he had to introduce Mrs. Green—currently gliding through the space, shaking hands and blowing air kisses—and he would be safe.

By seven forty-five, dread knotted his stomach. As he fiddled with the cuffs of his borrowed shirt, he told himself to get over it. He'd done this before. For years. And half the students in any given lecture hall hadn't been interested in anything he had to say. The people here would indulge him at least. And if he blew it completely, he could hide out in Brian's den or Seb's apartment for the rest of his life.

"You look like a man who could use a drink." Seb appeared before him, holding two wine glasses.

"Is it that obvious?" Martin took a glass and swallowed a big mouthful. The wine was red and a little more bitter than he usually liked, but any port in a storm, as it were.

"Just think of it as completing the look. Besides, if you've got a glass when you make your speech, it will give you something to do with your hands." Seb had changed into a checkered shirt and a paisley bowtie. He went to say something else, but Penny walked up to him, pulling a tall bearded man behind her.

"Hey guys!" she said, smiling wide. "Tim wanted to say hi! Seb and Martin, this is Tim, my husband. Tim, this is Seb and Martin." She said it like they were a unit. Batman and Robin. Sherlock and Watson. Seb and Martin.

Tim shook their hands and smiled politely. He had the distinct look of an introvert being tugged along by his extroverted partner when he'd much rather be at home or back in his kitchen.

"All set?" Penny asked.

"As much as I'll ever be." Martin took another sip of his wine.

"Just do what I do," Tim said.

"Picture everyone naked?" Penny laughed.

"No, muffin." Tim laughed. "That's what you do. Pick one person in the back of the crowd and pretend you're only talking to them."

"I'll be in the back," Penny said. She wore a multitude of bracelets that jangled as she bobbed up and down in her high heels and party dress. "I'll wave so you can see me."

Martin felt green around his edges as he walked up to the front of the room. He turned to face the group of milling attendees, chatting amongst themselves without seeming to notice him at all.

"Good evening, everyone," he said. The ambient noise didn't change. This had been his least favorite part of teaching. Getting a room of flighty undergrads to settle was always a chore.

He cleared his throat. "Good evening."

A few people glanced at him, but otherwise, there was no perceivable change.

Behind him, a trumpet pealed. One of the musicians played a complicated fanfare that reverberated through the whole room. As the last note died, the bookshop went silent. The trumpeter gave Martin a wry salute and sat back down.

Martin cleared his throat. "Good evening, everyone."

The crowd murmured "good evening" in response.

"On behalf of Dog Ears Book Shop, the Seacroft Town Council, and the . . . " He was distracted by movement at the back of the room as Penny flailed wildly against the wall. Her bracelets jingled, sounding not entirely unlike a Christmas tree falling over, with hundreds of tiny glass ornaments crashing to the floor. The commotion was enough that the next word out of his mouth evaporated and fear shivered down his spine. On behalf of the store, the council and the—who was the third group? Little fireworks of panic went off in his stomach. Someone stretched out to grasp Penny's frantically waving hand and pull it back down. Martin followed the motion and found the white-blond outline of Seb's head.

Look at someone at the back of the room.

"On behalf of Dog Ears, the town council," he tried again, "and the Seacroft Blues Festival organizing committee, we'd like to thank you for coming tonight. This event could not be possible without the efforts of a few important people, who I would like to take a moment to thank."

By the time Mrs. Green joined him, he was weak and noodly.

Martin made his way quietly along the side of the crowd. He detoured to the bar and took a glass of wine, then grabbed a second one in case Seb wanted it. The wine wobbled in the glasses as his hands shook, but when he arrived, Penny, Tim, and Seb greeted him with enthusiastic congratulations. Seb took the glass with a smile while Penny clapped Martin on the back.

"Good job," she hissed while Mrs. Green continued to speak. "You only looked like you were going to throw up twice."

Martin gave her a wobbly smile, then jumped as someone's hand slipped into his.

"You were great," Seb said, twining his fingers around Martin's.

The event wrapped up a little before ten. The winner of the silent auction was a middle-aged man who seemed very excited to receive Seb's donated piece, a carving from a children's book. A number of illustrated cats peered out indignantly at the observer.

Carol Anne refused to let Martin help them clean up, so he found himself standing in the middle of the bookshop a bit awkwardly, unsure what to do. He was too awake and energized to go home, but there really wasn't much going on in Seacroft on a Thursday night.

"Can I talk to you for a minute?" Seb appeared at his shoulder. His bow tie was undone, and the top button of his shirt was open.

"I think you already are." Martin grinned. Seb gave him a wink, then turned up the nearest aisle and made his way to the back of the shop. Martin followed him, winding their way up the stairs to the apartment.

"Can I get you something to drink?" Seb asked.

"Just a water." He'd had a couple glasses of wine. He wasn't drunk by any means, just in the warm soft moment where everything was relaxed.

Seb brought over two glasses and handed one to Martin, then sank onto the couch. Martin joined him, perching on the edge of the cushion.

"Cheers." Seb held up his cup, and Martin clinked his own against it.

Seb took a long swallow from his glass before he set it down. "We get along pretty well, don't we?"

Martin smiled at the remembered warmth of their hands linked together. "I think so."

Seb picked at a piece of lint on his knee. "You know I don't get along with my family."

Martin blinked. Where did Seb's family fit into this conversation?

"You've mentioned it."

Seb took Martin's hand in his again, tracing little circles around the palm. His lashes were as pale as the rest of him, fluttering down as he followed the movement of his thumb.

"There's a party at my parents' place next weekend. It's my grandmother's birthday, an overnight thing. First a dinner with my family, then a party the next day."

"Sounds fancy."

"You don't know the half of it. My sister is planning it, so it's going to make this event tonight look like a backwoods picnic. There will be more food and more booze than an entire village could eat in a month."

"And you're going to go?"

"I need a date."

Martin gaped.

"Wanna go?" Seb ran his free hand through his hair.

"Me?" Martin's heart picked up, harder than when he'd been about to make his speech.

"Yeah." Seb nodded. "Honestly, you'll fit in better than I ever have. You can talk to my dad about symposiums and humanistic theory and whatever crap it is that you people talk about when you get together."

Martin cast his eyes to the ground. So much for that idea.

But Seb squeezed Martin's hand, making him look up again.

"Sorry. I didn't mean that. What you do isn't crap. It's kind of cool, actually, and I can tell it's important to you. My dad, though—It's complicated." Seb eyes were soft. "Please? Come for the weekend?"

Martin was a fool. An idiot ten ways from Sunday and—He sighed. "Okay. I'll talk to Mrs. Green about getting next weekend off."

Seb smiled widely at him. Martin was going to lead himself to his own slaughter, but somehow, he couldn't stop.

He gave Seb a short smile. "I should head home." He turned to leave but was pulled off balance as Seb tugged him back toward the couch.

Their kiss was a collision. Martin stumbled, and Seb caught him, pulling Martin into his lap. Seb angled his head so that their lips fit together more closely. He tasted like wine, bitter and sweet, and his lips were as smooth as Martin imagined. Seb's free hand slid around him, under the suit jacket, and the warmth of his palm spread under Martin's shirt.

Martin leaned into him, letting his hand come to rest on Seb's ribs, feeling the breathing body underneath. Seb's breath on his cheek made him tremble.

Seb pulled away before the kiss could get too heated. He grinned and nipped at Martin's chin, making him shiver. He nuzzled at Seb's cheek, trying to find something to ground himself.

"I've been wanting to do that all night. For weeks, in fact." Seb kissed him again. Martin shuddered under his lips, as Seb's words swirled something complicated inside him. Joy. Relief. A puff of need that curled around his heart like smoke before sliding lower.

"I'm glad you took the initiative." Martin's breathing slowed until it synced with Seb's, calming him further.

"Can I ask another favor?" Seb's voice was low in Martin's ear.

"Yes." Martin's own voice was hoarser than he'd expected.

Seb rubbed their cheeks together before biting gently on Martin's earlobe. "Ask Penny if you can borrow this suit again next weekend. I love looking at you in it."

14

———

$\mathcal{T}$he following weekend, Martin pulled his duffle and the hanging bag with the borrowed suit in it out toward the front door. The late October wind rippled around his ankles as he stepped outside. Movement caught his attention, and he turned to find Brian hunched over a sheet of paper. He wore only a gray T-shirt. Martin was cold looking at him.

"Bit late in the season to be out here without a jacket," he said.

Brian's mouth twisted into an angry sneer. "Thanks, Smarts. Did they teach that to you in your master's program, or did you have to get the PhD to figure that out?"

Martin squared his shoulders. Since the night Brian made dinner, things had been better, and Martin wasn't going to start his weekend with a fight.

"Seb should be here in a minute. Can I get you a coat?"

Brian didn't say anything. As Martin moved closer, he couldn't help but read over his brother's shoulder. The paper was an official-looking document with the words "Separation Agreement" written across the top in block letters.

"Is that from Jess?" Martin slid onto the seat next to Brian, careful not to get too close.

"No, it's from the president. He wants me out of the country by midnight. Yes, it's from Jess." The paper fluttered in his shaking hands.

"That looks serious."

"I didn't think she'd actually do it."

Martin stared beyond the porch to the street in front of the house. When Brian and Jess had bought the place, Brian sent everyone he knew a picture of the two of them, standing proudly next to the SOLD sign on the front lawn. Martin was finishing the second year of his graduate program. He was living in a shoebox apartment and making most of his meals from a hot plate, and his big brother had seemed so settled. Brian and Jess's beaming smiles looked happy and certain as they got ready to build a life together.

"I know I haven't been very . . . " Martin tried to think of the right word, "available since I came here. You've done a lot more to support me than I have to support you. But if you ever want to talk about what happened, with you and Jess, I mean, you know I'll listen."

He didn't expect Brian to say anything. He was all set to go get his brother a coat before Seb's car pulled in, when Brian said, "I can't have kids."

"What?"

Brian's eyes were red-rimmed when he turned. "I can't. I'm shooting blanks."

Martin tried to piece this together. "How long have you known?"

"Over a year."

"And Jess knows?"

Brian's smile twisted again. "She knows. We both knew there was a problem. We tried for a long time. But my . . . er . . . equipment always seemed to be working right, so when she finally convinced me we should see a doctor, I assumed the problem would be with her."

"And it's not?" Was that too personal a question? Should Jess be here to tell him about this?

"Nope. The doctor said she wasn't getting any younger, but with viable sperm there was no reason to think she wouldn't be able to . . . You know."

Martin leaned back in his chair. The timing was terrible. His brother was finally talking to him, and he was about to leave for the weekend.

"Well, there are lots of ways to make that work, right? You can't be the only ones who have trouble with this kind of thing." Martin had certainly never planned to find a nice woman and make a bunch of kids, but he'd still like to be a father someday. "I mean, there's adoption, or you could find a sperm donor. Some of it's expensive, I think, but if it's really important to you . . ."

Brian shook his head. "We looked at that. All of it. I told her I couldn't do it."

"Do what?"

"Raise another man's kid."

This was so much more complicated than Martin had expected when he'd come out onto the porch. "And you told Jess that?"

"It didn't seem right, you know? I mean, if we adopted some kid, who knows what could happen?"

"What do you mean? "

Brian shrugged. "There are so many risks. Jess gave me some stuff to read. There's a lot of things we might not know, about history and medical things, with an adopted kid."

"It's not like having a biological child would be any more of a sure thing. Look at you and me."

Brian glared at him. "Thanks, Smarts."

"No!" Martin sighed. This was difficult, but Brian was obviously hurting. "I mean, we're pretty different, even though we had the same parents. Nothing's for sure, no matter how you do it. That's all I'm saying. And adoption wouldn't be your only option."

"Jess looked into all that. A sperm donor—" Brian's eyes widened. "It was my job, wasn't it? My job and I couldn't get it done. Looking at some other man's eyes in my kid for the rest of my life . . . I couldn't do that."

Martin faltered as he tried to choose his words again, but Brian kept talking.

"Anyway, you can imagine how that conversation went. Jess has always wanted to be a mom, and if I'm not the guy, then she —" He held up the separation agreement again, letting it flutter in the wind.

The photo swam into Martin's mind's eye again. Was that why they bought the house? It had always seemed big for the two of them, with an extra bedroom in the back and a finished basement they never put furniture into. The backyard was big enough to play catch, the kitchen table large enough to fit a whole family around. Was that what Brian and Jess had imagined when they had their picture taken?

The house was still there, but Jess, it seemed, was gone.

"That's a lot of bullshit." His words surprised him as much as they surprised Brian, if his brother's face was anything to go by.

"Excuse me?"

"You can't raise some other man's kid. That's bullshit, Brian. I'm sorry for saying it, but if that's how you feel, then I can see why she left your sorry ass."

Brian snorted and shoved at him. "You sound funny when you swear."

"You know you don't ever have to meet him, right? The sperm donor or whoever. It's not like he shows up and sleeps with your wife and then you have to invite him for dinner once a year to celebrate the conception of his kid. He's just a test tube of semen."

Brian squirmed. "It would still be weird."

"Do you remember Dad?" Martin asked. "Because I don't, not really."

"Sort of. He came a few times, for birthdays and stuff, but he stopped when you were still pretty little. Is this the part where you tell me he was never a real dad, just a sperm donor, and that real dads are the guys who show up day after day?"

"That was going to be my point, yes. I don't know about you, but I would have loved a real dad. You're not raising someone else's kid unless that's how you want to see it."

Brian folded the paper and put it back into its envelope. "That's what Jess told me."

"She was always my favorite sister-in-law."

"She's your only sister-in-law."

A blue hatchback pulled into the driveway. Seb popped out of the driver's seat wearing a pair of dark aviators and his leather jacket.

Martin stiffened. It didn't seem right, giving Brian a pep talk and a pat on the back and then heading off for the weekend.

"Go on." Brian gave Martin a tight smile. "It's good to see you like this. Go. I'll be fine. Nick's coming by tonight. First round at The Dugout is on him."

And the second, and the third, no doubt. Martin grabbed his suit and duffle and went down to the car, surprised when Seb came forward to greet him with a quick peck on the cheek. He waved at Brian over Martin's shoulder.

"You did that on purpose," Martin said.

Seb smiled broadly in Brian's direction while he took Martin's bag. "Just want him to know what we're up to this weekend."

———

Seb slid into the driver's seat and pulled the car back onto the road. He'd been looking forward to having Martin to himself since the moment he'd finally kissed him. In the week that followed, he'd flirted outrageously. Martin, predictably, adorably, blushed and stammered, but in small stolen moments at the back of the store turned out to be a decent kisser. They'd only been caught once, by Cass, whose eyes had nearly bugged out of her head before she'd squeaked and hurried away.

It was either his good mood, or possibly the underlying tension from the idea of seeing his family, but Seb didn't notice Martin had barely spoken—even less than usual—until they were on the highway, leaving Seacroft in the rearview mirror.

"Want to pick some music?" Seb asked. Martin wordlessly flipped the radio on, scrolled through the dial for a moment, and then went back to staring out the window.

"Everything okay?"

"Yeah." Martin sighed and leaned his head back against the car's leather headrest. "Except it's possible I haven't been the best brother in the world lately."

"Well, you've had some shit to work through. And as far as you've told me, he hasn't exactly been a poster child for big brother of the year either."

Martin fiddled with the knobs on the car's dash, turning the fan up and down until he turned it off altogether. "My brother's having a tough time. Ending a marriage is never easy, but I think it's harder on him than I realized. He said some things, just now, that I wasn't expecting to hear. Makes me wonder what else he hasn't told me since he's been too busy taking care of me."

"Hey." Seb put a hand on Martin's knee. "At least he's talking to you. That's more than most of my entire family will do."

Martin gave him a glum smile. "But you're going to see them now."

"Call me brave or stupid. I'm just glad Oliver tracked me down to say my grandmother was sick."

"Are you closest to your brother then?" Martin grazed his fingers over the back of Seb's hand for the briefest second before he quickly folded both his hands in his lap. Seb grinned. He was a tactile person, always had been. Now he had the option to touch Martin freely, and he wanted the connection pretty much all the time. Wearing down Martin's reserved restraint would be fun.

He ran a finger over Martin's ear, smoothing down a curl of hair threatening to fly free.

Martin shivered under the touch. "You're avoiding the question."

Seb growled and put both hands back on the wheel. "Ollie and I were close when we were growing up. He was my big brother. Whatever he did, I wanted to do it too. He played sports, I tried out for the team. He got elected senior class president, I ran to get on the student council too. I wasn't always successful —sports were never really my thing—but I wanted him to see me, you know? To know I saw him and how amazing he was, and that I wanted to be the same."

"And did he?"

Seb made a face. "When Ollie came out right before he went away to college, I think that was the happiest day of my life. Because my mom cried and said it didn't matter. And my dad hugged him, and he said they would support Ollie, no matter what. And I just about burst, because I knew it was all going to be okay. I'd known forever I was gay. And they said they'd support him, and I thought that meant they'd support me too when I was ready to tell them."

"Brian outed me to our mom. He didn't mean to," Martin said quickly when Seb went to protest. "We were joking around at dinner one night. He had his first serious girlfriend. I was giving him a hard time about it and brothers . . . you know. He kind of let it slip out. He looked so embarrassed when he said it. My mom smacked him for not letting me tell her when I was ready. And then she smacked me for thinking it was something that needed to be kept a secret." He smiled at the memory. Seb thought of Martin's smiles as something hidden, a little private. He was glad to be part of them more and more often and definitely wanted to see more of them. But then the smile shifted as Martin glanced across the car. "I gather that wasn't quite what happened with your family."

The happy little thrill over Martin's smiles faded. Seb sighed. He could make a joke and change the topic, but it didn't seem right. He'd brought this up, and Martin deserved to know at least some of what had happened since they were driving into the lion's den together.

"It seemed okay at first," Seb said. "Maybe my first mistake was telling them while I was still in high school. Oliver waited until right before he went away for college, but I didn't want to wait. I had a boyfriend, Kevin McCreery. I didn't want to have to hide when he came to the house, so I told my parents about him. It wasn't like when Ollie told them—there weren't tears and hugs—but they seemed to understand. But I guess the difference between me and Ollie was his big gay escapades were happening in a college dorm somewhere, and mine were happening in their house."

Martin's eyes widened. "Did they catch you with—"

"Not like that. But Kevin was out and proud and had been forever, so he didn't think anything of holding my hand at the dinner table or calling me 'babe' when my parents could hear. And I wanted him to like me, so I pretended not to see the way my dad looked at us."

The lane markers on the highway rolled by as they drove. Seb hesitated. He was telling the truth, but not all of it.

"Actually, I think my only real mistake was not being Ollie. He was the good son. He got good grades, went to the right school, got a good job right after graduation. My dad probably even thought Oliver's boyfriends were the right kind of gay. Good looking guys with good last names and good jobs. My dad could introduce as 'Oliver's friend' and let people assume what they wanted."

"And yours weren't the right kind?"

"Not even a little." His boyfriends were moody twinky types with long hair, piercings, and often a chip on their shoulder bigger than Seb's. He took a few of them to the house, but even introducing them as "Sebastian's friend" would never have hidden who they really were.

"I've probably never been the right kind of anything." It hurt to say it. "I barely got through high school. The only reason I got into college at all was because Dad pulled some strings at Watersmith, where he worked. I don't know what he thought I would do there. He put me in a business program, but I took all the fine arts classes I could get myself into in my first year, and in my second year they let me switch into the BFA program. He was pissed that no one in the registrar's office consulted him before they made the change."

"But you got in on the merit of your work then, not because of who you were." Martin ran a hand down Seb's arm. He caught it just as Martin went to pull away, lacing their fingers together. He held their hands on his thigh while he drove.

It was hard to say where his relationship with his family all went wrong, buried in so many years of disagreements and small failures.

"He didn't speak to me the whole summer between my freshman and sophomore years, and then after that second year, when I told him I dropped out, he didn't talk to me for another six months. The only reason he finally did was to thank me for coming to Parker's wedding. Like not coming had been an option." Realizing his attendance hadn't been considered mandatory was still painful.

"Parker's your older sister, right?" Martin squeezed his hand, pulling Seb out of his funk.

He was going for his grandmother. He had to focus on that.

"Yeah. I've got two older sisters. You'll meet them both. Gillian is the eldest. She's twelve years older than me. She got married while I was still in middle school, so we've never had much in common. Parker is between Gillian and Ollie. She's six years older than I am and four years older than Ollie. She's the only one who still lives in town. She's married to Jason, who's a real estate agent and an ass. They've got three kids and two golden retrievers. They're irritatingly perfect."

"What's Gillian's husband's name?" Martin asked.

Seb glanced at him and smirked. "Julian."

"Gillian and Julian?"

Seb let his smirk turn more evil. "The heart wants what the heart wants. And Gillian's heart wanted Julian. Gillie and I don't have a lot to say to each other, but don't think I didn't bring that up as much as I could through my teenage years."

Martin chuckled, almost a real laugh. Seb wanted to praise him for it, like one of Parker's golden retrievers. How much he enjoyed seeing those little unguarded moments of Martin's happiness surprised him.

"What about your mom?" Martin said. Seb's urge to rub his tummy popped like a bubble.

"My mom has done everything my dad has ever wanted. She's not a robot, but doing everything my dad's way was the agreement from the beginning, I think. If you're paying attention, you'll notice there's six years between Gillian and Parker, and then there's all three of us afterwards in six years together."

"I'm a historian," Martin said, "but even I can do that math, yes."

"Well then do this math. My parents got married in May, and Gillian was born in November the same year."

"Oh."

"Yup. My parents were poor undergrads who, let's assume, got carried away in the throes of young love. One and one makes three, as it were. So they got married and my dad probably promised my mom that if she stuck with his plan, they'd live a big happy life with a house full of kids someday."

"Sounds like it worked out, though."

Three out of four functional children was close enough?

"The point is, my mom got on board and never looked back. My dad calls the shots and she delivers."

"So she never stood up to your dad for you?"

Seb scratched at his ear. It was complicated. "She probably did. I mean, she did. When he'd lecture me about getting my grades up, she'd stand by him because what mother doesn't want her son to do well in school? When he told me I was throwing my life away if I left college, she said she just wanted me to be happy. But her idea of happy was a degree and a steady job and a houseful of kids. Security. So it's not like she chose my dad over me at some point. She just ... "

"She didn't get it," Martin said. It was close enough to the truth. "My mom's a little like that."

Seb raised an eyebrow. "But you're the poster boy for success. She must be so proud of you."

Martin's gazed dripped with dark humor. "I'm sleeping on my brother's couch and putting my PhD to use in a used bookstore."

Seb waved him off. "That's just temporary. Baby steps, remember?"

"My mom never went to college. She married my dad when she was twenty and divorced him before my second birthday. She's worked minimum wage jobs her whole life. When I went to college, she was proud of me. When I stayed in college to study dead Germans ... " He smiled his secret smile. Seb really wanted to pull over and kiss him. "She's proud of me, but she doesn't understand why I do it."

Seb consoled himself by pressing Martin's knuckles to his lips.

"Maybe we can switch. If you like them, my family is yours."

15

$\mathcal{M}$artin enjoyed the drive, but nervous energy zipped under his skin as they pulled off the highway. The population sign by the exit said the town was a little bigger than Seacroft, and Seb told him the number didn't count the eight or so thousand students who attended Watersmith. The downtown was bright and bustling. Everyone was pink-cheeked and cable knit, like Mount Garner before it turned gray and unwelcoming.

Seb drove with the confidence of someone who knew the town, signaling for turns Martin couldn't see until they were already at the intersection and making his way through quiet residential streets that all looked the same.

The farther they drove, the bigger and older the houses got, and the more Martin's pulse thrummed behind his eyes.

"The campus is right down there." Seb pointed down a tree-lined street as they made their way. Martin could have guessed that anyway. It was a Friday in October, and the sidewalks were full of students in Watersmith sweatshirts.

Picture perfect.

A few more blocks and they turned onto another street,

where the houses were even older and the properties spaced even farther apart.

"You grew up here?" Martin asked, forcing back his nerves. The neighborhood around the campus at Mount Garner was different. Newer, but not as well maintained. Here, the houses were old brick homes, some of them three stories. One had a garage bigger than the house Martin's mother rented while he and Brian were growing up.

"Don't get swept away by the Georgian glamor," Seb said. "They're drafty as hell in the winter."

They pulled into the last house on the street, a bit smaller than the ones they'd passed but still impressive. A Watersmith flag flapped lazily from a pole at the top of the circular driveway.

"Good thing I brought Penny's suit," Martin said, gazing out the window.

"We should get you one of your own. I'm going to need you to wear that a lot in the future." Seb leaned across the console and kissed him hard.

"What was that for?"

"You looked nervous, and I've been wanting to do that for the last hundred miles."

"Delayed gratification makes everything better?" Martin tried to will the color in his cheeks to go down before he had to go inside to meet Seb's family.

"I'll remember that." Seb's expression said he wasn't talking about kissing. It did nothing to help the state of Martin's face, or the way the air was suddenly too warm and his clothes too tight.

The front door to the house opened, and a tall man with sandy blond hair stepped out onto the porch. He waved and said something they couldn't hear inside the car.

Seb gave a heavy sigh. "Here we go. Say the word and we'll turn this car around."

"You don't mean that."

"I really do." But he undid his seatbelt and got out of the car.

"I was giving you another thirty minutes and then I was coming to get you," the man said as they approached. He was taller than Seb, and his hair was darker, but he had the same blue eyes and full mouth. He wore pressed khakis and a collared shirt with the sleeves rolled halfway up his forearms. Compared to Seb's worn leather jacket and faded jeans, he looked like he could run a bank.

"Ollie, if I weren't coming, you know I'd already be a hundred miles in the other direction by now," Seb said. The brothers hesitated for a second before they pulled each other into an awkward hug. Oliver glanced over Seb's shoulder toward Martin.

"You must be the doctor." His smile was easier as he held out his hand for Martin to shake.

"Dr. Martin Lindsey, at your service," Seb said.

Martin couldn't help the nervous flutter in his chest at Seb's proud smile, or the teasing look in Oliver's eyes, but he put on his bravest face. "It's nice to meet you. Seb's told me a lot."

"No he hasn't," Oliver said. "But he didn't tell me much about you either, so at least we're both starting from the same place."

Seb opened the rental car's trunk. "We're not going to stay long, but we'll be back for dinner. I just wanted to drop off a gift. It's kind of fragile, and Kenneth will kill me for driving this far without packing it properly. Then Martin and I are going to go get checked into the hotel. I thought I'd give him the grand tour. Is dinner casual tonight, or do we need to dress up?"

"It's casual," Oliver said. "But listen, Seb, there's a bit of a problem."

"What kind of problem? Martin, can you take one end of this?" Seb was busy pulling a box about the size of a small TV from the back of the car.

"Aunt Karen called a little while ago. They're on their way up."

"Aunt Karen is my dad's youngest sister," Seb said for Martin's benefit.

"What's in this?" Martin's arms trembled under the weight of the box.

"It's a gift. From both of us."

"Both of us?"

"Seb, are you listening?" Oliver followed them into the house.

"Aunt Karen. She called. Continue," Seb grunted as they made their way into a wide front hall.

"Jeanine decided she was coming at the last minute."

"That's my cousin," Seb said. "She's seventeen."

"She's twenty," Oliver said. "And she's bringing her boyfriend."

"Ollie." Seb's face was strained. Whatever was in the box weighed more than it had any right to. "This whole family chronicle is fascinating, but can you please show us where to put this before we drop it?"

Oliver lead them down a hall into a bright room furnished in warm woods and plush carpeting. A table was set up by two French doors, and they placed the box on it with an ominous rattle.

"Seriously." Martin stretched until something in his spine popped. "What was in that?"

"Just a little something for my favorite grandmother." Seb smiled, blue eyes flashing, before he turned to his brother. "Is Nana going to be at dinner tonight?"

"No, she's resting. She'll be here tomorrow. But Seb, I need you to listen." Oliver waved his hand impatiently.

"Can I go get a drink of water first? We've been in the car for hours."

"Seb!" Oliver's voice rose, and Martin froze in place.

Seb sighed. "If I die from dehydration, it'll be your fault."

"Drama queen," Oliver muttered. "You're not here five minutes, and you're already irritating the shit out of me."

"I told you not to invite me." Seb grinned.

"Karen's coming with Uncle Richard. Jeanine announced this morning she's coming with her boyfriend. Karen's got a room booked at the Bluewater Inn."

"Isn't that where we're staying?" Martin asked.

"So what's the problem?" Seb said. "Karen's not my favorite person, but I'm grown up enough to make small talk if we pass each other on the way to the ice machine."

"They need another room for Jeanine and the boyfriend."

"So?"

Oliver ground his teeth. "Are you being dense on purpose?"

"Ollie, I really don't see what this has to do with us."

"The Bluewater's sold out."

"So Jeanine and her boy toy can stay somewhere else. They'd probably prefer it actually."

"Everywhere's sold out." Oliver ran a hand through his hair. "It's homecoming at Watersmith this weekend. That's half the reason Parker picked this date for the party, since everyone we know will be in town already. But all the accommodations are sold out for fifty miles."

"That's their problem."

"You're such a brat!"

Seb raised his hands in the air. "What are you trying to say? You obviously want something from me. We've booked a room with two double beds. You want Jeanine and her boy—"

"Please don't call him a boy toy again." Oliver ran a hand through his hair.

"Boyfriend to stay with us? That's just weird. Martin doesn't know any of these people."

Martin took a step back at the mention of his name. Something was building between the brothers, and he didn't want to be in the middle when the storm broke.

"I wouldn't ask you to do that," Oliver said.

"Then what?"

"I'm asking you to stay here."

And there it was. Seb's expression turned so thunderous Martin wished for an umbrella, even though they were indoors.

"No."

"Seb, please."

"No." He shoved his hands into his pockets. The look on his face said he'd punch his brother otherwise.

"It's just two nights."

"Come on, we're going." Seb turned and grabbed Martin's elbow.

"Going?" Oliver trailed after them.

"Back to Seacroft. I'll stop at Nana's on the way out of town and apologize."

"Seb, come on. We're all adults. You can sleep here for two nights."

"I told him I would never step foot under this roof again. You think I can do two nights?"

Martin didn't ask about the "him" Seb was referring to. They were walking so fast Martin nearly stumbled. He checked over his shoulder, and his pulse picked up more at Oliver's pained expression. The pressed, confident persona was gone. Instead, there was real distress in the man's eyes; a wordless plea for help.

Had Brian ever looked at Martin like that? Had he been too caught up in his own swamp of fear and apathy to notice?

His feet slowed down. Seb's grip on his elbow slipped.

"What's wrong?" he said.

"We should stay." Martin fought not to tug at the sleeves of his coat. He fought to look like he meant it.

"What?"

Oliver stared at them helplessly, like all his cards had been played out and now he had nothing left to hold his hurricane little brother in place.

"It's just a bed to sleep in," Martin said. "Who cares if it's at a hotel or here? Didn't we come all this way for your grandmother and her party?"

Seb's mouth pressed together until his lips were so tight they were nearly white.

"You don't have to stay in your room. You can both sleep in the main floor guest room," Oliver said. "It's the farthest from Mom and Dad, and bigger too."

"We're not sleeping together," Seb said.

Martin flushed, first from embarrassment at the casual way Seb said it, and then from a sting of disappointment.

"You're not?" The sad look on Oliver's face gave way to confusion.

"The hotel room had two beds for a reason."

"Oh." Oliver said, and then understanding hit him. "Oh! I'm sorry. When you said you were bringing a date, I assumed—"

"You assumed wrong."

Another twist of disappointment swirled in Martin's chest. They hadn't talked about sleeping arrangements. Not that he didn't want to sleep together, now that he thought about it. Not that he hadn't thought about it before, but to hear Seb say it . . .

"We can put Martin in the guest room. It'll give you some more privacy." He smiled at Martin. It was a charming smile, likeable. Martin could see why Oliver had been successful in life, with a face like his and a smile like that.

"Why can't Karen's spawn stay here again? Why are we the ones who have to give up our hotel reservation?" Seb protested, but the fire had gone out of him.

"Two words. Thanksgiving 2009."

Seb nodded. "Technically, that's four words. Or possibly five."

"Asshole." But Oliver was smiling again.

Seb ran his hands through his hair, making it stand up from his scalp in white blond streaks like lightning. "Our original agreement still stands, though. You keep Dad away from me. I will be civil to everyone, and I will sleep in his house, but we are out of here first thing on Sunday morning."

"Fine. Yes, fine, I'll run interference. Let me show you guys to your rooms."

———

In his childhood bedroom, Seb unzipped his bag, shaking. Fuck Oliver for keeping this from them until they were already here. Of course, he'd basically proved his brother's need for secrecy by nearly storming out anyway. But then he'd felt Martin's hand on his arm and seen Oliver's lying, miserable face.

He'd make the effort, at least until someone else pissed him off.

Ollie said he'd show Martin to the guest room. When Seb was small, it was the den, and then converted to a bedroom when his great-grandmother lived with them for a few years before going to a nursing home. After that, it was reserved for guests, with its own en-suite bathroom.

He didn't like leaving Martin alone in the house, where members of Seb's family could be lurking around any corner. He set his bag on the bed and headed downstairs.

Martin was pulling a shirt over his head as Seb pushed open the guest room door. Navy waffle knit covered the line of his spine, an enticing path that Seb's fingers itched to trace. He grinned and knocked against the doorframe. Martin jumped and spun, cheeks pink and hair askew.

"Most people knock and then wait." He pulled the shirt the rest of the way down. It still hung loose on him, but the body underneath was lean and strong, not weak or thin.

"Most people close the door before they take off their shirt in a strange house."

The corner of Martin's mouth quirked up. "Oliver said everyone else was out."

The edge of Seb's earlier adrenaline still clung to him, making him think nasty things about Martin and his shirt.

"So you were waiting for me then?" He tugged at the hem, pulling Martin closer. Martin barely hesitated as their lips met, and Seb laughed as he tasted him. Martin sighed as Seb's hands slid around his body.

"Were you waiting for me?" he asked again.

Martin didn't reply, but he deepened the kiss, his tongue pressing against Seb's lips. Seb nipped at it before he opened his mouth and let Martin in. Surprisingly, as the professor became more comfortable around Seb in this way, he did indeed turn out to be a great kisser, with the right mix of Martin-esque hesitation and determination.

Seb's earlier tension faded. He concentrated on the feeling of Martin's hands on him and Martin's tongue in his mouth. As he pressed their bodies together more fully, Martin gasped. The sound sent a thrill of surprise and desire through him.

Behind them, someone cleared their throat.

Martin jumped back like he'd been electrocuted. Seb growled as he turned to face their audience.

Oliver stood in the doorway, looking sheepish.

"Asshole," Seb muttered.

"Are you sure you don't want to reconsider your sleeping arrangements?"

It wasn't like that, not really. They hadn't discussed it. Not that he didn't have hopes and aspirations, which would have been easy enough to figure out in the privacy of their hotel room, but he always wanted to give Martin the choice. No need to move too fast.

Although, with that kiss . . .

"What do you want?" he said.

"People are going to be arriving soon. Before they get here,

160

there's . . . " Oliver hesitated. "There's one more thing I need to talk to you about."

"Fine." Seb needed a moment longer with Martin. "We'll come find you in a bit."

"No. I need to talk to *you*."

Something was up. Oliver was definitely looking nervous. Seb gave Martin's hand a squeeze, eyes tracing his face, then sighed. "Fine. Lead the way."

Oliver pushed past them both to the tall patio door at the far end of the room. He slid it open, then stood aside to wait for Seb. "It won't take long. Martin, make yourself at home. I'll bring him back."

Seb paused long enough to kiss Martin again, silently telling him to hold that thought. He didn't care if the whole family was there to watch.

Oliver led him out over the back lawn to the small pond in the corner. When they'd been little, their mother kept Japanese carp in it, white and bright orange ones that sucked at the surface of the water for pellets. Then one summer, a snapping turtle took up residence in the pond, and the fish disappeared, one by one.

"This better not be a lecture about propriety," Seb said when Ollie slowed. "You were all set to put us in the same room, and everyone knows I'm a big old queer, so it's not like anyone's got any right to complain about who I kiss."

"Don't be a child." Oliver ran a hand over his head. Seb thought again that his brother looked tired. Older. His hair was longer than it had ever been. His shirt was pressed but untucked. He was the same Oliver, but less tidy.

"Did you bring anyone to this shindig?" Seb asked.

"No. I'm not seeing anyone right now."

"Couldn't convince Cooper to come, just for old time's sake? You two were practically married. Sometimes I think Mom and Dad liked him better than you. Remember that time he broke his ankle when we went skiing for spring break? Mom was hysterical. They definitely liked him better than me. Did he become the fourth Stevenson child after I left the last time?"

"Just stop talking for a second!" Oliver walked away, running his hand through his hair again in an old nervous habit. When he'd stopped biting his nails in junior high, he needed something to do with his hands, and his hair became the unfortunate victim. Stevenson hair came from tough stock, which was just as well because otherwise Oliver's would have given up the ghost a long time ago.

Seb smiled and bit his lip, while his big brother paced. He'd promised to be civil. He hadn't promised to not poke the buttons he'd learned to press over the years.

"I need your help," Oliver said finally.

"Okay. Parker got you tying chair covers in the morning?"

"No. Well, yes. But that's . . . " Oliver did another lap around the pond.

Anticipation made the hairs on Seb's neck stand up. This was going to be big. And if Oliver was asking him for help, he was desperate.

"Did you get some nice girl pregnant? Afraid of telling Mom and Dad you've sullied the Stevenson name?"

"Oh, for fuck's sake." Oliver spun on his heel and started marching back toward the house. Seb laughed and trotted after him, tugging on his sleeve.

"Okay, okay. I'll stop. Tell me what's up."

Oliver paced a few more laps at the edge of the pond. Seb waited.

"I'm leaving the firm."

"Say again?"

"My job. I'm quitting my job."

Seb nodded. "I figured that's what that meant. What do you mean though? You love that job."

Oliver smiled bleakly. "How would you know?"

Seb went to answer and then snapped his mouth shut. He had a bunch of smartass comments, but Oliver wasn't wrong. Seb didn't really know much about his brother's life at all.

"When?"

"At the end of the summer."

"Next summer?" Seb asked. Oliver always liked to be the man with the plan, but telling Seb about this almost a year ahead of time was excessive.

"No." Oliver sighed and hung his head. "I turned in my notice in August. I'm done next week."

Seb considered this. "What are you going to do after that?"

"I need more balance in my life. No more ninety-hour weeks. I'm starting my own business. Wellness consulting."

"Wellness what?"

"It's like life coaching, but with a focus on nutrition and work-life balance."

Seb snorted. "Sounds like a lot of new-age crap to me."

"You cut up books and call it art, and people pay you for it."

"Now you sound like Martin."

"He seems like my kind of guy."

"Not really. You like them taller and with a better tan."

They stared at each other, a few feet apart on the lawn where Oliver told his parents he was gay, and where Seb sucked off his prom date after their high school graduation party. His father nearly found them, and they'd had to hide out in a garden shed.

Evil glee exploded like fireworks as realization hit Seb.

"You haven't told Dad yet, have you?" The guilty expression on Oliver's face said Seb had guessed right. "You haven't! What do you think he's going to say when you tell him you're giving up your prestigious law career to tell people they need to eat more yogurt and meditate?"

"Shut up."

"What do you think he's going to say?"

"I don't care." Oliver scuffed a loafer in the grass.

"I don't believe that for a second. If you didn't care, you'd have made him proofread your resignation letter as a giant fuck you."

"No. That's what you would have done."

"Damn right I would. What? You think he won't notice? When you stop going to the office? When you start coming to the house in socks and sandals?"

"You're such an ass," Oliver said, but he was laughing now.

"So what do you want me to do? Soften the blow? Distract him from your earth-shattering news by giving Martin a hand job at the dinner table? You know I'm happy to make Dad squirm. I don't think Martin's into exhibitionism, but we're still getting to know each other."

Oliver's hands were in his hair again. "You promised you'd be civil this weekend."

"This is me being civil. I haven't told you your business plan sounds like you're going to be brewing artisanal kombucha for hipsters who can't afford it. Or that work-life balance is a myth slackers use to justify fucking off the clock at five under the guise of being dedicated to their family."

Oliver's eyes narrowed. "Were you always such a cynic?"

"Since the day my father called me a fag, and you didn't say anything to back me up."

It slipped out. Seb hadn't meant to say it. Not now. Not to Ollie. To his dad maybe, if Philip tried to make another right-eous stand in the family home, but not to his brother.

Oliver's face turned sad. His chin and shoulders dropped. "I'm sorry."

"Yeah. Me too." Whether he was apologizing for his outburst, or the years he'd spent treating his brother like some kind of a traitor when they were all crushed under their father's unyielding thumb, Seb wasn't sure. "I only ever wanted to be like you."

"Yeah." Oliver's voice was rough at the edges. "I know."

Seb smiled at him. "And instead you get to be a loser outcast like me!"

"You're not a loser."

"Never have been. But I don't know. Wellness consulting sounds like a one-way ticket to Loserland if you ask me."

Oliver shook his head and laughed, then pulled Seb into a hug, squeezing until Seb chuckled and returned it.

"I'm sorry," Oliver said into his shoulder. "About back then. With Dad. I should have said something."

"You should have." Seb slapped him on the back. "Don't think I'm not reserving the right to kick your ass at some undetermined time in the future."

"Understood."

"Can I go back to my date now? You interrupted something good there."

Oliver laughed. "You're sure you're not sleeping with him?"

"Not yet."

"That elusive artist charm?"

"He's a good guy."

"He looks like a scarecrow."

"You should see him in a suit." Seb turned, but Oliver squeezed his shoulder.

"There's one more thing."

Seb rolled his eyes. "Yes, Columbo?"

"I'm moving to Seacroft."

16

$\mathcal{M}$artin watched Oliver lead Seb out across the lawn. He hoped Seb listened to whatever his brother had to say. Oliver was obviously agitated, and it would be just like Seb to make a joke out of everything and get punched in the face for his trouble.

When they didn't come back right away, Martin took the opportunity to pull his suit out of its bag and stash it in the closet. No need to iron out more wrinkles than were absolutely necessary.

They were only staying for two nights, so it didn't make sense for him to unpack everything, even though there was an empty dresser in the room. He hadn't seen Seb's suit at all. For a moment, he worried the whole weekend was going to be more informal than he'd been led to believe. He would be the only one to show up in a suit, just because Seb liked to look at him in it.

Seb seemed to like a lot of things about Martin. His skin heated at the remembered press of Seb's lips on his and the friction of his body moving shamelessly against Martin's, even though the door had been wide open for anyone to see.

He hadn't felt interested enough in life to be attracted to

anyone else in it for a long time. Now that he was, he wanted Seb to come back soon to continue what they'd started.

Except Seb didn't come back. After a while, Martin considered going after them, but he didn't want to disturb them if they were discussing something important. Eventually, though, sitting like a lump in the strange guest room started to feel too much like the endless days he'd spent in bed, so he gave up waiting and went to explore.

Down the hall from his room was a small library, warm and elegant like the rest of the house. Floor-to-ceiling bookshelves held books on every subject imaginable. It reminded Martin a bit of the bookstore, although the Stevenson's library was noticeably better organized.

A significant portion of the shelves were dedicated to literature and history, understandably so. There were several of Dr. Stevenson's publications—Martin recognized the ones he had read himself—as well as books written by many of Martin's colleagues, friends, acquaintances.

And there, wedged between significantly weightier material, was Martin's one thin book.

They'd decided to publish his thesis. Martin hadn't been convinced it was the right idea. He'd always felt it was incomplete, not conclusive enough to really contribute anything to the study of Bergmann's life and works. His supervisor pushed the idea, though, and the book happened. Not that it had been a roaring success of any kind. Martin wasn't even listed as the first author. From time to time, he'd get a fraction of a royalty check from the university, but mostly, he didn't think about it.

Except there it was. His book, with his name, on the shelf of one of the giants of the modern academic world. He hadn't read it in a while. His own copies were in boxes in Brian's basement, collected hastily when Brian cleaned out Martin's office at Mount Garner and never looked at again.

The complete summation of his life's work to date didn't feel very heavy.

"Can I help you?"

In the doorway stood Doctor Philip Stevenson.

Martin fumbled. He stammered. He nearly dropped the book. "I came with Seb."

Dr. Stevenson's lips thinned. "Is Sebastian here?" He was bigger than Martin remembered.

"Yes." He managed to speak. "He's outside. With Oliver."

"I didn't think we'd see him until tomorrow."

"Oh. Oliver told us there was a dinner tonight." What if that wasn't true? Or they weren't invited? Seb had been on edge since they'd arrived. If dinner didn't go according to plan, Martin would be back to sleeping on Brian's couch tonight.

Dr. Stevenson glanced down at the Martin's book. "Doing a little light reading?"

"Oh, well. I was surprised. Bergmann isn't exactly—"

"Are you familiar with Bergmann?" Dr. Stevenson stepped forward. He took the book from Martin's hand and flipped through the pages.

"Yes. Well. That is—"

"Not a lot known about him. A bit of a controversial figure at the moment. Some say he never existed at all. That he's been made up to be some kind of poster child for LGBT persecution by the Nazis. Others disagree as to how many of the poems that have been attributed to him are legitimate."

Martin heard all these arguments before. Bergmann was a real person with a real story, and not just some mid-century propaganda figure.

"But the research shows that—"

"And really, from a literary standpoint, there's not much to the poetry, even if he did write them. They're fairly rudimentary in style, structure, and word choice. Particularly for the era.

There's not much of significance to them, other than the way the poet died—if, indeed, he wrote them at all."

Every word was like a punch to Martin's gut. He'd heard this all before, but to hear it from Dr. Philip Stevenson, *the* Dr. Stevenson . . . If this was his feeling on the matter, then what hope did Martin have for anything but languishing in obscurity like Bergmann himself?

"I'm sorry," Dr. Stevenson said. "We haven't even been introduced. I'm Philip." He held out his hand like people shook it every day.

"Martin. Er . . . Dr. Martin Lindsey."

Philip's grip was firm, but his confident smile slipped. His gaze dropped to the book he held, a finger running down the cover until it stopped below Martin's name.

His laugh was big, as big as he was, filling the whole room. Martin clenched his jaw and flexed his toes in his shoes to keep from flinching.

"Oh my!" Philip said. His slap on Martin's back was solid, making him cough. "Well played. A little vanity never hurt anyone."

"I didn't mean—"

Philip's blue eyes twinkled as he laughed again. For a minute, Martin could see Seb in them. There was very little else to link the two men. Philip was big and solid where Seb was long and almost lithe. Philip's face was ruddy, and his hair, though gray now, had been dark from what Martin remembered. Seb's skin and hair were so many shades lighter. The only thing that showed any sign of their relation was the eyes.

"Lindsey, eh?" Philip scratched at his beard. "Where are you working?"

"Well, I was at Mount Garner, but . . . " Martin coughed before he could admit to his idol that he was working part time at a used bookstore, because that was all he could manage these days.

"Mount Garner?" Philip's eyebrow arched as his smile turned mischievous. Another thing Seb inherited from his father, then. "What a mess that is. It will take a long time to recover after that whole fuss. And you're still there?"

"No." Martin wanted to take his book back. Or grab another one from the shelf. Anything so he would have something to do with his hands. "I'm on . . . sabbatical, at the moment."

"That's fortunate. Good timing on your part." Philip put one big arm around Martin's shoulders. "And you came with my son? That seems unlikely. Maybe there is hope for him yet. Are you thirsty? How about a drink?"

He led Martin out of the library. Martin was torn between flattery at the attention and outright terror, like a princess being dragged down to the ogre's cave.

Would it be too much to hope Seb would come rescue him?

———

It was hard not to be out of sorts after Seb's conversation with Oliver. The idea of his brother living in his town made him twitchy, which compounded all the twitch from being back at the family house. And then there was the simmering sexual frustration, wanting to get back to Martin to see if the professor would let Seb kiss him again. Properly. Behind a closed door.

He found Martin still in the guest room, sitting in one of the floral armchairs and reading a thin hardcover book.

"What's that?" Seb asked.

"My book." Martin flipped through the pages, frowning like he thought there should be more of them.

"You brought a book?"

"No, I wrote a book."

"You did? That one? That's amazing!" Seb came around to peer over his shoulder, but Martin shut the book.

"It's nothing special. There should be whole volumes written

170

about Bergmann, but it's a start, right? It probably won't ever go farther than one publication run for the university market." He smiled ruefully up at Seb. "In a few years, you'll find a copy in the back of Dog Ears, cut it up, and sell it as something new for more money than I'll ever make on all of them."

"Don't say that. You wrote a book!" It hurt that Martin couldn't see what an accomplishment that was.

"I met your dad."

Seb froze, his eyes darting around the room in instinctual panic. Not that he expected Philip Stevenson to be lurking behind a curtain, but his nerves were nearly shot, and he needed at least forty-five minutes with no more surprises.

"And?" he said, hoping he didn't sound too nervous.

"He called my book inconsequential and poured me a drink." Martin smiled crookedly, happy and sad at the same time.

Seb knew the feeling, and Martin's reluctance to show off his book made more sense. Seb was ready to stalk down the hall and punch his dad for it, but he'd promised Oliver—again— he'd behave, at least until after Oliver broke his big news to the family.

Seb squeezed Martin's shoulder. "Did he at least give you the good whiskey?"

"I asked for a vodka soda." Martin turned the book over in his hands again. "But he's got good vodka too."

Dinner was always a formal affair in the Stevenson household, even when they said it was casual. Seb's mom was an outstanding cook, and dinner was French service, as she liked to call it. Everything was carved and plated in the kitchen and brought out to the table in individual portions, like they were in a restaurant.

That night was an especially elaborate affair given all the people gathered. There were the six Stevensons—Philip and Seb's mother Nora, Gillian and Parker, Ollie and Seb. Then there was Gillian's husband Julian—Seb still had to fight back a smirk as he introduced them to Martin—and Parker's husband Jason. And Martin. Gillian and Parker's combined five children were excused from the family festivities for the evening. Just as well because that would have been too damn much quality family time for Seb.

"So Martin," Jason said once salads were served. "Parker says you're a doctor? What do you practice? I have a cousin who is a urologist in Jacksonville."

Martin wiped his mouth with a napkin and cleared his throat. "I'm not that kind of doctor."

Seb glanced at Oliver, who glanced at Parker, who shrugged. Seb said he was bringing a doctor, and he'd said it to cause a stir. He hadn't expected the news to make it as far down the family grapevine as Jason.

"Martin and I have quite a bit in common," Philip said from his place at the head of the table. "He specializes in the historical side of the spectrum, but we are both men of knowledge."

Philip claiming Martin as one of his own made Seb's spine tense.

"So how did you two meet?" Parker asked. Her smile was kind. Seb tried to tell himself she was being polite, not nosey. Martin cut into an endive, and little splotches of color formed just above the collar of the shirt he'd put on for dinner. He probably didn't want to talk about the bookstore. Seb pressed his knee against Martin's and took the lead.

"One of those gay hookup apps. Doctors Without Borders. Something like that." He used the practiced social smile he'd perfected years ago with his family. It irritated the shit out of most of them. "Isn't that how you two met, Gillie?"

"Oh for god's sakes," Gillian said. His eldest sister was a cardiologist in Charleston, but she and Julian were part of a group of practitioners who ran a clinic in Guatemala. She also looked like an owl, with wispy hair that wasn't light enough to be blond or dark enough to be brown, and wide eyes set under heavy brows perpetually judging the people around them.

"How was the drive?" Nora asked. Seb's mom could always be relied on to redirect the conversation before the second course could be delayed.

The second course turned out to be seared fish. Pink, with golden brown skin and roasted grapes. Seb was dubious, but Martin looked pleased.

"Oliver," Philip said, once everyone had resumed eating. "I saw Cooper the other day."

"Cooper?" Martin asked Seb quietly.

"My brother's ex." He didn't bother to pitch his voice as low as Martin's. "Good as arm candy at gala dinners, and he knew his way around a Porsche. Not good for much else."

"Cooper is a very talented lawyer." Philip's eyes held a spark of challenge, one Seb knew exactly how to stoke to a flame if the need arose.

"He's not my boyfriend anymore, Dad," Oliver said.

"That doesn't mean you two can't be friends," Nora said. "We've known his family for years. You were friends for ages before you dated."

Oliver nodded, eyes on his plate.

"What happened between you two anyway?" Seb asked.

"It's complicated." Oliver forked a grape into his mouth.

"Complicated? Does that mean you can't even be Facebook friends anymore?" Seb couldn't help the dig.

"Facebook." Jason laughed. "No one uses Facebook. My kids will tell you it's for old people. It's all pictures now. Instachat and Snap-App."

Parker smiled at her husband. The smile said she knew he was wrong, but wasn't going to correct him.

But Seb could.

"I'm coming up to Charlotte next week, Oliver," Philip said as Seb was about to launch his retort. "I'm having dinner with Dr.

Fisher—you remember him—but I thought I could stop by your office and we could have lunch together."

A blind person could see the panic spread across Oliver's face, but the family's collective eyesight appeared to have deteriorated significantly over the years.

Oliver was gripping his knife like a weapon. "I could meet you somewhere. You don't need to come all the way to the office."

"No, no, I'll have the car. I can park it in your visitor parking for free while we eat."

Cheap bastard.

Oliver appeared to be on the verge of losing consciousness. His knife trembled, and he threw a desperate look at Seb.

Coward.

Seb felt for him, though. Announcing his holistic lifestyle makeover to this room of his nearest and somewhat dearest was never going to be easy. The thought of their father strolling through Oliver's soon-to-be former office and hearing the news that way had to be even more terrifying.

Seb sighed. Time to dig his brother out of this one. He'd collect his reward later.

"I've got a show coming up in six weeks." His opening line was unimportant. He needed to wait for someone to take the bait. "I've been invited to exhibit some of my work as part of a tribute to Arlene Schiller."

"Seb, that sounds great!" Nora said.

"Sebastian, don't interrupt while I'm talking to your brother." Philip regarded him like a fly buzzing around a picnic.

Seb forced his smile and continued undeterred. "It was supposed to be a collaborative show, but Schiller had to back out."

"Do you get paid for something like that?" Jason asked.

Bingo.

"Oliver—" Philip tried again.

"Some. It's exposure mostly, but shows like this usually net a few sales after the fact," Seb said. "Kenneth says it's good for my career. Probably the biggest show I've done so far."

"Sebastian—"

"But you don't get paid? Is it even a real job if you're not making money? What kind of sense does that make?"

Seb narrowed his eyes. Jason always made it too easy. "About as much sense as my sister keeping you around even though we all know you're a Class D moron."

"Seb!" Parker said.

"Sebastian!" Philip's knife clattered to his plate.

Seb smiled blithely across the table at his father. "Yes, Dad?"

"Apologize to Jason."

Martin's leg shifted against Seb's, possibly in warning, but Seb knew exactly what he was doing. Too bad Martin would witness this, though. Things were about to get loud. The Stevensons were yellers when they all got together.

"Jason." He slipped his hand into Martin's. "I'm sorry you wouldn't know good art if it bit you in your sagging ass. Seriously, man, with what you make in commissions, a gym membership shouldn't be that hard to manage."

"Sebastian!" Philip's voice dropped another note lower.

"It's fine, Seb." Oliver's voice was quiet next to him. "You can stop."

Seb winked at his big brother. Oliver never understood this. The only way to escape was to commit to the very end.

"Seriously?" Jason's face was several shades pinker than the fish on his plate. "That's the best you can come up with? You're going to insult my ass?"

"I've seen a lot of ass in my time," Seb said.

"Sebastian, that is enough!" His father pounded the table.

"Yours isn't all that great. I remember."

"Seb!" Parker's voice rose above the others.

"Seb, stop." Oliver's hand was on Seb's knee, squeezing so hard the pain radiated up his leg.

"You asshole," Jason growled.

"It's okay, Jay." Seb took a bite of his dinner. "Everyone gets experimental. I'm always happy to help a brother-in-law out."

"You didn't!" Parker said. It didn't matter if she was talking to Seb or Jason.

"That is enough, Sebastian." Philip's face was purple. Murderous.

Seb squared his shoulders. Now they were getting somewhere. "Dad. Do you know who calls me Sebastian? Just you. No one else. It's Seb, Dad. It has been since I was ten. It's like you don't want to admit who I am or something. That I don't get to make my own choices."

"You've made your choices."

The table around them went silent. Seb stood his ground. "I have, Dad. Repeatedly. Yet you choose not to recognize them."

"I'm supposed to recognize that you've thrown everything I've ever offered you back in my face? That you continue to embarrass this family? You want praise for that?"

"Philip," Nora said. Philip ignored her.

"Everything you've offered me?" Seb said. Oliver's hand on his knee was a claw, and even Martin's hand around his had gone tight, but Seb pushed on. "You told me how it was going to be and then kicked me out when I didn't do things your way."

"We gave you every kind of support you needed. And you rejected it."

Seb had to laugh at that. Was that how his father saw it? "You didn't offer support. You offered a straightjacket."

"He has dyslexia." Philip turned to Martin. "Did he tell you that?"

"You make it sound like it's contagious." Seb's insides boiled. That wasn't Philip's story to tell.

"Do you know his *art*," the word was a sneer, "is an extended metaphor for revenge against me and my life's work? Your life's work too. Those poems you work so hard to prove your dead German wrote? He'll cut them up and sell them."

"You've never understood." Seb's voice dropped. His work wasn't some coping mechanism or a shout into the void about the unfairness of the way his brain was wired. He created new words, new works from unwanted goods. That was his *art*.

"We tried to help him." Philip was still speaking to Martin, probably seeking backup. "Accommodations could have been made."

"I didn't need accommodating." Seb sneered. "I needed you to see I wasn't like you!"

"Because you never even tried!" Philip banged on the table again.

"Dad!" This was from Oliver.

"You were determined to fail at everything we ever asked you to do."

"Fail? Because I don't work a job with a salary? Because I don't come here to talk about my mortgage and my retirement plans? Because I bring men to the house instead of women?"

"This has nothing to do with that. We have always supported your and Oliver's choices."

"Dad." Oliver said again. Seb would have bruises where Oliver gripped him.

"It's not a choice, Dad! We're gay! Your sons are gay."

"Dad!"

"You think I care about—"

"Dad!"

"What?" Philip's glare seared its way across the table to Oliver.

"I quit my job to make artisanal kombucha."

17

"It's not like it used to be," Seb said, after dinner. They were on the patio, staring out over the dark yard. Seb had a whiskey in his hand. Martin sat on a cold patio chair, nursing another vodka soda.

"It went better than I thought it would." Oliver sipped his own rocks glass.

"That was better?" Martin asked.

The brothers chuckled. The dark sound made Martin shiver.

The dinner reminded him of his first lecture at Mount Garner. *Don't look them in the eye*, they said. *They'll know if you're nervous. Don't let them see you sweat. They smell blood in the water.*

His students smelled his blood from the moment he'd left his office, two floors up from the chaos of the lecture hall. He wasn't supposed to be teaching that semester, but he'd been asked to stand in for a week to cover for a colleague with pneumonia. The freshman students, already mid-semester and bored, took one look at him, and before he even opened his mouth, he knew it was a lost cause.

The difference between his first lecture and dinner with the Stevensons was that, at Mount Garner, he had fought to be seen and heard over the roar of the crowd, whereas at the dinner, sitting next to Seb, Martin desperately wished to vanish.

Everyone started shouting at once. Philip redirected his fury at Oliver. Parker pointed fingers and hurled insults, sometimes at Jason, sometimes at Seb. Gillian and Julian tried to break up Philip and Oliver, and Parker and everyone, and Nora kept asking if someone could pass the wine.

"I noticed Mom bought new dishes," Seb said.

"I think we've broken so many of the other ones over the years that she didn't have enough to serve all nine of us." Oliver pulled a cigarette pack out from his pocket.

"How does that fit with your holistic lifestyle?" Seb asked.

"I'm going to quit."

"How did the dishes get broken?" Martin was pretty sure he knew the answer.

"You should have let me handle it." Seb glared at Oliver.

"Handle what?" Oliver said through clenched lips as he lit the cigarette. "I really thought he might kill you this time."

"Nah. We've said everything we were ever going to really say to each other years ago."

Martin had seen it coming. He didn't even know what it was, but he'd felt the shift, like the quiet moment before rain started. One minute, they'd been talking about dinner and Oliver's ex-boyfriend, and then something in Seb's face changed. His pale skin went taught around his eyes and his jaw. The color rose on his cheeks as he leaned into the table.

And then Seb walked into the no-man's land of a family dinner, armed with nothing but a tilt of his head and words aimed to wound.

"Did you really sleep with Parker's husband?" Martin asked.

Oliver laughed around an inhale of his cigarette.

"No." Seb leaned in to kiss Martin, quick and hard. Everything about him was kinetic in the watery glow of the floodlights that lined the yard.

"Then why—"

"Because Seb can't even spell subtlety," Oliver said. "It's the silent b. Gets him every time."

Seb punched him in the arm, making Oliver yelp and his whiskey slosh over the edge of his glass.

"First blood." Seb grinned. "Doesn't matter what it's about. If you draw first blood in a confrontation, you start with the upper hand."

"But Parker—" Martin tried to say.

"Knows it's not true. Jason could only get straighter if I shoved a stick up his ass." Seb snorted. "I really thought she'd have divorced him by now, though."

"She's got the kids. You know Parker." Oliver tossed back the last of his drink. "She wears the pants in that relationship. The pants, the boxers, and the combat boots. She'll leave when she's good and ready."

They laughed, clapping each other on the back. Oliver's hair was darker against his skin on the shadowy patio, while Seb's nearly glowed. But at night, all cats were gray, and they stood shoulder to shoulder. Sadness slithered through Martin as he watched them commiserate. What must growing up together have been like for them to congratulate each other on getting through a meal without a broken dish and discussing the end of their sister's marriage like they'd run out of small talk?

Seb glanced over his shoulder. He must have seen Martin's thoughts on his face because his easy grin turned serious. "You okay?"

"Yeah." Martin pulled himself to his feet, faking a stretch. He was an intruder in all of this, and it was time to go. "It was a long day. I think I'm going to head to bed."

"Already?" The rest of Seb's smile faded. "It's kind of early."

Martin took a step back. Anxiety thrummed under his skin as the edge of adrenaline from the most dysfunctional dinner he'd ever been to wore off.

"I'll see you tomorrow." He needed some space to think, and despite the sprawling backyard, he wasn't getting it here. He turned, leaving the Stevenson brothers to themselves.

———

The bed was comfortable, but it still wasn't his. Martin stared at the dark shape of the dresser. He'd been trying to sleep for an hour.

The dinner replayed over and over in his mind. The yelling, the insults, the way Oliver and Seb laughed it all off when it was over. Nervousness spiraled in a loop from his brain to his chest and back again. He shouldn't have been there, at dinner. He shouldn't have come at all.

Once again, *should* was such a useless word.

There was a scraping sound.

"Martin."

Martin's breath caught.

"Hey, are you awake?"

He lay still where he was.

The patio door slid in its track, and Martin silently cursed that he hadn't thought to lock it. He held his breath, then squeezed his eyes shut at the sound of Seb's footsteps on the carpet.

He was asleep. Seb needed to think he was asleep.

"We're pretty fucked up," Seb said quietly. "I can't even imagine what that must have looked like to you. Zoo animals have better manners than we do."

"No shit," Martin said.

"You *are* awake!" Seb's voice rose in the dark.

Martin growled, pulling himself upright against the headboard. He fumbled until he found the lamp by the bed and turned it on. Seb sat across from him in the floral arm chair. Mud streaked the sleeve of his leather jacket, and his feet were bare, but he grinned at Martin. Normally, that grin was charming, but tonight it flared an emotion close to anger in Martin's chest. He didn't deserve to feel like this, and it was Seb's fault for bringing him into such a volatile situation.

"What am I doing here?" Martin let his irritation show. "Huh? Why did you invite me?"

Seb's smile fell. "I'm sorry." Shadows played over his face.

"Do you want me here at all? Or was I part of some big *screw you* to your parents?"

"No!"

"What happened to being civil? What happened to leaving at the first sign of someone looking at you funny?"

"Oliver needed me." Seb twisted his hands in his lap. His earlier frenetic energy vanished.

"To do what? Start a yelling match at dinner? Imply you were sleeping with your brother-in-law? What was it you thought he needed you to do?"

"To be me, okay?" Seb's features hardened.

"What does that mean?" Martin's fists clenched against the comforter.

"That's who I am to them." He beat at his chest. "The fuck up. Screwed up Sebastian, who can't be normal, who can't be like everyone."

"Are you really dyslexic?"

"That's what you're getting out of all of this?" Seb paced the room, and the energy charged around him.

Martin sighed. This wasn't what he'd wanted. He was still reeling from the whole evening, but he hadn't meant to direct his frustration at Seb. He pulled the covers away and stood, trying to get in front of the other man. "Just calm down." The last thing either of them needed was for Seb to go storming into the house looking to pick another fight.

"There's nothing wrong with me," Seb's voice rasped.

"I never said there was."

"It's not a disease. He says it like I have syphilis."

"He doesn't think that."

Seb's eyes flashed cobalt in the dim room. "How would you know?" He continued to circle like a caged tiger. Martin fought the flutters in his stomach that told him to run. He'd never seen Seb like this, the confident persona shattered to pieces.

Martin held his ground. Seb was hurting. Martin needed to stay. "Hey." He held his hands out wide. "Hey, it's okay."

"It's not." Seb grabbed at big handfuls of his hair. "It's not okay. Why are they like that? Why do they make me so crazy?"

"Families do that."

"Does your family do that?" Seb glared at him.

"My family is me and Brian and sometimes our mom. We don't have the critical mass to be like yours."

"Critical mass? What are we, some kind of bomb?" Seb's face was pained.

"I wouldn't be surprised if there's a crater where the dining room used to be in the morning." He took another step forward.

"Screw you," Seb said, but there wasn't any heat behind it. He hunched in on himself, arms curled around his sides. The Seb who swaggered through the bookstore was nowhere to be seen.

Martin was close enough to smell the leather and sweat scent of Seb's jacket. Another step, and their toes bumped together. Martin's arms were still wide. To his surprise, Seb closed the rest of the space between them, burying his face in Martin's shoulder and wrapping his arms around Martin's waist.

"Fuck, I'm so sorry." Seb breathed it against Martin's skin. His hands wrapped all the way around his body. Martin relaxed and slid his own arms around Seb, one hand resting in the middle of his back, the other on his neck where the white-blond hair was fine and soft.

"It's okay." Martin's anger evaporated as Seb shuddered against him.

"We're horrible. You shouldn't have to see us."

"It's fine. I'm not sorry I came this weekend."

"Well, I'm sorry I brought you."

———

Martin smelled like laundry detergent and drug store deodorant. Seb wanted to drown in it. Burn his senses out with it, so the last few hours went up in a puff of cotton fresh-scented smoke.

He'd been giddy, buzzed on that one glass of whiskey and the evil thrill he got every time he went toe to toe with his dad.

But the disappointment in Martin's face as he'd left Seb and Oliver on the patio made holding onto his good mood impossible.

Now he pressed into Martin, fighting back tears while Martin smoothed a hand over his hair and murmured soft things.

"I just . . . " Seb said. "I see my dad, and something inside me snaps, you know?"

"Do you want to talk about it?"

"No."

Martin pulled away. Seb wanted to tug him back just as quick, but let him cross the room and sit on the bed. Martin wore a ragged T-shirt and soft pajama pants. He scrubbed his hands over his face. "What are we even doing here? Why did you come if you knew it would be like this?"

Seb couldn't help but sit on the edge of the mattress. He rested his head on Martin's shoulder. "Because my grandmother was sick, and my brother is more scared of my dad than he is of me." His head bobbed when Martin laughed.

"And what am I doing here?"

Seb nuzzled in farther, wrapping one arm around Martin's shoulders to keep him close. "I like a challenge?"

"I think you proved that tonight."

"I was an ass tonight. That's not much of a challenge. But you push me, whether you know it or not. You make me want to try harder, be kinder. Maybe I thought your being here would force me to be a better version of myself. The one who isn't cynical and quick to shoot first. I want different things when you're around."

"What things?" Martin coughed quietly and Seb buried a knowing smile in Martin's T-shirt.

"That too." He kissed the soft cotton. "But I don't have much. In Seacroft. I don't know if you've noticed. There's my work and my apartment, and I have Cass because she wouldn't leave me alone until I agreed to help her. Everyone else, though . . . I just skim."

"Everyone else loves you."

"They don't know me." And wasn't that a kick in the teeth? He'd lived in Seacroft for almost four years. He had acquaintances, people he passed on the street who waved hello, but that was it.

When Martin's fingers slid under his jaw, tipping his head up to press their lips together, relief poured over Seb. If Martin let him go on much longer, he would have spilled every wish, every fearful secret he'd ever held. Seb kissed him back, shutting his eyes, trying to push away the ache, the lingering nervous energy from that freak show of a dinner. He focused on Martin: his clean washed scent, the pressure of his mouth.

The kiss turned hungry, recovering some of the heat from earlier in the afternoon, before Seb's head filled with his family and their endless crises.

He shifted, coming up to his knees and climbing over Martin until he straddled his lap. He shed the leather jacket and let it fall to the floor, then buried his fingers in Martin's hair while his tongue pushed into Martin's mouth.

"Is this a good idea?" It had to be. Seb arched as warm hands curved over the small of his back. His dick twitched, and he rolled his hips.

"I'm not sure." Martin's eyes were bright. He was all crooked lines—his nose, his jaw, his smile.

"Should I go? Let you go back to sleep?" Seb would, if Martin told him to. It was the least he could do, after everything.

The most he could do, though . . .

Martin stilled, his hands on Seb's skin, his mouth slightly open. Seb waited, counted to five, listened to the soft sound of Martin's breath as it brushed over his chin. When he didn't say anything, Seb put a hand on Martin's shoulders and went to climb down. It was enough. After a night like this, one good kiss would have to be enough.

Martin moved so fast Seb didn't see it coming. He only had time to think the professor was stronger than he looked before Seb was wrapped up in his arms, turned, and pushed onto the bed in one motion. He stared up, wide-eyed and gasping, as Martin came down over him, body pressed along Seb's.

He groaned and pulled at Martin's shirt, trying to shift so more of them aligned. Martin's heavy weight on top of him was unexpected but welcome. It grounded him, brought him more into the moment, where before he'd been about to fly apart at any second.

"There is nothing wrong with you," Martin whispered in his ear, his voice harder than Seb expected. His arousal grew at the sound. "And there is nothing wrong with me either. I am not broken. You don't have to treat me like I am."

The last part was a declaration, maybe not even meant for Seb. He found the hem of Martin's T-shirt, then the warm skin underneath, and Martin growled at the contact.

"I wasn't—" Seb's words were cut off when Martin's mouth found his again. Martin was wiry, all hard angles and bone against Seb's body, but he was strong. One hand gripped Seb's hair and tugged his head gently to one side so Martin could nibble on his jaw.

"I don't," Seb tried again. "I don't even know what you like."

"It's been a while."

"How long is a while?"

"Longer than months, less than never."

Seb laughed and pushed until they rolled, so that Martin was on his back and Seb sprawled half on top of him. Martin's shirt was rucked up, exposing the stretch of skin and hair that had first caught Seb's imagination. He ran his fingers over it, making Martin suck his stomach down in reflex. Seb trailed his hand up under the shirt until he found a nipple. He flicked a finger over it, and Martin grunted softly.

"Take your shirt off," Martin said.

Seb smiled. "Want to do it for me?"

"I want to watch you."

The statement made heat flood Seb's throat while his groin tightened. Martin's hand was on his own belly, fingers turning in slow circles. Seb stood, focused on undoing the buttons of his shirt. He slid it off and gripped the hem of his T-shirt. Martin watched him through heavy-lidded eyes as Seb pulled the shirt over his head, shivering in the cool air of the bedroom. Silver barbells pierced each of Seb's nipples. He toyed absently with one as he took in Martin on the bed.

Martin pulled himself up on his elbows, grasping his own shirt to tug it off by the collar. Wiry. But strong. The hair on his stomach trailed up his torso. His collarbones were deep grooves, showing the width of him and the muscle that ran from his shoulders over his chest.

"I want to touch your piercings." That Martin didn't ask but simply stated made something flash inside Seb—hot, then molten. As he came to stand between Martin's knees, his dick lengthened inside his jeans. His own knees trembled when Martin took one of the silver barbells between his thumb and forefinger, flicking and pinching. The sensation made Seb flinch, then put his hands around Martin's face and pulled him up until their mouths were on each other. Seb wanted him, and every tugging sting as Martin pulled on the piercing again fired his need even more. Gasping, Seb collapsed to straddle Martin's lap again.

He held all of himself tight, barely balanced on the edge of the mattress. Martin seemed more interested in playing with the piercings than in holding Seb up. His teeth nipped at Seb's lower lip while his fingers explored. It was almost like Seb wasn't there, like Martin was so focused on a single task he had gone somewhere else, but each flick of his nipple made Seb pant. The piercings were a fun idea a dozen or so years earlier, but few lovers were interested in them since. Feeling the rigid length of Martin's erection under him, he ground down with his hips and slipped a hand between them.

Martin grabbed hold of his wrist and pulled it back up, twisting it behind Seb's back. He bit at Seb's lip harder this time.

"Do you want to be in charge?" Seb asked. "Is that it?"

Martin sucked on the bitten spot as he brought Seb's other hand around behind him, so both his wrists were clasped together. "I saw you." Martin said it like Seb hadn't spoken. He licked at Seb's nipples, making him groan and arch.

"When?"

"When you decided to protect Oliver at dinner. I saw you make the decision."

"I don't want to talk about that." Seb ran his fingers down Martin's back, letting his nails scrape, watching the line of goosebumps that rose up.

"You were like a warrior. You knew you'd get hurt, but you went in anyway. You took the blows because Oliver needed you to. I thought . . . " His eyelids fluttered, and he pressed his forehead against the center of Seb's chest, hands roaming over his skin.

"You thought what?" He couldn't imagine what Martin was trying to say.

"I thought maybe you might like not being the one to make decisions for a little while." He pulled Seb's head down to kiss him. "Let me be that person. Let your guard down."

Seb moaned. Yes. He wanted that. He wanted this: Martin, to not think, only to feel and be here. But uncertainty lived just under the desire. He didn't know what Martin liked, and if he was trying something because he thought Seb would get off on it, it wasn't necessarily a good idea.

"You want to play some 'naughty professor' thing? Because I can try, but I sort of thought after what you told me about—"

"Stand up." Martin's eyes narrowed.

"What?"

"Stand. Up."

Seb scrambled off, his heart squeezing with regret. He shouldn't have brought up the professor thing.

"Take your pants off."

The way Martin set his chin made Seb's chest squeeze again, but in a different way. The blood in his body traveled south in a hurry.

"Pants off," Martin said again. Seb's hands shook as he complied. "One button at a time. That's it." There wasn't much light in the room, only the one bedside lamp, but the white line of Martin's teeth was visible as he grinned. His hand was back on the hollow of his stomach, fingers moving in slow circles again.

Seb went to shuck his pants and underwear, but Martin shook his head. "Just the pants."

His erection definitely liked where this was going. Seb pulled his pants off, kicking them to the side. Martin leaned back, bottom lip in his teeth.

"I was not expecting this."

"You didn't know me. Before."

Before?

Oh.

Martin's hand slid lower, his fingers moving from slow circles to soft lines up and down the shape of his cock in his pajamas.

"You wanted to know what I like," Martin said.

Oh boy, had Seb ever wanted to know.

"I like it slow. I like to watch. I like to touch. I don't like to be worried about all the things that could go wrong, and it has been a very long time since I felt like I could do that."

He wasn't talking about sex. Or not simply sex. But if it was going to happen like this, if Martin needed to feel in control, to feel safe, in order for this thing between them to work tonight, Seb was totally on board with it.

"I—"

"Touch yourself." Martin gripped himself through his pants. "I want to touch you, and for you to touch me, but . . . I want to see what you like first, so I know what to do. Show me."

Well then.

"Doing your research? Very studious of you." Seb's hand moved over his own chest. He flicked at the piercing as his other hand roamed lower. He watched Martin's hand while he did it, focusing on the long fingers playing over the place where Martin's erection was pitching a not-so-little tent. Seb hissed when his own fingers grazed the tip of his cock, pressed snug in the elastic of his briefs. Tugging at his piercing, he ran his palm down the front of the soft cotton.

He hadn't done this for an audience in a while. Usually, there wasn't time. A few kisses, a fumble with a zipper, and someone was on their knees or face-down before anyone remembered the niceties.

Martin's hand slipped into his pants.

"I really want that to be my hand." Seb gasped.

"I do too. We'll get there. Show me what it would be like first. I want to know."

The whole time he palmed himself, Seb kept his eyes on Martin. He pulled his cock free of his briefs and wrapped his fingers around himself. Martin's mouth was open slightly, and his tongue darted out to swipe at his lower lip while he watched.

Seb worked himself slowly. The more he watched Martin watching him, the more he wanted this to go on for hours. He slid his hand up, running his palm over the crown of his dick. He flicked at his nipple and trembled.

"Yeah." Martin tugged his pants off, and Seb bit his lip on a protest when Martin's underwear went with them, even though he hadn't let Seb do the same. But then it didn't matter, because holy fuck, Martin was beautiful. He was long. All of him. Legs, arms, his torso, the heavy cock that moved in and out of his hand. His thighs were muscled, and fine hair swirled over them. Seb wanted to run his palms over them while he licked at Martin's cock. He wanted to feel those legs around his body.

"Come here."

Seb stumbled forward like he was on a string. He stopped between Martin's knees. Strong hands gripped his hips. Martin pressed a kiss to Seb's stomach, inches above where his cock started to leak. Then Martin slipped lower and licked at the crown. "Show me what you like. So I know what to do."

Seb did, and oh god, it was good. Martin's breath brushed against the hair at the base of Seb's cock while Martin watched and then took over, stroking him, his other hand flat on one of Seb's ass cheeks to hold him in place. Seb pinched his nipples, letting his hands wander as he watched the flushed head of his cock pumped in and out of Martin's hand.

Martin's mouth on him was a hot shock that made Seb tremble, and he gripped at Martin's hair as he swallowed him.

"Oh." He gasped as Martin's tongue swirled around him. "Oh god, yes. That. Just keep doing that."

Martin had a whole suitcase of hidden skills. The voice. The things he could do with his mouth. As he sucked, his fingers played over Seb's balls, and Seb nearly drew blood digging his fingernails into Martin's shoulders to stay upright.

"More. Please. You're doing great," he said.

Martin pulled off him with a wet slide. Seb's hips followed him. Seb bent and kissed him, pushing at his shoulders. They tumbled to the mattress. Seb was lightheaded, and his heart pounded in his ears as he settled against Martin's body.

"I want to be inside you." Martin frowned, like that desire was a problem in need of solving. "Or you inside me. I don't care. But I don't have any lube."

And wasn't that a kicker?

"I have some upstairs," Seb said.

Martin laughed between kisses. "You said we weren't sleeping together."

"We weren't when we got here. That doesn't mean I didn't have aspirations."

"Upstairs is far." Martin bit at his neck, making Seb grunt while his hips kicked forward.

"Something to aim for next time."

Seb pulled himself up to kneeling and stared at Martin, laid out in front of him. He was scruffy and flushed, and Seb wanted to do so many things to him to see him writhe.

"Tell me what you're thinking," Martin said.

Seb had to clear this throat as arousal took him over. "I want to know what you taste like."

Martin's grin twisted. "So find out."

"You sure?"

"I'll tell you to stop if I need to."

Seb couldn't help himself as he dove back for Martin's mouth, because the other option would be to stare up at the ceiling and babble out an incoherent prayer thanking whatever force had brought Martin into his life.

Martin's hands were in his hair, pulling and then tugging down. Seb got the hint. He braced his shoulders against the backs of Martin's thighs, pushing them up until Martin was open to him. Seb swiped his tongue against Martin's hole, then up the crease to his taint. Martin groaned above him. Just as well they weren't upstairs, because, lube or no lube, Seb was going to make Martin do that again, loudly.

He sucked Martin's cock into his mouth, loving the taste of him on his tongue. The cotton laundry smell was gone, replaced with an earthier musk that tickled his nose as he went deeper. Martin shifted under his hands, shuddering with need. Seb hollowed his cheeks and bobbed his head. He closed his eyes, not wanting to see anything around him, nothing that would distract him from the taste of Martin and the feel of the hands still threaded into Seb's hair.

"Oh, that's amazing." Nothing Martin said since this started sounded like a question, and his confidence was driving Seb crazy. He'd do anything for Martin when he was like this. Martin bumped against his throat. Seb swallowed, taking him deeper, and Martin grunted, but then he tensed.

"Wait. Too fast," he said. Seb froze, looking up the flat, angular lines of Martin's body. "Too fast. I'm not—" His chest rose and fell with shallow breaths. He pulled himself up to his elbows and reached down, fingers trailing along Seb's lips. "Your mouth is beautiful. All of you is so—But I—What if I . . . "

Seb crawled up Martin's body to kiss him. They rolled, legs tangling together and sheets twisting around their bodies until they were wrapped up in each other.

"I want more." Seb gasped as Martin licked at his throat.

"More?" Martin gripped their cocks together, jerking them slowly.

"That's good too. We can do this if you're more comfortable with it, but I really liked sucking you off. It's okay if it's fast. I want you to come in my mouth." He wanted to know everything: what Martin looked like, tasted like, sounded like, as he let go and came apart.

They untangled themselves, shifting and repositioning until Seb sat against the headboard, and Martin knelt above him. His cock hung, thick and heavy, and Seb cursed the lube situation again. He wanted that inside of him. He wanted the stretch and the burn, and the weight of Martin on top of him and pushing into him at the same time, so close they were almost one person; the best parts of each of them together.

Martin stroked himself. Seb could let him do that all night. Sit there and watch as Martin's skin flushed and his hips thrust, until Martin's come painted Seb's skin. He'd like that.

"You can tell me to stop anytime you want to." He opened his mouth, pressing his tongue flat against his lower lip.

"I don't think I'll need to." The mattress creaked as Martin braced on the headboard. Pre-come glistened at the tip of his cock, and Seb licked it off, making Martin hiss.

Seb lapped at him, waiting, encouraging. "I want you in me. In me, on me. Everywhere. Just as you are. I want you to come down my throat. Is that okay?" Anticipation swirled inside Seb, making his heart pound and his dick pulse. Martin clenched his jaw, and he nodded. Seb warmed. He would make this good—so good—for both of them.

Martin was still tentative, at first. It was all new, and Seb could tell he was feeling the situation out, even while lust made him brave. Seb kept his mouth open, jaw slack, letting Martin explore, while concentration furrowed between his eyebrows. Eventually, Seb tightened his lips, wrapping them around his teeth and picking up the pace. Martin's breathing went ragged. Seb sucked, using his hands to pull Martin's hips back and forth, showing him how far he could go.

When Martin finally took over, Seb closed his eyes. This was what he wanted. To be used, a little. To give Martin control and pleasure, in the safety of this dark room together. He let Martin fuck his mouth, and he worked his own cock, spurred on by

Martin's heavy breathing and the hot weight of the other man's dick pressing back against his throat.

He ached, leaking in his fist. Saliva pooled and spilled over his lips. It was messy and perfect. Seb wished he could tell Martin how perfect it was, but Martin was clearly lost in it now. His hips pumped, and his gaze was glassy, while a flush spread over his collarbones.

"Oh god," Martin groaned. Seb wanted to praise him, tell him how amazing he felt. "That's . . . " Martin gasped. "That's good." His rhythm faltered for a moment and then picked up, harder. Seb choked, but hummed when he could breathe again.

Martin felt powerful against him. Strong and demanding, and Seb had helped him get there. Seb was so turned on by the idea. He leaked all over his fist, and Martin murmured praise as his spine curled. His head dropped between his arms, his mouth inches from Seb's head.

"So good. This is so good. Thank you. You don't know . . . " He was babbling. Seb closed his eyes and took it all in. Took everything Martin gave him.

"That's—That's . . . " Martin made a choked sound, and then he was coming, hot and salty. Seb wrapped his free arm around Martin's hips, holding him tight in his mouth while he pulled on his own dick in short, rapid strokes. He hummed and swallowed while Martin pulsed in Seb's mouth, just like he'd asked. Seb's orgasm ripped out of him, splattering against his belly and the inside of Martin's thighs. He panted when Martin finally pulled out of his mouth.

———

They collapsed. Or rather, Martin collapsed, and Seb went with him, wrapping his arms around him. Martin kissed him, tasting himself on Seb's lips. He wanted to chase it.

"In the future," Seb gasped, "there will be lube."

Martin laughed, kissing lazy trails on Seb's skin. He needed to wash off, but he didn't want to get up. Lightening sparked under his skin. He'd never done anything like that before, and the sight of Seb's burning gaze while Martin's cock had disappeared into his mouth would be seared onto his brain forever.

"So that was good then?" he asked.

"Unquestionably. But next time, I want to ride you until we both can't remember our names."

Martin groaned. His cock was soft and spent, but the image of that made him want to see if he could revive it quick enough to give that a try tonight.

Seb traced his fingers along Martin's spine.

"Thanks for coming," he said. Martin couldn't help the laughter that rumbled out of him, and then he laughed harder when Seb swatted at his shoulder. "Not like that! What are you, fourteen?"

"You're welcome." Martin kissed him before sliding off the bed. He found towels in the adjoining bathroom and did his best to clean himself off, then carried a wet towel out to Seb to do the same.

Seb was beautiful. Pale and a little freckled.

"Stay here tonight?" Martin asked, feeling brave. He bent to pick up Seb's discarded underwear.

"Kenny was right," Seb said. Martin froze. He checked over his shoulder as he straightened. Seb sat up on the bed. He'd pulled the comforter and sheet aside, one corner draped over his knee. His grin was lazy and self-assured. Classic Seb.

Clearing his throat, Martin said, "Right about what?"

"You have a spectacular ass."

Martin slid into the bed and wrapped himself along Seb's side. He idly played with one of the silver piercings as he situated himself in this new element of their relationship. "What's tomorrow going to be like?" he said.

Seb's hand, which had been making little circles on Martin's bicep, stilled.

"More of the same. But different. Everyone will be on their best behavior for the party."

"Everyone?"

"Even me."

"That's not what I meant."

"Even me." Seb kissed Martin's forehead.

"So you all just pretend like nothing happened?"

"Some will. My mom. Gillian. Parker will be too busy making sure it's all perfect to get too passive aggressive. Ollie will most likely be hungover, based on the way he was going when I left him, and my dad . . . " He let out a long sigh. "My dad and I will steer clear of each other and pretend like the other one's not there."

"That's the plan?" It seemed sad.

"Well, there was the part where we get our act together and I ride your dick until we both can't walk."

"Maybe we should start with that part. Get everything off on the right foot."

Seb kissed him again, then turned onto his side. He shimmied on the mattress until his back was pressed against Martin's front, and he pulled Martin's arm around him and held the palm to his chest.

18

_____

There *was* a morning ride, but not the kind Seb
hoped for.

It was outside.

With Oliver.

Who pounded on the bedroom door at seven-thirty.

"Come on, lovebirds! Daylight's burning."

"I hate him," Seb grumbled. He rolled and snuggled against
Martin, rubbing his cheek in the ticklish hair on his chest.

"You don't hate him," Martin said.

"No," Seb agreed. "He might be the only one I like."

"Come on, Seb! We're going for a run!" Oliver said.

"I don't run!"

"You used to!"

Seb cursed and licked a trail between Martin's nipples,
making him shiver.

He pushed Seb's head away gently. "Do you have a bike?"
Martin asked, loud enough to be heard through the door.

There was a pause.

"I can get one. Or two. One for each of you!"

"Traitor," Seb said, but Martin was already rolling away from
him and walking his fabulous ass to the bathroom.

The ride was longer and farther than Seb expected. He ached when it was done, and still not in the good way he wanted. Martin, however, appeared to thoroughly enjoy their campus tour and Seb's narration of his childhood haunts. By the time they got home, his cheeks were flushed and his smile easy.

They needed a shower. When he suggested it, Martin blushed furiously, which made Seb smile and press him up against the garage wall to kiss him silly. They were both half hard, and Martin's hands were sliding under Seb's belt when Oliver reappeared at the garage door with a polite cough and a raised eyebrow.

"Parker needs help moving some furniture in the living room," he said.

"I hate you," Seb growled as he pulled himself away from Martin.

"No, you don't." Oliver smiled a shit-eating grin at him. "Martin, my dad wants to see you."

That stopped them both in their tracks.

"What about?" Seb asked. Oliver shrugged.

"I need to shower first," Martin said.

"It didn't sound urgent."

"You don't have to go," Seb said, but Martin squeezed his hand and smiled.

"I'm a guest. It would be rude."

"Were you there at dinner last night? Ignoring a summons is pretty far down the list as far as rude goes."

"I'm sure whatever it is, it won't take long. I'll see you soon." Martin kissed him and disappeared down the hall toward their room.

Seb followed Oliver through the house.

"Did he say what he wanted?" he asked.

"He asked to see your friend. That's all he said."

Seb gritted his teeth. His friend. His boyfriend, maybe. The man who fucked his mouth in his parents' guest room. Friends didn't do that.

He could go find his dad. Martin would be in the shower. Seb had time to intervene.

"Oh for goodness's sake, Jason, put it down before you hurt yourself!" Parker's voice snagged his attention as they entered the house's formal living room.

Jason stood at the table by the window, his hands wrapped around Seb's gift. His face was pinched like he was passing a kidney stone while he tried to lift it.

"Put it down!" Seb said.

"I've got it," Jason said.

"Put it the fuck down!" Seb strode across the room in three big steps. He'd punch the asshole, only Jason would drop the box and it would shatter.

Fortunately, his expression was enough for Jason to see he meant business. He paled and stepped aside after he set the box back down gently.

By the time Seb had relocated the gift where Parker wanted it, and then helped her retie bows on a few dozen chairs in the garden, and then moved the gift again because the original table had been a better idea after all, and then found a garbage bag after one of Parker's golden retrievers escaped from the room in the basement where they were stashed and collided with a caterer carrying a tray of glasses, and then . . .

By the time Seb was ready to go find his father and ask him what the hell he wanted with Martin, Martin was standing in the living room. He wore Penny's suit, although he'd gone for a pale blue shirt instead of the white one. Seb looked forward to peeling him out of it later.

"You look awesome." He kissed Martin in greeting, but Martin barely returned it. When he pulled away, Martin was staring dazedly over Seb's shoulder. "What's wrong?"

"Nothing."

"Come on," he said. "I have to get changed."

Seb took his hand and pulled him gently down the hall. He'd brought his things down to the guest room earlier in the morning while Martin was getting dressed for their impromptu bike ride.

Martin floated after him silently. He didn't react when Seb closed the door, or as he pulled the henley he'd worn outside over his head.

"Okay, seriously." Seb grabbed his clean shirt from the closet. "You're making me nervous. What happened?"

"What happened?" Martin ran a hand over his hair, making it swirl in fluffy patterns off his scalp.

"Did my dad . . . " Seb's pulse kicked up a few notches. Philip was ferocious, a lion in his home. But he wouldn't say anything outright offensive to Martin. Would he? "What did my dad want?"

"It's fine." Martin waved him away. The subtle vibration coming off of him didn't stop, though. "He was in his office. Invited me in. Asked about my book again. He—"

"What?"

"I think he offered me a job?"

———

Martin knocked gently on the doorframe. Philip Stevenson sat with his back to him in a heavy leather chair behind a heavier wooden desk.

"Yes?" He smiled as he turned around in his seat. "Oh good. Oliver found you. Come in!"

The room was like the library: wall-to-wall bookshelves filled with a veritable collection of European literature.

"Did you have a good ride? Oliver said you went around the college."

"Yes, it was very nice, thank you."

"Have a seat."

Martin slid into one of the two club chairs across the desk. Having something so formal set up in someone's home seemed odd, but he supposed if anyone was going to do it, Philip Stevenson was the most likely candidate.

"How did you like the campus?" Philip said, and Martin frowned. Philip couldn't have asked him here to talk about this. They could chat about the scenery over cocktails at the party.

"It was very pretty. Busy today. You could see them setting up for the football game." He didn't know much about football, but Philip smiled, so it must have been an appropriately safe answer.

"Yes, the homecoming game. We always play the team from Hume College. They always lose. It's how the narrative is supposed to go."

"Oh." Martin hadn't even given much thought to the narrative of football games.

"Do you know Edward Scott?" Philip asked.

The spit in Martin's mouth dried.

"I think you know I must." Edward Scott was the president of Mount Garner College, so anything else Martin could say would be evasive or an outright lie.

Philip smiled at him, and Martin had the distinct impression he might be a mouse with his tail caught under Philip's paw. "Edward and I went to college together. I spoke with him last night. I mentioned you were here this weekend with my son."

Martin wasn't sure if Dr. Scott knew he was gay, but it should have been irrelevant, particularly since he was no longer employed by Mount Garner.

"Edward said it's been very difficult, what with everything that happened last spring."

Martin nodded. To say more would invite the panic rippling along his ribs to spread farther, like it always did when he tried to talk about those last months.

Except when he'd told Seb. He trusted Seb to keep his secrets and help him when he needed it, and in exchange, Seb had made him feel more powerful than he had in years.

"According to Edward, you took it especially hard." Philip's eyes narrowed. Every inch the predator.

"As you said, it was a difficult few months." Despite his growing courage, Martin wished Seb was there to tell his dad to fuck off. He'd do a better job of it than Martin ever could.

Philip's smile grew. He was toying with him, but Martin didn't know what his endgame was. They were strangers for all intents and purposes. Some common colleagues and one horrible dinner barely made them acquaintances.

"You said you were on sabbatical," Philip said.

Ah.

"I did."

"Edward said your time away was a little more permanent than that."

"I'm not sure—"

"We all have our moments of . . . " Philip waved his hand. "Weakness."

The word stung.

"I'm not—"

"I read your book." Philip's change of topic made Martin's head spin.

"Oh?"

"Last night." Philip shifted in his chair, the first time he'd shown any discomfort. He seemed to catch himself and smoothed a hand over the blotter on his desk. "After that unpleasantness, I had some time on my hands, more time than we'd expected given we'd planned an evening with family. Sebastian and Oliver . . . " He coughed. "I read your book."

"All of it?" It wasn't an encyclopedia, but he'd like to think it would take more time to get through than a little light bedtime reading would allow.

"The parts you wrote." Philip's smile grew as Martin froze. He *was listed as the second author while his thesis supervisor had taken the first place. Martin had regretted it for years afterward. But for Philip to know they had written the chapters separately . . . that was extraordinary.*

"Oh please," Philip said. "I've known Bernard almost as long as I've known Edward. You think I can't recognize his long-winded verbal diarrhea masquerading as historical interpretation? It's not even analysis. He's just paraphrasing."

Martin shook his head. Not that he disagreed, but criticizing him when he wasn't there seemed unfair.

"Your chapters, though." Philip leaned back in his chair. "Very interesting. One might almost say insightful."

Well, don't hurt yourself with the praise, *Martin thought. What he said was,* "Thank you."

"Edward said you were an astute young man generally. He was sorry to see you go."

This time, Martin's thanks were genuine, if a little bit stammered.

Philip smiled, warmer now. "Professor Emeritus, that's what they call me now. I'm sure Sebastian told you I've retired."

"He did, sir, yes." *Martin couldn't help but notice that, even after the night before, Philip still called Seb by his full name.*

"Watersmith was our home for a long time, though. The new dean of the history department, Angela, you've met her?"

"Angela Friedman?"

"Yes."

"No, I haven't." *Like everyone, Martin knew of her, but they'd never had a conversation.*

"I could speak to her. If you like. Obviously, Sebastian might not understand, but I know how much work you've put into getting as far as you did. It would be a shame to see it end there. There's a position opening up in the spring. Primarily research, with one course to teach a semester. Officially, we'd have to post it, but Watersmith has always relied heavily on the recommendations of its faculty, both current*

204

and . . . " The lion smiled his toothy smile. "Former. A few good words from me could . . . "

───────

"Don't you fucking trust a single thing he says to you." Seb tugged on his bowtie with such force the whole thing unraveled. He cursed and kicked at the dresser. The mirror behind it rattled. "I knew I should have gone with you."

Martin came forward, his hands trembling as he raised them. They were steadier than Seb's, though, and he had the bowtie redone in seconds. "I told him I had to think about it."

"Well, you think yourself into a 'no.' He never gives anything freely."

"It does seem a little weird, given that we've just met."

"He's testing you. It's what he does. He tests people, looking for weaknesses."

"Looking for the sick antelope at the watering hole?" Martin slumped.

"You're not an antelope." Seb leaned in to kiss him. Why the hell were they here again? Kissing Martin would be a much better use of a day than dealing with his dysfunctional family and their perpetual chess game, and it could be done at home.

"He knew. About me. About why I left." Martin's eyes dropped to the floor.

Seb swore. He pressed their foreheads together and wrapped a hand around the back of Martin's neck. "It's nothing to be ashamed of. If he thinks it makes you weak, he doesn't know you at all."

Someone knocked on the door.

"Jesus, I am going to put a fucking bell on you," Seb snarled.

"Everything okay in here?" Oliver had also changed, going for his lawyer best in a designer suit. Silver cufflinks peeked out from the edges of his sleeves.

"It's fine," Martin said. "We were just coming."

"Dad offered Martin a job." Seb ignored the startled look Martin gave him.

"It's a trap," Oliver said, face serious.

"That's what I said."

"Thanks, guys." Martin stared glumly at his shoes.

"Is the party starting?" Seb turned his attention to Oliver, because they couldn't make this immediately better, so a distraction was as good as anything.

"Nana's car just pulled in."

"She's not still driving, is she?"

"No, Gillie went to get her."

"It's adorable that you still call your grandmother Nana." Martin's smile was back.

Seb kissed him quickly for it. "What else are we supposed to call her?"

Seb was surprised how nervous he felt as they came down the hall. In all of the chaos of the past twenty-four hours, he hadn't thought to ask Oliver for an update on their grandmother's health. Would she be different? Frailer? Smaller? He imagined her, wheeled in by some medical attendant, a tank of oxygen at her side. She'd lift one bony hand like the queen she had been, and he'd fall to his knees and apologize for staying away so long. He was so sorry.

But then she was there, or rather, they were there: Seb, with Martin's hand tucked securely in his. His family clustered in the front entranceway: his siblings, his parents, his nieces and nephews, aunts, uncles, cousins he barely recognized. There was a lot of cooing and hugging, and Seb hovered at the edge of it all, waiting nervously for a glimpse of her. The noise of so many people talking echoed off the high ceiling above them, and it felt like it was pressing him out of the room.

And then the sea parted. There she was, like he remembered her. She walked with a cane now, but she was impeccably dressed in a peach-colored suit and her favorite pearl necklace. Her hair was a shade whiter than the last time he'd seen her, but in his eyes, she was every inch as perfect as he remembered.

He couldn't help the stupid smile on his face as he bent to kiss her.

"Seb." Her grip on his shoulders was firm. "You've been gone too long."

And then she was being trotted away by doting family.

Seb hadn't expected the tightness in his throat, but he was grateful when Martin came up behind him and linked their arms together.

"That was her?" he said in Seb's ear.

Seb sniffed and smiled. "That was my Nana."

19

Getting a chance to actually speak to with his grandmother was nearly impossible. Parker pulled out all the stops, which included inviting close to a hundred people. On top of that were almost a dozen hired staff for the day: people to pass around finger sandwiches and glasses of wine, and then different people to carry all the empty dishes and spent paper napkins away again when the guests were done.

"How many of the people here are you related to?" Martin asked.

"Just the natural blonds."

Around two o'clock, Seb finally found his grandmother, seated by herself in one corner of the living room. He took the chance and tugged Martin along.

She greeted him with a smile. Her hands on his cheeks were cool. "You are the nicest surprise we've had at this party," she said. He couldn't help but smile back. "Who's your friend?" she asked.

Seb pulled Martin up and wrapped an arm around his shoulders. "Martin Lindsey, meet my grandmother, Alice Stevenson."

"You can call me Dinah." She held out a long-fingered hand, decked out in the large emerald ring she'd always worn.

"Dinah?" Martin frowned at Seb.

"All the eldest daughters in her family are called Alice," he said. Using her real first name had seemed safest. It was more formal, and she'd like that. "After a great-great-grandmother or something. Too many Alices means my Nana is a Dinah."

"I never met the woman. I hear she was a heartbreaker, though. Four husbands, fifteen children. That's why there are so many of us Alices now." She gave them a conspiratorial wink. Her voice was gravelly, the way it had been when Seb was small and she would take him to museums or leave him in peace to work on whatever new masterpiece his grade-school heart could dream of.

"It's very nice to meet you," Martin said. "Seb's told me a lot about you."

"He's told me nothing about you. He's been negligent." She still held on to Martin's hand, but turned and gave Seb's arm a reassuring pat to say she didn't really mean it. He appreciated that, but they both knew it was true. Without Martin as a buffer, she'd be bending his ear.

"Seb." Her eyes were the same color as his. "My glass is empty, and your young man is looking thirsty too."

Seb raised an eyebrow at Martin, who was blushing furiously. Thirsty. One way to phrase it.

"I'll be right back." He bent and kissed his grandmother's cheek, then kissed Martin too for good measure.

There was a line at the bar set up in the dining room. Parker lurked nearby, looking pinched.

"Nana wants a G&T," he said. She barely glanced at him, continuing to hover. He could see her mental wheels turning as she counted and recounted the people in line. "Is that okay?"

"Why wouldn't it be?"

"How would I know? Is she on medication? Something that can't mix with alcohol?"

"She's got pills for her arthritis. Nothing else."

"They didn't give her anything in the hospital?"

Parker's attention snapped toward him like a laser. "When was Nana in the hospital?"

"Oliver told me she was sick."

"When?"

"Ten days ago? He called me and—"

"She wasn't in the hospital."

Seb opened his mouth to argue and then clacked it shut again. He narrowed his eyes, but Parker stared back at him, the same bored stare she'd given him when he was eleven and she was seventeen and he'd asked if he could go to her "grown up" high school parties with her.

Stewing, he shuffled his way up the line. He chewed on his lip, broke apart the puzzle in his head, and reassembled it until it made sense. The picture was so much clearer now, the seams between the pieces so much snugger.

He found Martin and his grandmother right where he'd left them. He handed them their drinks, then watched his grandmother for a minute, trying to see anything to contradict what he was pretty sure he knew now.

"Everything okay?" Martin asked.

"Fine." The word was a tight syllable on his lips. He knelt next to his grandmother. "How are you doing?"

She smiled at him. "Lovely. Your sister has put together a great day. And Martin here was telling me about the young woman you've been helping. It's so good to see you doing that. I wish you'd had someone when you were making those decisions."

She wanted to talk about his dad. She couldn't help herself. Philip was her only son, and the distance between him and Seb had always been a difficult spot for her.

He wouldn't let her distract him. "Oliver said you were sick."

"When?"

"A couple weeks ago. A respiratory infection, he said?"

"Oh that. It was just a sniffle. I don't know what everyone was so worked up about. They wanted to take me to the doctor's, but I said some tea and a little gin and I'd be fine. And I was! I knew you were coming. Oliver told me. I had to be in fighting shape to see you!" She patted his cheek and then sipped her drink.

Seb gave her hand another squeeze, then stood. "I didn't get a drink for myself." He slipped away before Martin could ask questions that would slow Seb on his new mission.

Oliver was out on the back patio under one of the propane heaters, laughing with a couple of their cousins.

Without bothering with niceties, he slung an arm around Oliver's shoulders. "I need to talk to you."

To his brother's credit, he gave no resistance. Oliver didn't ask what this was about. He let Seb march them across the yard to the old shed in the far back corner, behind the pond.

"They'll find my body sooner or later," he said as Seb pulled the moldy old door open.

"Shut up and get inside."

Oliver didn't look overly worried. "If you're going to punch me, you're better to do it out here. The shed's cramped. You won't be able to wind up so well."

Seb shoved him through the open door. He flicked on the light switch, and the one bare bulb in the ceiling flooded the small space with ugly yellow light.

They stared at each other: Seb scowling, Oliver trying to maintain a serious facade, but mouth trembling as he fought down the grin.

"She's dying, Seb." Seb dropped his voice to sound more like Oliver's, wobbling dramatically and pressing the back of his hand to his forehead.

"I never said she was dying." Oliver's grin escaped its confines.

"She keeps asking for you, Seb."

"She did. You've been her favorite since you learned to hold a crayon the right way down."

"Crayons work from both ends." He shook his head. "Don't distract me! You told me she was sick."

"She *was* sick."

"You said she was in the hospital."

"She should have been."

"She said it was just a sniffle."

"She also weighs ninety pounds and thinks three gin and tonics is an appetizer. You can't believe everything she says!"

No one had ever needed punching as much as Oliver did in that moment. "You lied to me."

"I used selected truths." Oliver rocked on his heels and grinned.

"*Selected truths.* Fucking lawyers." Seb paced in the tiny area of the shed. "You could have told me! Said she wanted me to come. I would have."

Oliver snorted. "I did tell you. You hung up on me."

"You'll have to be more specific. I've been hanging up on you for years."

"You threw a laptop across the room rather than listen to me!"

"Don't be dramatic. I knocked you off the table."

"See!" Oliver shoved a finger at him, the edges of his cocky self-assurance crumbling. "That. That right there is why I had to lie."

"What?"

"You! You, asshole. You're so fucking stubborn, you'd argue with me even if you knew I was right!"

"No, I—" Seb snapped his mouth shut.

"She did ask about you. Every time I talked to her, she asked if I knew if you were coming. It would have broken her heart if you weren't here Seb. And you, you stubborn, selfish asshole, you wouldn't even let me speak long enough for me to tell you that."

"But I said, last time I was here, after Dad—"

"Dad? Do you know why you hate him so much? Why you two fight whenever you get within shouting distance of each other?"

"Because he's a controlling asshole?"

"Apple doesn't fall far from the tree, does it?"

"Don't compare me to him."

"Oh my god! You're exactly the same, the two of you. So stubborn and you refuse to see it! I could be pissing on both of you, and you'd swear it was raining to prove you were right."

"That is a truly disturbing mental image, Ollie."

"Would you shut up and thank me already?" Oliver's voice cracked on the last word.

"Thank you?"

"I did this. Me." He thumped his chest. "The first thing she asked me when she walked in the door this afternoon was if you were here. And I got to say yes. That is the best gift I could have given her." He was out of breath as he smoothed his hand over his hair. "I did it. I got you here, so you could be the center of attention, just like you've always wanted. And instead, you're arguing with me in a fucking garden shed in October. It is fifty-five degrees out, and this suit is not made for that. Can you please punch me so we can go back inside?"

The shed fell into damp silence. Oliver huffed and put his hands on his hips, fanning out the back of his jacket. Seb tried a few times to say something. Argue. Snap back with a witty retort.

In the end, he held his arms out wide.

"What are you doing?" Oliver said.

"Come here."

Oliver hesitated.

"Don't look at me like that. Come here and hug it out." Seb came forward and wrapped Oliver in a hug.

"You're an asshole." Oliver squeezed him so hard something in Seb's spine went *pop.*

"It's genetic apparently."

"I love you."

"Love you too, man. But I'll love you less if you break a rib."

Seb got waylaid on the way back into the party by his Aunt Karen, who cornered him and wouldn't let him go until she'd thanked him no less than a dozen times for giving up his room at the Bluewater Inn. Then she insisted on reintroducing him to his cousin Jeanine, who might have been twenty but looked way too young to be shacking up in a hotel room with the giant on her arm. The guy said he played defensive tackle on their college football team, and Seb believed him.

By the time he wiggled his way through the crowd, speeches were underway. Philip was telling a story about a family road trip when he was a child. Seb had heard it before. It ended in a tent with a leak so big they were floating by the time Dinah finally announced the vacation was over.

A hand on his hip was the only warning he got before Martin slid up against his side. "Where'd you go?" His smile was loose, and there was a glass of wine in his hand.

"I had to go bury a body in the backyard." Seb pulled Martin close to him and nuzzled against his neck. Martin laughed and pressed a kiss to his hair. Being this close to Martin was warm and safe, and it seemed impossible that they had waited so long to get here when they fit so well together.

His father's speech ended. Gillian took her turn. Then Parker. Oliver stood up, the golden son. What would it be like a year from now, when his custom suits were replaced with hemp? Oliver's speech included the time he and Seb had run away from home when then were eight and ten. They'd gone about two blocks before realizing their plan involved leaving the house, but not a destination. They went to their grandparents', where Dinah fed them grilled cheese and chocolate milk until their mother came to get them. Ollie left out the part of the story where Philip had been so furious he'd thrown out all the toys they'd taken with them and refused to replace them. Dinah's face shone as she listened to Oliver recount the whole adventure. This wasn't the moment to dwell on old hurts.

"And now I'd like to introduce my brother."

It took Seb a minute to realize that Oliver meant for him to make a speech.

———

When Seb's hand slipped out of his, Martin almost didn't understand what was happening. But then Seb was crossing the open space, cutting through the crowd gathered around to share stories and well wishes. Instinctively, without Seb's solid presence to bolster him, Martin slipped back between the people, or else they moved forward, and he stayed where he was. There seemed to be a lot of collective breath holding as Seb bent to kiss his grandmother's cheek.

"Well, this is embarrassing," Seb said as he turned. "Because Oliver totally took my story. Except he implied that we were brothers in arms on that little escapade, and I want to make it very clear, for the record, that Ollie was the mastermind, and I was just following orders."

Quiet laughter rippled over the group, while Oliver called they would have to agree to disagree.

"My grandmother." Seb's smile was warm as she took his hand in hers and patted it. "My grandmother took me to see my first play when I was nine. We went just the two of us. Do you remember?"

Dinah beamed up at him. "*Alice in Wonderland.*"

"*Alice in Wonderland*. It seemed like a really big deal, because usually we went to see you and Grampie as a family, all six of us, but here was this time where I got to spend the whole day with just you. I thought it was going to be boring, though. Because I was nine and *Alice in Wonderland* is about a girl, and those things together mean it's going to be boring. But then it wasn't. It was..." He tensed as he stared out over the crowd, his defenses starting to come up, warding off the invisible judgement radiating off his extended family.

It was unfair that Seb couldn't even let himself have this moment.

Martin's hands trembled. The last time he had been this uncomfortable in this suit, he'd been the one standing at the front of a crowd of people, trying to make himself heard. He had been so nervous until he had seen the bright shape of Seb in the back of the room. Then he talked to Seb like he was the only person there.

He shifted, finding an open spot where he had a clear line of sight. The movement must have caught Seb's attention because he turned, and his blue eyes locked on Martin's. His head tilted, and the tension in the straight line of his shoulders started to relax.

"It was magic. There were puppets. Everything in Wonderland was puppets. After the play, we went backstage, and you could see them. They were papier-mâché, and they had been made from the pages of old books. Do you remember?" He looked down at his grandmother, who nodded.

"I wasn't much of a reader. I wasn't very good in school at all. But that day . . . I thought, here is something I can do. Here is the way I can find magic in those books." His eyes were shining as he turned back to Martin. Seb chewed on his lip and ran a hand along the back of his head, like the next part made him nervous.

"When I heard there was a party, I wasn't sure if this was the kind of shindig that involved gifts. But the other thing my grandmother taught me was to never come to a party empty handed. So I brought you something."

Behind the chair where Dinah sat was a small end table, probably meant to sit next to the chair, but moved out of the way to make more room for the afternoon. Seb pulled it out and set it in front of her. He turned, and Oliver started forward, but Seb spoke directly to Martin. "Can you help me?"

The box, the one they'd hauled in from the rental car, sat on another table by the door. It was just as heavy as the day before, but now Martin had an idea what was inside, and it felt even more precious.

They set it on the little table, barely big enough to hold it. Oliver joined them and helped Dinah to stand and pull the bright wrapping paper off the package. Inside was a heavy pressboard container, which explained a lot of the weight. Seb released a latch on the bottom with a snap. He gestured to Martin again, and together they lifted the top off, leaving the contents on the base.

A gasp sounded in the room, and Martin had a moment of disappointment that he couldn't see whatever was inside at the same time as everyone else. He was setting the box down, but when he stood, it didn't matter because everyone around him was enchanted, and there was lots of time to catch up.

On the little table was a square case with glass panels on all four sides. A small peaked top was finished with a wooden knob, and the same warm wood made up the base. The first thing he noticed was the little frowning man standing at the corner, back to the glass. He looked like a beach ball in a jockey's cap, and the frown made Martin recognize Tweedledee.

Inside the glass, a black and white illustrated Alice looked up at the Cheshire Cat in his tree. Seb had split the image out, so the cat was set deeper into the case than Alice. Enhancing the depth was a forest of cut-out trees, each one made from faded yellow pages of text. It was a diorama, but under Seb's skillful blade, it had life.

The crowd murmured again as Seb grasped the knob at the top, and then the whole creation turned slowly. The square case had been divided, wooden panels running from the corners, into four compartments, each one triangular. Each compartment showed another cut-out scene from Alice's adventures. The Cheshire Cat. Alice playing croquet with a flamingo. The caterpillar on his mushroom. The white rabbit disappearing down a hall of increasingly small doors. All made from black-and-white illustrations and Lewis Carroll's printed words.

"It's Alice for Alice," Seb said. He kissed his grandmother's cheek and turned his creation again.

The room broke into applause. Oliver shook Seb's hand and then helped their grandmother back into her chair. Seb slipped his arm through Martin's and squeezed.

"It's beautiful," Martin said into his ear.

Seb grinned and kissed his cheek. "I think she liked it."

"Everybody liked it. You did good." They moved back into the crowd.

"I did, huh? Kenneth's going to be pissed though."

Martin frowned at the mention of Seb's agent. "What do you mean?"

"That was supposed to be the last piece for the Schiller show, and I just gave it to my grandmother."

20

---

*A*fter his speech, there was a certain amount of glad-handing as people came up to Seb to talk about the Alice piece and ask about his work. It was gratifying, and he managed to bite back most of the snappy answers about how they'd never had an interest in his art before. Maybe they just needed to see it up close. He wore the battery out on his phone sending texts with information on the Schiller exhibit and contacts for the representative at the Diving Bell Gallery.

Gillian took Dinah home as the last of the guests trailed out. Parker made noises about dinner, but the extended finger foods in the afternoon had most of them groaning and begging off.

Oliver, Seb, and Martin found themselves in the family den. The TV was on, but the food coma meant Seb wasn't sure what they were watching. He was pressed against Martin's side, head on his shoulder. Oliver laughed at the screen from time to time, but none of them were really watching.

"When did you make that?" Martin whispered.

"It took a few weeks."

"A few weeks? That's all?"

Seb grinned and burrowed a little closer. Martin's jacket was off, and the stiff cotton of his shirt crinkled under Seb's cheek.

"It only takes a few weeks, provided things like sleeping and eating aren't much of a priority." Seb wrapped an arm around Martin's body. "Thanks for coming this weekend. I'm not sure we could have escaped homicide without your moderating influence."

Martin smiled down at him. "Weekend's not over yet."

"Hey." Oliver growled as he paused whatever movie they were watching. "If you're going to talk through the whole thing, go somewhere else."

Seb bared his teeth, and Ollie flipped them off. Martin pulled Seb close again, and he settled, dozing for a while. The movie was one of those loud exploding ones Oliver had always liked. Seb thought they were boring and had long ago learned to sleep through most of them. When he woke, his head was in Martin's lap, and Martin's fingers played in his hair.

"Hey." Martin's voice was soft.

"Hi." Seb curled and stretched like a cat. He rolled until he could kiss Martin's palm.

"Jesus, go find a room before you set the couch on fire with the eye fucking." Oliver's disgust didn't carry much bite.

"Are you sure you have to move to Seacroft? It's a nice place. I'd hate for your attitude to corrupt it."

"You're moving to Seacroft?" Martin's hands stopped moving, and Seb nuzzled against him.

"Did you miss that detail?"

"When was I supposed to get it?"

"During the yelling match otherwise known as dinner last night." Oliver turned the movie off.

"Yeah," Martin said. "I must have missed that."

"I still don't understand why it has to be Seacroft." Seb ran a hand underneath Martin's untucked shirt, rewarded by a sharp inhale as Seb skimmed over his belly.

Oliver looked pointedly away and rolled his eyes. "We—I did

the research. The town has the right demographics to support the kind of business I want to run, and the revenue from tourists in the summer will support it through the quieter off season. Plus, it's a little farther away from here, and by *here* I mean Dad, which, as you've proven all these years, isn't necessarily a bad thing."

"That last part is the most honest thing you've said in days."

Oliver grinned at him.

The house was quiet. Parker and her family had gone home, taking Gillian, Julian and their brood with them, and Seb's parents had never been night owls. Oliver made noises about going out in search of more entertainment on a Saturday night, but Seb threw a glance at Martin, and the sleepy flicker in his eye said staying in was the better choice. Seb wrapped his hand around Martin's and wished his brother a good night.

It was different, the second time. Seb followed Martin into the guest room, instead of sneaking in through the open patio door. Their kisses were slow and lazy, where the night before Seb had been a ball of frenzied energy in search for an outlet. As they undressed each other, Seb took the time to taste Martin's mouth.

"I love the way you look in this suit," Seb breathed as he pulled the belt from Martin's waist.

"I could leave it on?"

"I like the way you look out of it even more." He ran his hands over the wiry hair on Martin's chest, gratified with a soft laugh as Martin's hands explored his body.

When they were naked, they fell into bed together. Seb was hard, but the ache from the night before was absent. Tonight would be easier.

Martin groaned as Seb thrust against his hip until Martin bent a knee to settle them more closely against each other. The ease that Martin showed like this, the way he wasn't shy about making noise or showing Seb what he wanted, had been unexpected yesterday. Tonight, it was dazzling. Seb wanted to make Martin feel safe with him for a very long time.

And he wanted Martin to come his brains out. But those two things didn't have to be mutually exclusive.

"This has, without a doubt, been the most interesting weekend of my life," Martin said.

"I'm just getting started." Seb flicked his tongue of the edge of Martin's teeth, then hissed when Martin's thumb brushed against his piercing.

"You think you have something to add?"

Seb ground against him, shifting until their cocks lined up. He slid a hand between them, grasping at them both. Lube was by the bed—he'd made sure it was there hours ago—but he didn't reach for it. They had lots of time.

His grasp wasn't tight as he stroked them together, but Martin rolled underneath him, thrusting into Seb's fist.

"Good?" Seb asked.

Martin wrapped his hand around Seb's. "Very."

"You're full of surprises, you know that?"

"That I like a hand on my dick? Not very surprising." It wasn't, but admitting it so openly—when talking about himself always seemed to be such a challenge—was the nicest surprise Seb had experienced all weekend.

He grinned and kissed Martin as he thrust, reveling in the press of their bodies together.

"Not everyone could have survived this weekend. Even fewer of them would let me take them to bed afterward. Most would have shown me the door."

"I need someone to drive me home tomorrow."

Laughing, Seb pumped their cocks at the edge of too hard as he nipped at Martin's lip. Martin chuckled, but then came back with a kiss that made Seb's toes curl and his dick start to leak against his fingers. Teasing gave way to heat in his chest and limbs.

"How do you want this?" He sucked Martin's earlobe into his mouth, which made Martin shake under him. Seb filed that away for future reference.

"I believe there was talk of riding." Martin squeezed Seb's ass. The motion slid their cocks together again. With some more kissing and little lube for good measure, Seb would be able to come like that. It would be slow and messy, which was okay with him. But the way "riding" had curled around Martin's tongue made him want to play that idea out first. They could go for slow and messy back at Seb's apartment. In fact, Seb would pencil hours of that into his schedule as soon as they were home.

He jolted out of that fantasy at the sensation of Martin's finger circling his rim. Oh. He clenched and bit at Martin's lip, letting him explore.

"What do you like?" Martin's breath was warm against Seb's throat.

"Is this more research?" Seb laughed and then grunted as the finger against his ass pressed in the tiniest amount.

"Last night was more of a review. This will be primary research. Hands on."

Seb bit back the joke about naughty teachers and extra credit, because Martin wouldn't like it.

"I like hands on." He rocked as Martin squeezed his cheeks again, kneading the muscle there. "And mouths. I like mouths. I'm—" Martin kissed him. "Not fussy."

Martin pushed him around, laying Seb out the way he wanted to. He wasn't rough, just focused, reminding Seb of how he laid out all his tools before tackling a new project at his work table. Make sure everything was just so, before he started in.

He found himself lying on his back, head resting on his crossed arms. Martin had him lift his hips and put a pillow underneath, changing the angle for better access. Martin brushed a hand across Seb's hip. The gesture was slow, fond, and it made him feel cared for, especially when Martin followed the same path with his mouth. His lips trailed over Seb's thigh and across the sensitive skin of his groin.

"Are we sure this is a good idea? In your parents' house, I mean?" It was a question, but the little puffs of his breath as he spoke tickled over Seb's balls, making it hard for him to object, even if he wanted to.

Seb reached down, found the hand that rested on his stomach, and squeezed. "How loud are you going to make me scream?"

Martin glanced up, gray eyes sparkling as he smiled his crooked smile. "There's another pillow there, just in case."

The words made Seb's stomach flip. In someone else, even from himself, it might have sounded cocky. A dare. From Martin, it sounded like a promise.

Seb's head rolled back as he felt the slide of Martin's tongue down the seam of his balls, over his taint, and then lower. Seb moaned in the back of his throat. Martin pushed his thighs apart, holding him exposed.

"You want this?" Martin said. "My mouth on you?"

"Yes please." Seb's thighs trembled, and they had barely even started. He used his hands to hold his legs open so Martin could explore more, which turned out to be a really good idea. Martin slipped a finger into his mouth and then pressed it gently against Seb's hole, watching him the entire time. Gasping, Seb had to close his eyes as Martin's head ducked lower and the gentle pressure of one finger was replaced by the warm flat of Martin's tongue.

It was good. Martin's tongue flicked over his ass, wet strokes and gentle stabs as Martin used the tip to curl against him and slip inside. Seb gritted his teeth and growled encouragement, especially when Martin's hand circled around Seb's cock and jerked him slowly. Seb let one hand slip, the thigh resting over the back of Martin's shoulder, so he could reach up and flick at the piercing in one nipple. The little twist of pain made him clench as Martin continued to work him up with his hand and his mouth.

"More." Seb was rewarded with a wet stroke as Martin licked him one last time and sat up, looking sheepishly pleased with himself.

"You've got hidden talents," Seb said, and Martin grinned as he reached toward the nightstand and the lube there.

"I was a poor student for a long time," he said, flicking the cap open. "When there wasn't money for condoms, we had to satisfy ourselves with other activities."

"Like ping pong?" Seb waggled his eyebrows, then hissed as one lube-slicked finger slid down the crease of his ass.

"Just like ping pong." Martin circled his hole again. After Martin's previous attention, Seb was loose enough that the first finger slid in without much of a fuss, and the second stretched just enough to make him hum as he shifted against the bed. His concentration was focused on the sensation of Martin's fingers sliding in and out of him, working him open, and Seb couldn't find the right place for his limbs. He grasped at the sheets and slid his heels restlessly. Martin shushed him gently, running his free hand up and down the inside of Seb's thigh while his other hand continued to move back and forth, the fingers twisting. Seb rolled with it, chewing on his lip, still conscious of the fact that this wasn't his house and someone could hear. Yesterday, he would have been okay with that. Today, he wanted this, him and Martin. He didn't want to share it with anyone else.

Martin added a third finger, and the pressure made Seb curl up on himself. His cock was hard and flushed against his stomach.

"More," he said again. The fingers twisted and flexed and found his prostate, and a gasp punched out of him. He pulled Martin up, pressing their mouths together, and Martin fell forward until both his hands were planted on either side of Seb's head, leaving him empty where Martin had been so diligently prepping him.

"More than that," he said against Martin's lips, and was rewarded with a soft moan.

"Show me."

It was Seb's chance to be bossy. He positioned Martin exactly as he wanted him, sitting upright against the bed's headboard. Martin was hard too, his cock bobbing eagerly as Seb found the condom he'd stashed underneath one of the pillows.

"May I?" he said as he held the wrapper between two fingers.

"You're never this polite with anyone else," Martin said.

Seb pouted, even as he pulled the foil apart. "It seems like the best plan before I stick your dick in my ass."

"You really aren't much for sweet talk, though, are you?" Martin laughed, then sucked in his breath as Seb grasped his cock and stroked him.

"I am an artist, but subtlety escapes me in most other media, yes."

"The silent b, I remember."

Seb unrolled the condom and slicked on more lube. Fumbling, they both laughed as he positioned himself, facing away from Martin, who tried to help. Somehow they wound up with four hands and one cock and generally too much going on down there, so Seb distracted Martin with a long kiss over his shoulder while he slowly pressed down.

The stinging stretch as Martin entered him had him throwing his head back. He shifted, retreating a fraction of an inch before sliding down farther. Martin's hands were on his ribs now, roaming, as he kissed along the ridges of Seb's shoulder blades.

"Oh, yes. Don't stop," Martin said.

"So good." Seb rocked his hips, trying to take more of him. Martin's hands tightened around him. "Just give me a minute."

"Take your time. I'm enjoying the view."

Seb bet he was. Martin's cock disappeared inch by inch inside of him. The pressure and the heat were amazing. To see his hole, stretched tight and taking Martin in . . .

He seated himself, cradled between Martin's knees. They both groaned as Seb clenched and rocked, trying to adjust to the last demanding inch.

Beneath, tentatively at first, Martin rolled his hips, and Seb shuddered. "Do that again."

Martin kissed him and obliged, and yes, that was good. They could do that for a while. Martin didn't seem to have any problems getting on board with that plan either.

They kissed, slow and heavy, like when they'd first come to bed. Martin's hand was on Seb's cock, but like before, without urgency. They moved against each other, Seb raising himself up and then sliding back down to feel every inch of Martin's length. He bottomed out again with a twist and made needy whimpers as Martin stroked against his prostate. Heat spread up his spine and across his chest.

"How many hours before the sun comes up?" he said as he clenched around Martin, making him shudder. He wanted to brand Martin inside his body. It would be a long slow process, but Seb could take it.

"I don't think we'll last that long." Martin shifted, sliding just a little lower to improve his leverage, and pressed up into Seb. The movement found another fraction of an inch he didn't know was there. Tiny stars burst under his eyelids as he let out a soft whine.

"Again," he said, and like before, Martin seemed only happy to follow instructions. Seb blew out a laugh.

"Something funny?" Martin said as he thrust up again,

harder. This side of him, not bossy, not dominant, but confident, sure of himself, was something Seb wanted so much more of.

"Not in the slightest." He sighed and gave himself to the rhythm that Martin set.

It was good. So good. But the angle wasn't enough to make him come, and his thighs shook. Martin kissed him before running a hand up his spine and pushing him forward, until Seb was face down on the bed, his ass propped up against his thighs. Martin followed, covering him with his body, knees spread wide as he thrust in hard.

Seb shouted, turning his head to bury his face in the mattress. Martin had promised him a pillow if he screamed, but the mattress would do. He shifted his hips to give himself enough space to grasp his cock and tugged in time with Martin's hard strokes inside his body.

Martin drove them on now, his breath hot on Seb's spine, grunting with each thrust, as Seb let out a line of curses and encouragement. Martin's hands were under his torso, lifting, pulling, until Seb was on his knees, hands planted on the mattress, and Martin kept going. Seb continued to jerk himself off and felt the warm weight of Martin wrapped around him. It still wasn't enough.

Martin's clever fingers found one of his piercings and twisted, driving the sensation from Seb's chest to his gut and lower to the small of his back where the orgasm built.

"Again," he said. Martin's mouth was on his skin, his dick in Seb's ass, while his fingers continued to draw little electric shocks at his nipples, and . . .

His orgasm was like the snap of a rubber band. Seb's mind went blank as his body locked down. Arched under Martin's weight, his hand grew slick with his come. Martin's strangled shout against his back was Seb's only warning before Martin tensed and shuddered. They rocked together, and Seb's arms gave out. Martin tumbled down with him, body still wrapped around his torso as his hips spasmed.

"Wow," Seb groaned.

"Yeah." Martin's laugh was hoarse. He slipped out of Seb with a grunt, and Seb took the opportunity to spread himself out, boneless on the mattress. There was a wet spot under his belly, which would be really gross in a minute, but until then, he was going to bask as his body sparked and tingled from his scalp to the tips of his toes.

Martin was in the bathroom, tidying up. Seb slipped off the bed, taking the soiled sheet with him. As he entered the bathroom, he tossed it in a corner and wrapped himself around Martin. He looked at them in the mirror. Martin pressed his cheek against Seb's and linked their hands together over his chest.

"The most interesting weekend I've had in a long time," he said, staring at Seb's reflection.

"I hope what we just did was more than interesting." Seb bit at his shoulder. Martin danced away but didn't get very far before he pulled Seb to him, wrapping them together for a short brush of lips that left them both nuzzling at each other.

"I'm an academic. Interesting is the highest compliment we know."

"Better than fascinating? I think fascinating is farther up the food chain."

Martin hummed and kissed him again.

"Fascinating is reserved for truly exceptional experiences."

Seb pouted. "That wasn't truly exceptional?"

"It was good. Better than good. But life changing? Paradigm shifting?" He made a skeptical noise.

Seb bit at his lip. "I love a challenge."

———

When Martin woke up, it was still dark. He was warm, curled under a soft comforter and wrapped around Seb, his cheek resting on the curve of Seb's spine.

He was hard too, and wasn't that something? As everything fell apart at Mount Garner, his libido had been the first thing to go. Not that anyone had been there to notice, but months passed where he hadn't felt even the smallest flicker of arousal. As if that entire part of him had been erased, to the point where he didn't even miss it.

Feeling need again was a relief, though, as he pressed his erection against the crease of Seb's ass. Seb sighed in his sleep, and then his hips rocked back, trapping Martin between their bodies. Martin kissed his bare shoulder, rewarded with a fuzzy sigh as Seb rolled against him again.

"I'm going to hurt in the morning," Seb said. Martin lifted his head to kiss Seb's cheek. He let his hand slide down over Seb's bare chest, then lower, following the thin thread of hair to the waistband of his briefs.

"I wouldn't want that." Martin found Seb's cock, half hard and growing, and stroked it.

"Very considerate of you." Seb rolled so they could kiss fully, long and slow, both of them still partly wrapped in soft sleepy warmth. Martin ground against Seb's hip, and Seb made happy noises in the back of his throat. He laughed as Martin rolled on top of him. Martin could get used to this, provided Seb's bed above the bookstore was big and comfortable enough for the two of them. Although, anything would be better than Brian's couch, especially if Seb was there.

Martin followed the path his hand took before, only this time with his mouth. Seb tunneled his fingers through Martin's hair as he pulled Seb's waistband down to free his straining cock.

Under the blankets and licking at the head of Seb's erection, he was only dimly aware of the sound of a phone vibrating. He was in a warm dreamy place where everything was dark and smelled like Seb, and phones had no place there. Seb's hips rocked under his hands, like he was rolling toward the side of the bed, and then they settled into place again. Martin took Seb into his mouth, loving the taste of him as much as he loved his own body wanting this.

"Hello?" Seb's voice was rough, and Martin pinched at the inside of Seb's thigh in annoyance. Clearly, they were involved in something more important than a phone call. He was rewarded by a soft smack on the back of his head. Laughing, he hollowed his cheeks in response and then let his tongue swirl around Seb's slit.

Seb's hips rocked again, pushing more of his length into Martin's mouth, and Martin murmured a happy groan. He sucked down as far as he could go, but then Seb's hips stilled. "Mrs. Green? Slow down. What's wrong?"

Martin's growing arousal paused at the mention of his employer. Why was Mrs. Green calling Seb? What time was it?

"Okay." The tension in Seb's voice was apparent now. Martin rolled off him and came up from under the covers. As soon as he was free, Seb pulled himself up to sitting.

"What's wrong?" Martin whispered, but Seb didn't reply. Martin flipped on the light on the table next to his side of the bed. The warm glow flooded the space around them, but the expression on Seb's face made his heart stop.

Seb was already rolling out of bed as Martin watched, snagging clothes from the floor. He pulled them on, the phone pressed between his ear and shoulder the whole time. "Okay. It's okay. We're awake. We're coming."

Martin grabbed his phone and checked the time. A little after two thirty. "What's wrong?" he said again.

Seb hung up, stuffing belongings into his suitcase. "Get dressed. We have to go home."

"Seb?"

"Get dressed. We're leaving in three minutes. You can ride naked if you want, but we're going."

Martin was out of bed in a second. He found the borrowed suit on the floor. "Would you just tell me what's wrong?"

In the shadowed part of the room the little bedside lamp couldn't reach, Seb's eyes were dark.

"There's a fire. We have to go."

21

The drive back to Seacroft was silent. Tense. Even though the highways were empty at that time of night and Seb drove well beyond the speed limit the whole way, it took forever. He hardly spoke. There was a fire. No one was hurt. That was all he knew. Martin watched the mile markers ghost by.

As they drove into town, it was still dark. It was fall, and the sun wouldn't be up until after seven. Martin didn't know what he expected. An orange glow on the horizon to light their way?

The first change was the smell. Seb had the window down, probably to keep himself awake after hours of driving, but as they got closer, the air changed. Martin should have thought of campfires, or Brian cooking chicken skewers in the backyard, but instead his stomach turned. It wasn't any of those things.

It was the bookstore.

There was no orange glow. There *was* the flicker of red lights spinning on the top of fire trucks forming a perimeter around the bookstore as it smoked and steamed. The smell was overwhelming here, making Martin's eyes water as they got out of the car. Puddles covered the street, even though the sky was clear, and Martin needed a moment to realize they were from the firehoses, not rain.

Dog Ears Book Shop was a ruin. The black-and-white sign that might have been a cow or a dog was scorched. The lettering faded into the blackened wood, so only the "D" on the front and the "P" on the end were visible. The front windows were empty sockets gaping at the sidewalk. It was too dark to see very far inside, but the counter where the cash register had stood was gone, and the shelves that ran to the ceiling closest to the door were charred pillars.

Upstairs, the street light outside showed the marks like giant claws on the brick where the flames and smoke stretched out from the broken windows of Seb's apartment, looking for more to consume.

"Seb." Martin could barely tear his eyes away. He felt too many things at once: the queasy twist of fear at what the rest of the bookstore looked like, the sadness for what this meant for both of them, the exhaustion of stress, and too many wordless hours on the road.

Seb's face was blank. His hands were jammed into his coat pockets, and he barely blinked as he stared up at his home. Martin linked an arm through his, but Seb didn't respond, either to pull him closer or push him away. He simply stared, his face turning strange shadows in the revolving lights on the street.

"Dr. Lindsey?" Martin barely recognized Mrs. Green as she came toward them. Her normally immaculate hair and face were covered in gray soot.

"What happened?" He took a step away from Seb, but couldn't make himself go farther.

Mrs. Green's eyes were wide. "I called you as soon as I saw what had happened. I was so worried Sebastian was upstairs!"

"We were away."

"It was a relief to hear that. But the store. The apartment." She glanced around them, but they were alone, the firefighters still working on the building. "Dr. Lindsey, I think it was my fault." Her voice was thin and ragged.

"What?"

A tear tracked a trail over her dirty face. "Seb, I am so sorry. Your home. Your work, I didn't—"

Martin put an arm around Seb's shoulders, but it was like hugging a statue. "Why don't you tell us what happened?"

"I . . . " She pulled her coat tighter against her chest. "I went in this evening—yesterday evening, rather—to do the weekly bookkeeping. I normally do it on Sundays, but I have a number of obligations today. I was only there for a few hours, but it was cool inside, and bookkeeping can be tedious. I made a pot of coffee. Dr. Lindsey." She gripped his arm. "The coffee maker has been a bit temperamental for years and it's possible I may have forgotten to turn it off before I went home. Do you think this—" She gestured at the blackened building behind her, and her voice cracked. "Do you think that's what caused this?"

Martin didn't know, and he didn't want to speculate. Mrs. Green seemed convinced, though, and she burst into tears right there on the street. Martin had to let go of Seb to console her. The whole time, Seb still stared dispassionately at what was left of his home. He really might have been a statue, except for the way his throat worked up and down, like he was also swallowing tears—or maybe a scream. Martin wished he would let it out.

After that, Mrs. Green seemed to decide Martin had some kind of authority and made him stand with her as the fire department asked questions and gave out information. They didn't comment on her coffee maker theory, but no one talked about arson or anything suspicious either.

Eventually, most of the fire trucks pulled away, and Martin convinced Mrs. Green to go home and get some rest. The sky turned gray and then pink, like the sun was finally ready to greet the day without knowing what had happened over the course of one night.

The daylight didn't make anything better. It illuminated the inside of the store, and everything was black and ash or sodden and gray. About halfway back was a hole in the ceiling, and only black was visible in the space that should have been the apartment.

Seb still didn't say anything.

People started to appear, residents out for a quick run before their day started. Business owners came and gaped at the sight.

Somewhere along the way, Brian arrived. "I heard about it when I got to work. How long have you been here?"

Martin shivered. When had he gotten so cold? "A few hours."

"Why didn't you call me?"

Brian drove them home. Brian's home. Martin's home, sort of. The whole time they drove, all Martin could think was that Seb didn't have a home. Not anymore.

"Do you want breakfast?" Brian said as they walked inside.

"Maybe?" The last thing they'd eaten was finger sandwiches at the party the day before.

"Is toast okay? We're out of eggs."

"Seb?" Martin checked over his shoulder. "Is toast—"

Seb was in the living room, standing next to the couch, still unfolded like Martin had been there all weekend. Seb took off his coat and let it drop to the floor. He pulled things from his pockets. Wallet, keys, phone. The screen flashed an incoming call as he set it on the coffee table. *Oliver*, it said. They were probably waking up—Oliver, his parents—only to find Seb and Martin both gone without so much as a note.

Seb dropped to the mattress like a puppet whose strings were cut. Martin was half afraid that Seb might be crying, and then half afraid when he realized he wasn't.

"Maybe we'll skip breakfast," he said.

"Are you sure? I can—"

Martin put a hand on his brother's arm. "We'll be fine."

Brian left them to go back to work. Finally being alone was a relief. He followed Seb's example, losing his coat and emptying his pockets. He toed off his shoes. He should have suggested Seb do the same, but the hard line of Seb's spine appeared taught enough to break. So instead, Martin lay down on the mattress and stared at the ceiling. A spider was making a web inside one of the pot lights.

Seb still hadn't moved. His body held too much tension for him to be asleep, but he clearly didn't want to talk.

Martin rolled, pillowing his arm under his head. He slid forward until his knees were tucked under Seb's, and his chest was pressed to Seb's back. He waited for Seb to push him away, but like on the street, he gave no response. When Martin slid his hand under Seb's soft T-shirt, his heart thumped steadily, like nothing was wrong.

Martin kissed the nape of Seb's neck and was rewarded with a shiver: the only sign of real life Seb gave him in hours.

It was enough.

They stayed like that until Martin fell asleep.

———

When he woke up, it was cold again, but different than on the street. Not cold that came from standing outside for hours in the dark. Just uncomfortable, like someone had stolen all the covers. Or like the body warming him wasn't there anymore.

A soft voice came from the kitchen.

Martin rolled, and the smell of smoke filled his nostrils, wafting off his clothes, his hair, everywhere. He stared at the ceiling. The spider was still there.

Seb was hunched over the kitchen table. His phone was pressed to his ear, and he held a pencil in his other hand, doodling on the back of an envelope.

"Okay," he said, to whoever was on the phone. "Yeah. No. Yes." Single syllables. He glanced up when Martin passed through the doorway but didn't return Martin's smile. "Yeah. I understand, Kenny."

Martin waited, but the conversation kept going, and eventually he wandered away.

The shower was good. He let the hot water roll over the back of his neck and down his spine. His suitcase was still in the rental car downtown, including his shampoo, so he borrowed the cheap stuff Brian liked. He soaped his hair twice, until the manufactured masculine smell covered the smoke.

He kept clean clothes in a dresser Jess must not have wanted in the old guest room. Thinking of Jess made him picture Brian, looking defeated on the front porch. Had that only been two days ago?

Clean and dressed, Martin checked the kitchen, but it was empty. Seb's phone was still on the kitchen table, showing another call coming in from Oliver. Martin hesitated. He should answer it, let Oliver at least know what had happened.

The screen went dark, and concern over Seb got the better of him. He made his way back down the hall to the den, where Seb was on the pullout again. His shoes were off, but the rest of him was in the same place as before.

"Seb?"

"I'm kinda tired." His voice was flat. The words formed little shards of ice in Martin's chest. He knew those words. He'd used them so many times.

"Oh. Okay." He lay down on the mattress again, their bodies making little squiggles against each other. This time, Seb squeezed his hand when he pulled them together. Martin listened and waited. In minutes, he felt the tension ease. Seb's body sagged, and his breathing evened out as he fell asleep.

His hair smelled like smoke.

———

They stayed in bed for the rest of the day. Seb didn't speak. Brian snuck home mid-day, and Martin gave him the rental car keys and instructions for returning it. Martin settled himself against the back of the couch and surfed channels with the sound off. At some point, Seb rolled over and buried his head in Martin's lap. Martin held him close. Seb was asleep again when Brian returned, carrying both their suitcases as well as a paper bag of fish and chips. Outside, the sun was down.

Martin managed to coax Seb out of bed and down the hall to the shower. He left clean clothes on the back of the toilet, because Seb didn't seem with it enough to do anything but put his smoky clothes back on.

Brian was setting out plates when Martin came into the kitchen. "How's he doing?"

Martin shrugged. "He made a phone call earlier. His agent, I think. He hasn't said much else."

Brian grunted, pulling the wrapped packages of fish and chips from the bag. "I hope Seb eats fish. It seemed like the easiest thing to get."

"It will be fine." Fine. He'd described himself that way so often when he'd been anything but.

The water turned off in the shower, and the silence made Martin tense. He wasn't ready to see Seb's blank face again.

"He looks like you did," Brian said as he unwrapped their dinner, "when you first got here. I thought you'd been brainwashed. You didn't say anything to me for the first week. You got up to go to the bathroom, and then you'd go back to bed."

The bathroom door creaked open. Martin and Brian stared at each other, listening to the quiet sound of Seb's feet coming down the hall. He didn't stop as he passed the kitchen.

"Brian brought us dinner." Martin's heart twisted when Seb flinched.

"I hope you like fish and chips." Brian sounded falsely cheery.

Seb's eyes were slashed with grief. "I'm not very hungry. I think I'm just going to go back to sleep."

The lump that formed in Martin's throat nearly strangled him. Had he looked like that when Brian brought him here?

"Hey," Brian said as he pushed his chair back. "Come have something. You need to eat." He moved across the kitchen and led Seb to the table with a gentle arm around his shoulders. It was such a familiar gesture. How many times had Brian done the same thing for Martin?

Seb allowed himself to be seated. Martin resisted the urge to cut the fish into pieces like Seb was a child, but maybe he should have because Seb took a few fries and left the rest untouched.

"How was the party?" Brian said. Martin could kiss his brother for trying.

Seb pushed away from the table before Brian and Martin were halfway through their meal. He didn't say anything, just shuffled out of the kitchen. A minute later, the pull-out couch's springs creaked.

"It'll be better in the morning," Martin said.

———

It was better. Or worse, depending how one looked at it. When Martin woke, for a second, he was at home at Brian's, and everything was okay. And then he rolled into a puff of smoke-scented air coming from the sheets, and Martin remembered.

The bed was empty.

The house was empty. A plate of cold bacon and eggs sat on the table, as well as a note from Brian saying he'd gone to work and to call if they needed anything.

"Seb?"

A short investigation showed Seb wasn't in the house, but maybe that was a good sign. If he was out, he had to be feeling better.

Martin took another long shower, pulled the sheets off the couch, and threw them in the wash along with their smoky clothes. He threw out the eggs and bacon and washed the single dish in the sink.

Then he started to worry.

Was this how Brian had felt when Martin had been at his worst? Seb left no note. No indication of where he'd gone. No sign that he'd had anything to eat. He'd had all of about four french fries last night, and nothing else for more than twenty-four hours.

If Martin had been like this when he'd first come to Seacroft, no wonder he'd lost weight.

He called Seb. There was no answer, which became obvious when Martin found his phone on the coffee table. The battery was dead, so Martin plugged it in and then went back to the den to wait.

Hours later, he was wearing a path up and down the hall pacing when Seb's phone rang. Martin didn't hesitate when he saw Oliver's name on the screen.

"Hello?"

"Martin?"

"Hi! Yes. Hi. It's Martin. Oliver, I'm sorr—"

"Where did you go?"

"I know. We—"

"It's not your fault. I don't know what set Seb off, but I'm sure you can only be an innocent bystander."

"You don't under—"

"But Parker's pissed that you guys ran off and—"

"Oliver, it's not—"

"And Dad's pissed that Parker's pissed, and mostly because he doesn't need much of an excuse to be pissed at Seb and—"

"There was—"

"And I don't care, really. But a phone call or a note would have been good."

"Oliver, would you shut up and listen?"

The phone went silent. Martin was breathing hard.

"You've been taking lessons from my brother," Oliver said, but he sounded nervous. Martin let the silence stretch, to make it clear he wasn't joking.

"We got a call, on Saturday night. Or Sunday morning. Anyway. There was a fire. The bookstore. It burned down."

More silence. Martin sat on the edge of the couch, which he'd folded up earlier when he'd stripped the sheets off.

"The bookstore?"

"Yes."

"Is it bad?"

Martin held the phone between his ear and his shoulder and put his face in his hands. "Define bad."

"Are you guys okay?"

Martin had the fleeting thought that he really liked Oliver. There had been so much trepidation on the drive up to see them, so many expectations about Seb's family and how the weekend would go. Martin hoped he could count on Oliver as a friend now.

The question, though. Were they okay?

"I don't know where Seb is." His voice cracked.

It all came out. Thirty-six hours of tension and exhaustion, grief and fear. Martin told Oliver everything, although there wasn't much to tell. The call, the fire, Seb truly looking like a ghost as he lay in bed or shuffled down the hall, and then disappearing altogether.

"It's really all gone?" Oliver's slow exhale was audible over the phone.

There was a sound. Martin's fingers went numb as the front door swung open and Seb walked in.

"I'll call you back." The phone tumbled out of his hand. He might not have even hung up, but it didn't matter because Seb was back. He looked tired. The skin under his eyes was purple, and his lips were drawn into a thin line when all Martin wanted to see was the casual smirk that meant Seb was there.

"Hey." Seb's voice crumbled like chalk.

"Where did you go?" he said.

"Nowhere."

"You scared me."

They stood there like that for a long time, staring at each other. Martin wanted to bury his face in Seb's neck and hold on, but he had no idea how to make any of what happened better. "Are you hungry? We need some food. I could order a pizza?"

A muscle twitched at the corner of Seb's mouth, like he was trying to rally the troops to smile, but that was as far as it went. "I think I'm just going to go to—"

"No." The ice that had formed in Martin's chest stabbed at him. "No, Seb. You've got to eat. You need . . . " His protest died in his throat. He watched, powerless, as Seb went to the living room and lay down on the couch, face in the cushions.

"Seb." Martin tried again, but Seb's hands came over the back of his head, covering his ears. It hurt to see him like that. It hurt to remember Martin had done the same, desperate to block out everything around him.

"Seb. Look at me."

It didn't work. He knew it wouldn't.

22

S eb woke up in pain. It was physical, though, which was a relief after what seemed like days of what felt like his organs had been burnt, along with all his belongings and most of his life's work.

Somewhere nearby, two people were speaking softly.

He groaned. His neck was twisted, and his left hand was trapped under his body, tingling with pins and needles as it tried to stay alive. He shifted and unwound himself. He'd been sleeping on a strange couch. Martin's couch. Martin, who watched him with sad gray eyes and secret smiles. Martin, who tasted like coffee and salt and—

Smoke.

The memory made his stomach cramp. One minute he'd been lost in the warm recollection of Martin's skin on his, his breath in his ear, and then—

Seb rolled. Closing his eyes and lying there until sleep came back would be easier. Sensation was coming back in his hand, and he shifted the pillow that was squashed in the corner of the couch to support his neck. Sleep. It would be better if he slept.

His stomach twisted. He might be hungry. Somewhere recently, he'd eaten french fries, but how recently, or where, or with who, he couldn't say. If he'd had anything to drink, even water, since his whole life literally turned to ash, he really wasn't sure.

He sat up, then braced himself against the couch cushions as his head spun. He stared up at the white ceiling, trying not to think. The memory was there, throbbing, just behind his conscious thought, and if he poked at it, he worried it would burst and drown him in what lay underneath.

Martin was in the kitchen. He had his back to Seb as he entered. Penny stood beside Martin, a glass of wine in her hand as she spoke to him quietly. He nodded and laughed at whatever she was saying. Her gaze shifted, and then her eyes widened when she saw Seb leaning against the doorway.

"Hey!" she said. "You're up."

"I'm—I was . . . " He didn't recognize the sound of his voice. "I think I'm hungry."

Penny smiled at him, and relief swept over Martin's face as he turned, and it made Seb wonder what had happened. It felt like only hours since he and Martin had been tangled in bed, loving each other, happy, but it had to have been longer. Everything was patchy, moments of shock and despair separated by long periods of nothing. He assumed he'd been asleep for most of those, but how long, and whether he'd been awake for parts and didn't remember, he wasn't sure.

"Come sit." Penny put an arm around his shoulders. He tensed under the weight, feeling brittle, but he let her lead him to the small table.

"Are you hungry?" Martin asked. "Penny brought some food from the diner."

"Sure. And some water."

Penny placed a glass down next to him, squeezing his shoulder. Martin set a plate of pulled pork and potato salad in front of him. The smell of it made Seb's stomach curdle. He drank more water and waited for the feeling to go away.

It didn't.

"On second thought . . . " He pushed the plate away.

"No. Please." Martin sat on his other side. His voice was sad.

"I'm sorry," Seb said. "I just . . . "

"You have to eat. Trust me, I know this. You need to eat something."

It was all so overwhelming. Their concerned faces. The smell of the food. The throbbing thing in his chest that told him nothing would ever be the same.

"The insurance adjusters came to look at the diner today," Penny said.

"Really?" Martin's hand slipped into Seb's. It felt like sandpaper on his skin.

"They said that even though there's no visible damage, there could be smoke damage in the walls."

"That makes sense. Can't be too careful, right?"

The chitchat was obvious. If they weren't pretending everything was all right, they were at least pretending life was going to go on.

Seb poked at the potato salad. It smelled faintly of eggs, and not in a good way, but he put a little in his mouth, and the people sitting around him let out a relieved exhale. He tried not to gag while he chewed.

"Can I get you anything else?" Martin sat at the edge of his chair, like he was ready to leap up at a moment's notice. His eyes held a streak of panic Seb hadn't seen in a long time.

How long had they been back in Seacroft?

"What day is it?"

"It's Monday." Martin tilted his head, and the panic drained, leaving sympathy in its place.

That wasn't any better.

Seb had called Kenneth at some point.

"It's not insured," Kenneth said.

"People insure art all the time."

246

"*Art that has been purchased or assessed. If it's your personal collection and you've never had it valued, it won't be covered. Who's to say how much it's worth?*"

It wasn't about the money. Not in the way Kenneth might have assumed. The pieces in his apartment, the pieces he'd kept, were the most valuable, but only to him. The books he painstakingly sliced out, word by word. The whole point of his work was taking something mass produced and making it unique, and in the process, he made something that couldn't be replaced.

But the insurance would at least have told him it was worth it. That someone else could still see the value of what was lost in a heap of ash and charred covers.

Egg-flavored bile rose in his throat.

"Seb?" Martin's worried face swam into focus, and he had to wipe tears he didn't know he'd been crying from his cheeks.

He swallowed down the sour taste in his mouth and sniffed, forcing iron into his spine. "I'm fine."

"You aren't," Martin said. "But it's okay. We'll get through it."

The words did little to fill the empty ache in Seb's chest. All he could see was the black nothing where his home, his studio, and all his work had been. It was gone. No amount of quiet sympathy and warm meals would make that better.

"We'll figure it out when Oliver gets here."

Martin's statement took a minute to filter through Seb's circular thoughts. When it did, it seemed impossible that he'd heard right. "Oliver?"

"Yes."

"He's coming here?" Seb's heart started to pound.

"Tomorrow. He couldn't get away from work today."

"Martin's been taking care of everything." Penny's smile, like everything else that was happening, was probably meant to be kind, but she obviously knew more about what was going on than Seb, which only made the roar in his head grow even louder.

"Ollie," he said again. Oliver was coming. Coming here. Seb had spent the last few days in bed, helpless and oblivious while his family—

"He was really worried. "

"You called him?" The question came out like a croak as Seb's throat tried to close over again. Oliver. The golden boy, the good son, was coming to rescue Seb and—

"He called me," Martin said. "Or, actually, he called you, but you weren't home and your phone—"

"You answered my phone?" Seb had lost everything, including his privacy apparently. Oliver was coming, and Martin couldn't even respect basic boundaries.

"He called and—"

"Is anyone else coming?" Seb really was going to be sick. If Oliver knew, the rest of the family knew. His sisters, his father. They knew. They'd had time to plan and organize while he'd been wallowing in pointless self-pity. Parker would treat him like another project. His father would stand at the edges of the bookstore's remains and shake his head like he'd known it would come to this all along. In this moment of loss and weakness, they would suck him back into the fold, and it was his fault for not seeing it coming.

"Hey." Martin came around the table as Seb pushed away from his chair. "Hey, it's okay. What's wrong? What do you need?"

Seb shook his head, shrugging away as Martin tried to wrap his arms around him. He needed an escape. They were coming. It was too late to stop them or protect himself from them.

"Seb?" Penny's sudden intrusion made the walls of the kitchen press in on him even more. He didn't want an audience. They couldn't see him like this.

Before the thought was fully formed, he was moving. His suitcase sat against the wall just inside the den, like it had packed itself and was waiting for him. He grabbed it, along with the traitorous phone that sat on the coffee table, and stumbled for the front door.

"Seb!" Martin called. "Wait! Where are you going?"

The cold air on his face should have brought clarity, but Seb pushed onward up the street. He needed to go. It was cowardly, but it was too late to make his stand with his family. They had the advantage, and the only thing left for Seb was to not be here when they arrived.

Footsteps chased after him.

"Hey!" Martin's face was flushed, and his eyes were wide as he caught up and stepped in front of him.

Seb hitched the overnight bag that contained everything he owned over his shoulder. "I can't."

"Stop! Just wait a minute."

Seb didn't slow. Martin's hand pulled at him, and he danced away.

"Where are you going?"

"What do you care?" Better than admitting he didn't know.

"Please." Martin was breathing hard as he tried to keep up. "Talk to me. I've been waiting for you to talk to me for days."

Seb wheeled on him. The bag fell to the ground with a thump.

"Days? You're so concerned, aren't you? How long did you wait before you went behind my back and called my brother?"

"He was worried."

Seb snorted when Martin didn't even try to deny the accusation. "He shouldn't be. He hasn't worried in years. Too busy protecting his own perfect image, while Seb the black sheep got on with his life. "

"He's your brother. Of course he cares."

"You think spending a weekend with them means you know them?" Seb's hurt boiled into rage, whipping up like the flames that had destroyed his life. He had nothing left to protect but himself. "You think they care about anything but themselves and their own perfect lives? They're just coming to gloat."

"You don't mean that."

"Where has he been? Huh? All these years? Since you're so tight now, maybe you can tell me. In fact, since you seem to get along so well, why don't you just forget about me? You're not really Oliver's type—he likes them to wear Gucci and bring a trust fund to the table—but maybe his good Samaritan act will extend to a pity fuck to massage his ego."

As Seb hurled words at him, Martin's shoulders slumped. The tiniest voice in the very back of his head said he needed to stop, but the fire was consuming him. He'd never known how to back down from an argument, and it was too late to learn now. His insides blackened like everything else in his life. He ignored the defeat rising in Martin's eyes. Why shouldn't Seb torch what had sparked to life between them? Martin had gone behind his back and, in the end, maybe fit better with Seb's family than he ever had.

"What are you saying?" Martin's voice was small.

"You can't help me!" Seb's voice echoed in the fading light of the street. "And neither can Ollie! And I don't want your pity or your judgement. So go jerk each other off and pat yourselves on the back that you escaped before I dragged you down and ruined your life."

"We don't—Seb, you don't mean that."

Seb was done talking. Pain bracketed the edges of Martin's mouth, and it was time to leave. Seb grabbed his bag off the ground and spun.

"Where are you going to go?" Martin called from behind him.

Seb didn't answer, and there was no indication that Martin was following him. He stalked down the street as his guts smoldered and went to ash, leaving his life trailing behind him.

23

The sucking loss at the sight of Seb's retreating back threatened to pull Martin under. Only Penny, standing anxiously on the steps when he returned to the house, gave him something to focus on and stay afloat.

Brian returned from work to find the two of them in the kitchen, Seb's untouched meal still on the table.

"He'll come back," Brian said. But he hadn't seen the look on Seb's face, or felt the wrenching pain of every word and accusation flung at Martin. Grief and rage twisted Seb into someone Martin didn't recognize.

Had he made a mistake in talking to Oliver? Or had admitting to it been the problem? If he'd said nothing and waited for Oliver to show up unannounced in the morning, would Seb have reacted any better?

He rolled, missing the nearness of Seb's body in the bed. The last few nights, it had been as if they were tethered together, with Martin holding Seb to the world while he mourned silently. Before that, something else pulled them together. Need and lust, yes, but Seb had been so careful, kind even. Martin wanted that back. Not just the sex, but the sense of connection, like someone finally cared about him after months of drowning in depression and the endless loneliness brought with it.

Brian watched him while they ate breakfast. Martin had to reassure him he would be fine before his brother finally agreed to go to work. He told Martin repeatedly to call if he needed anything, reminding him of those first weeks in Seacroft, when Brian treated him like he might break under the slightest pressure. He was better now, though, sturdier. He had to be, in case Seb came back.

Just before noon, a knock sent his heart off on a runaway train. He raced to answer it, forming apologies and promises as he pulled the door open, and the train skidded off the track.

It was Oliver.

He must have seen the crushing disappointment on Martin's face, because his own smile faded. "He's not here, is he?" he said.

Martin didn't have to ask who he meant. "I don't know where he is."

They drove downtown, because Oliver wanted to see the bookstore. The area was cordoned off, and several dumpsters had been placed on the street. Crews were loading heaps of old material into them with shovels.

"Holy shit," Oliver said.

"More or less."

They parked and went to the diner, because Martin couldn't bear the idea of going back to Brian's. Carol Anne and Penny were both there and made a big fuss when Martin introduced her to Oliver.

"Sit! Sit!" Penny shuffled them to a table near the cash. "Do you want something to drink? Coffee? Tea? Are you hungry? We're trying a new coconut crusted catfish this week. I'll get you some. On the house."

"She's very friendly," Oliver said when they were alone again.

Carol Anne appeared with water and a basket of rolls, then pulled up a seat. "How's Seb?"

Martin shook his head, and her eyes widened.

"I'll find him." Oliver gave her a confident smile. It hurt that Oliver was saying it, because Martin didn't even know where to start. A sense of failure was sinking in. From the moment they'd come back to town, he'd wanted to help Seb so badly, and now he was left to powerlessly wait.

"I don't understand," he said. "He hardly spoke for two days, and then I mentioned that you'd called and it was like raising him from the dead."

"I probably should have warned you not to say anything. He —We—It's complicated. I could blame it on fiery artistic sensibilities, but that wouldn't be fair. We never made it easy on him."

"I saw you all at dinner. I don't think any of you know how to make it easy for yourselves."

Oliver wiped a crumb from his chin. "That's somewhat true. It's especially tough when Seb and my dad are in the same room. They've never understood one another. And then a few years ago there was this fight. Seb came to the house for my dad's retirement party. He brought a guy with him, someone we'd never heard of. Seb didn't even seem to know him very well. He might have found him on Grindr right before he drove up. Dad could tell it was a stunt, and he started picking on Seb. He never could resist pushing Seb's buttons, but once Seb was old enough to push Dad's back, it always ended in a shouting match. I don't remember all of that last one, but Seb called Dad a bigoted snob, and Dad said he didn't need a fag flaunting his lifestyle under the family roof, and . . . " Oliver shrugged.

"He didn't tell me." The anguish on Seb's face at the thought his family might come to see him in Seacroft suddenly made more sense.

"For all his bluster, Seb's a really private person. He doesn't trust easily, and he'll strike first if he thinks someone's trying to hurt him."

"First blood," Martin said, and Oliver nodded.

"He's learned to hide most of his insecurities under mountains of cynicism. You could drill for years and never strike oil with him."

None of that made Martin feel better. The contrast of Seb, swaggering through the shop like king of the world, and the shrunken figure he'd become in the last few days played over and over in his head. "I could have helped."

Oliver's smile was kind. "If he was going to let anyone help, I think it would have been you. He's different with you. I don't know him as well as I probably should, but I could see the way he looked at you this weekend. There was care there. He wanted to make sure you were okay, even when he couldn't stop stoking the shit show that is our family. He cares about you, trust me on that."

Martin's throat hurt the longer Oliver spoke. He'd like to believe that Seb cared about him, but . . .

"He left."

"He's hurting, and he doesn't know what to do with everything he's feeling. He's been putting distance between himself and the people and situations that hurt him for years, so that's his go-to response." Oliver put a hand on Martin's arm. "You haven't done anything wrong. He'll come back when he's ready."

Martin wished he could believe him.

———

Seb wasn't sure how they got to the loft door. Kenneth was a hundred and eighty pounds of nearly dead, intoxicated weight draped across his shoulders.

"This isn't my apartment," Kenneth slurred as Seb propped him up against the wall and fished through his pockets for keys.

"It totally is. Don't be an asshole."

"But I don't want to be at my apartment. I want to be at Anton's apartment." He hiccupped, and Seb had to move fast as

Kenneth slumped toward the floor. But his dismay over not being in his fuckboy du jour's bed vanished as Seb ran his hands over Kenneth's clothes and then in the other places he might have stashed a key.

Giggling, he pulled Seb closer, nuzzling at his neck. "You're pretty." His breath smelled like the fruity vodka drinks he'd spent all night drinking at the club. "You've always been so pretty."

"Get off me!" Seb found the single key, deep in the front pocket of the skintight jeans Kenneth had poured himself into, and shoved him away. Cursing, he fumbled until he managed to get the lock open and swung the door wide.

"We should go to Pete's Gate! Anton always goes there after the other bars close. We could still catch up to him. He'd like you, trust me."

"Shut up and get inside." Seb ground his teeth as the last of his patience wilted.

Clubbing had been Kenneth's idea, and Seb should have seen it for the mistake it was from the outset. But he'd been tired and numb, and letting someone else make plans and decisions had been a relief, so he hadn't given it much thought.

Kenneth spotted Anton almost from the moment they arrived and proceeded to drink himself under the table while rambling on about how much he missed him and what he would do to win Anton back. Of course, he'd done none of those things, and Seb finally found him nearly passed out in the bathroom shortly before last call.

And that was how he wound up dragging his oldest so-called friend up to Kenneth's apartment at dark o'clock without the benefit of a buzz or someone to help him take the edge off through the night.

Not that he wanted anyone. Certainly not Kenneth, and not one of the guys who had come up to him with a smile on their lips and sex on their minds. The hands on his body when he'd tried to dance felt like fire against his skin, burning trails all the way to his heart which screamed at him to get out. Every face looked the same, and none sparked his interest.

At night, all cats are gray.

Seb didn't want to think about the hands and the body he really needed right now.

Kenneth was unconscious by the time Seb had him sprawled out on the couch. He poured a glass of water and set it on the coffee table, then headed to the bathroom.

Steam filled the room as he stripped out of the jeans and T-shirt he'd worn. He was tired, but he stank of booze and the film any bar packed to its fire code capacity left on everyone inside.

The water was hot enough to scald his skin, and he stood under its spray, head bent, letting it slide the grime off his body, wishing it could take more with it.

Exhausted and heartsick, he'd arrived at Kenneth's the day before. Kenneth took one look at him and forced him into bed, despite Seb's protests that he'd hardly done anything but sleep for days. Kenneth went full-blown mother hen on him, or, as best he could anyway. His cooking skills were limited to heating chicken noodle soup in the microwave and serving it on a tray with saltines. Seb pointed out he was homeless, not sick, but Kenneth didn't care.

Seb had still been awake deep into the night, long after Kenneth had fallen asleep in the other room. When he checked his phone, he had streams of missed calls going back days, mostly from Oliver. The one call Martin had answered was a green checkmark amidst the red list. The more recent calls from Martin and Oliver, the ones since he'd left Seacroft, came less and less frequently as the day went on.

He'd been wrong to insinuate anything going on between Oliver and Martin. He shouldn't have said it but hadn't been able to stop himself. They were together now, though, talking about him like a wounded bird that needed care.

He didn't need anything from them. He'd never needed anything from anyone but himself.

There had been voicemails too, but Seb didn't bother to listen to them or the cold comfort they offered.

He'd finally fallen asleep as the sun was rising, which meant it was late in the afternoon when Kenneth ripped the blanket off him and told him to get his ass out of bed. "Come on, princess. Moping won't help. We're going out."

"Out" meant drinks, then dinner, then more drinks, then dancing. Seb enjoyed himself at first, but the longer he let Kenneth drag him from one bar to the next, the more he wanted to go home, wherever that was.

Now, back in Kenneth's apartment, he shut the water off in the shower. The bathroom was warm and steamy as he stepped out and dried himself. His hands on his body made him think of Martin's hands doing the same thing in his parents' guest room bath. He blocked out the ache from the memory of Martin's lips on his skin.

Kenneth was still snoring on the couch, so Seb left him there and let himself into the spare bedroom. He slipped into clean briefs and lay down, even though he knew sleep would escape him.

On his night stand, the phone flashed with a text message from Oliver.

Call me.

He stared at it, chewing his lip, then finally flipped through screens until he got to his voicemail.

"You have three new messages," the automated greeting said.

"Seb?" Martin's voice was breathless, and the flutter of wind over the receiver said he was outside. He might have left this message minutes after Seb had walked away from him. "Seb, I'm sorry. I shouldn't have talked to Oliver. But you wouldn't talk to me. Please come back."

Seb deleted the voicemail. The next one played.

"Hi, it's Martin again. It's morning, and you're not—Oliver is still coming today. I know he wants to talk to you. We could meet you at the diner if you—I don't know. Call me if you can."

Seb stared at the ceiling as he listened to Martin's sad voice, and regret pricked at his skin. Martin didn't deserve this; he only wanted to help. It was better that Seb had left before Martin was consumed by the disaster Seb left in his wake.

The third message was from Oliver and came in while Seb was out with Kenneth.

"Hey, it's Ollie. I came to see you, and you weren't there. I saw Martin, though. You were an ass to him, I hope you know that. I also know you're hiding out at Kenneth's. If that's what you have to do, that's fine, but call Martin and tell him where you are. He's worried, and for whatever reason, he cares about your dramatic ass. You can give me the silent treatment, but he deserves more than that. I'll come down there to drag you back to Seacroft if I have to, and then—"

Seb deleted the rest of it.

He thumbed back to his texts and hit reply to Oliver's last message.

I'm fine. Don't call me again.

He flipped through a few more contacts until he found Martin's and hesitated. He wanted to send the same message, but he owed Martin more. Or less. If he said nothing, Martin would get on with his life.

He's worried, and for whatever reason, he cares about your dramatic ass.

No one had cared in a long time. The realization hurt. Oliver might, but overcoming decades of sibling squabbling and family baggage was hard. Kenneth cared, but only when and how it suited him.

Martin, though . . . Seb could still feel the warm press of Martin's leg against his thigh, trying to warn him off as he launched himself toward making a spectacle over a family dinner. He could see Martin's eyes reaching for him across a crowd as Martin stammered his way through a welcome speech meant for the community and delivered entirely to Seb, like he was some kind of lifeline.

Martin cared, but he'd settled his hope on the wrong person. *I'm not who you think I am.*

He sent the message before he could second guess himself.

24

I'm not who you think I am.

It had been days and that was the only response Martin received. He didn't even know what it meant. He'd called Seb's phone twice and texted more than that, but there was nothing else.

I'm not who you think I am.

He'd spoken to Oliver, who had been vague and said Seb was fine, but he wasn't ready to talk or come back yet.

A week after the fire, Martin ran into Cassidy outside the diner.

"Where have you been?" She clutched at his jacket. "I tried to change the beginning of my essay. It's a disaster!"

Settling into the task was hard. Every time he tried to read what she'd written, or remind her of something they'd talked about, he remembered their last conversation had taken place in the bookstore. He already missed those rainy afternoons in Seb's apartment, reading quietly while Seb and Cassidy bantered in the background and fashioned new stories out of old books and paper no one wanted anymore.

"It's not the same, is it?" Cassidy asked.

"What?" Martin stared blankly at her laptop screen.

"This?" She gestured at the bustling diner. Customers and waitstaff flowed around Cassidy and Martin like a rock in a wide river.

"Do you think the knitting circle would come hang out here?" he said.

"I bet they would!" Cassidy's smile didn't last long before her green eyes turned serious. "Have you heard from Seb?"

Martin could only shake his head.

Cassidy misses you. He sent the text as he went to unchain his bike. If Seb wouldn't reply to him, he might talk to Cassidy. She had known him longer than Martin. Maybe she would be enough to pull him back.

Helplessness gnawed at him as he rode back to the house. It wasn't the same weight pressing down on him as it had been through his last days at Mount Garner. Before, he had an unshakable conviction that everything was broken, and he could do nothing about it. Here, he knew what had gone wrong.

He missed Seb, but all he could do was send text messages into the void.

The house was quiet as he pulled in and stashed his bike in the garage. Nothing to suggest anything out of the ordinary.

Except in retrospect, there were clues.

If he'd been paying attention, he might have noticed the back door was open even though he and Brian always kept it locked. If he hadn't been trying to mentally force his phone to do anything but show the same text message over and over, he might have seen the pile of clothes on the floor in the hall. If he hadn't been worrying that Seb might never come back, he might have heard the sounds coming from the kitchen.

In the end, none of these things happened, and so Martin was completely unprepared for the sight of Brian's naked ass, clenching as he thrust into a woman whose legs were wrapped around his hips, on the kitchen table.

"Holy shit!" Martin threw his arm over his eyes like he'd witnessed an explosion and flung himself back into the hall.

"Jesus!" Brian's voice was just as surprised. There was a scuffling sound, and the woman yelped.

"Smarts! What the hell?" Brian appeared. His shirt was off, and he was doing up his belt. "Have you never heard of knocking?"

"I have to knock in my own house? I'm allowed to come in without announcing myself!"

Brian had the decency to look apologetic.

"And you have a bedroom!" Martin's eyes widened. "I mean, a little discretion would be good in any case, but really? The kitchen? I eat on that table!"

Brian nodded, head hanging down. For a second, it looked like he might be fighting back tears, or trying not to be sick, but then his shoulders gave a telltale tremor, and Martin's horror grew.

"Are you laughing?" he asked.

Brian shook his head, but a giggle escaped. His brother doubled over, his whole body shaking with it.

Movement caught Martin's attention; a woman with long brown hair peeked out of the kitchen.

"Jess?" He blinked and tried not to recoil as she stepped into the hall.

"Hey, Marty. Sorry about that."

Her hair was a mess. She wore a knee-length denim skirt twisted to one side, and she had wrapped a red and white striped dishtowel around her chest.

"It's, uh . . . " He very studiously stared anywhere but at his perhaps-not-so-former sister-in-law's breasts.

"Nice to see you too. Excuse me." She scooted between the two of them and out the way Martin came in. Then he saw the clothes on the floor which she snatched up and darted into the laundry room, slamming the door shut as she went.

The brothers stood in the hall, silently staring at each other. Martin's pulse was still jumping in his throat.

"So." Brian scratched at his chest. One shoulder was covered in bite marks.

"Yeah." The residual embarrassment pressed in on Martin, and he fled to the porch.

A few minutes later, the front door opened, and Brian and Jess, both fully dressed again, appeared.

"Sorry again, Marty. About before." Jess stood on her toes to kiss Brian for longer than they probably should have for two people who spent most of their time yelling at each other. They murmured soft things to each other that made Martin's heart hurt, and then she hopped down the steps. Her car was parked on the street. Martin couldn't understand how he hadn't seen it before.

Brian came to sit next to him. Neither one spoke for a bit. The last time they had sat like this was right before Seb arrived to pick Martin up, when Brian received the separation agreement.

"So," Martin said when he realized Brian wasn't going to make the first move. He'd make the last one, though—Martin would make sure, because it involved sanitizing every surface in the kitchen.

"So."

"Was that just some kind of farewell thing you straight people do? Or should I take this to mean the separation is off?"

Brian chuckled. "It's on an indefinite hold."

"What brought that on?" Martin coughed on a lump that felt suspiciously like disappointment, which was unfair because his brother deserved to be happy.

"She called. Said she was sorry, and . . . " Brian laughed softly. "No. That's not true. I called her. I begged. Told her everything."

"Everything?" Martin raised an eyebrow.

"That I was a selfish prick who couldn't get his head out of his ass to see how much she was hurting over this. That I'd been too stubborn to move beyond my own ego. That I loved her and it didn't matter if we had kids or not, or if we had them some other way, as long as she—" It was Brian's turn to cough. He sniffed and ran his hand over his eyes. "I love her, Smarts, and . . . and that's it, I guess. I'll do whatever she wants me to do, as long as I can be with her."

Martin's smile was thin but sincere. "Is she moving back?"

"We're . . . " Brian's returning grin was shy. "You weren't supposed to see that, before. It was kind of a spur of the moment thing. We're going to take it slow." His eyes widened, as if a thought had just occurred to him. "But even when she moves back in, that doesn't mean you have to go! If nothing else, she'll bring all the old furniture, so you can have a real room instead of the pullout. You know you've got a home here."

Martin nodded, but he couldn't make himself speak. He didn't want to stay, not if it meant being the third wheel in Brian and Jess's happy reunion.

He missed the apartment above the bookstore, even though it had never been his.

"Did you hear from Seb?" Brian must have developed mind reading as a skill, along with humility.

Martin shook his head. "Please don't make this the part where you tell me I need some big gesture. Where I have to call him and pour my heart out that I miss him and need him and that I want him to come home. Because I've tried that, and it hasn't helped."

"Well, it worked for me." Brian stretched and wrapped one arm over Martin's shoulder, giving him a gentle squeeze.

"Seb isn't Jess. And I can't give him back what he lost."

"Then what can you give him?"

Martin frowned. "What?"

"If you care about him so much, and he's disappeared

264

because he's lost everything, what do you have that might get him to come back?"

"When did you get so astute?"

"When I realized my wife was going to leave me if I didn't stop being an immature jerk."

He had a point.

"I won't miss lying to her on the phone about where you are."

Brian winced. "Sorry about that. And don't change the subject. We're talking about your love life, not mine."

"Believe me," Martin grimaced, "I have seen more of your love life this afternoon than I ever wanted to."

"I'll put a sock on the door next time. The look on your face. I don't think I'll ever forget it."

Martin laughed. "Might need a flashing light. I completely missed Jess's bra on the floor when I walked in."

"So what are you going to do?"

"Jesus. You convince your wife to take you back and suddenly you're the love doctor."

"Two doctors in the family! I'm as surprised as you are. I didn't know I had it in me."

I'm not who you think I am.

Who did Seb think he was? There were so many versions of him. The ghost, the charming artist everyone wanted to know, the lost son only good for making a scene. Which one was Seb?

"You've got your thinking face on," Brian said.

What Martin had was a headache. And possibly an idea.

25

---

*K*enneth pulled Seb out onto the street. It was raining, not enough to get wet, but definitely enough to be cold within thirty seconds. Seb flipped up the collar of his jacket.

"See? I told you this was a good idea." Kenneth grinned, pulling a pack of cigarettes from one pocket.

It had been a not bad idea. After several more unsuccessful attempts to get Seb to enjoy himself in the club scene, or possibly for Kenneth to "conveniently" show up at the same places Anton frequented, Kenneth suggested a weekend in Asheville might be their best bet.

Kenneth splurged on a hotel, although Seb had suggested an Airbnb would have been the more economical choice. He'd expected Kenneth to set them up for another night of clubbing, but his friend surprised him with a dinner reservation and last-minute theater tickets. He'd done something similar back when he'd booked Seb his first show. A city dinner and a show hadn't been in the cards for either of them at the time, but Kenneth went all out on a two-for-one special at a diner, followed by a community theater production of *Rent*. It hadn't been fancy, but the sentiment had been there.

Seb's phone vibrated. Oliver had been texting a few times a day. *Persistent bastard.* Seb checked the phone long enough to see it wasn't Oliver. It was Martin. That was almost worse. He could give Oliver the cold shoulder, but the longer Seb stayed away, the more he regretted how he'd left things with Martin. He missed his quiet warmth beside him in bed and his gentle care when Seb's mood turned too dark.

He didn't bother to read the message. Next to him, Kenneth took a drag on his cigarette.

"So after this," he exhaled a long stream of smoke, "I'm thinking drinks at a rooftop bar. We can flirt with whoever stops by, but we're sleeping alone. Deal?"

Seb groaned. "You talk a good game now, but we both know the first pair of dark eyes and a designer watch that looks at you the right way will have you on your knees in the bathroom."

Kenneth made an indignant noise. "I said I wasn't going to bring them back to the hotel. What happens in the bathroom stays in the bathroom." He put the cigarette to his lips again and inhaled.

Seb watched the end glow red, flaring and consuming the paper and tobacco. Kenneth continued to lay on the terrible jokes and innuendo, but Seb responded mechanically, watching the cigarette burn and shrink. His books had done the same, abandoned and dancing as the fire took them away.

Martin's frightened face appeared in his thoughts, the afternoon in the apartment when Seb found him with that first piece in his hand. He'd said Seb was corrupting someone else's work.

The cigarette glowed.

Seb's pulse picked up.

"You ever heard of anyone doing an exhibit with fire?" he asked.

"They do it at the circus all the time. I could get you some chainsaws too."

"No, I'm serious!" His mind creaked slowly to life. Sluggish at first after a week of spiraling sadness, but gaining momentum. He thought of the way Martin had pulled his life back from the abyss and how he spoke so passionately about his dead poet whose work had nearly disappeared.

There was an idea. Inspiration. It hovered at the edge of conscious thought.

And then that one warm ember vanished as his phone buzzed again.

He scowled at the screen and whoever had dared to interrupt him.

"Who is it?" Kenneth asked.

"It's my brother." Or else someone had hacked Oliver's phone because the message was a link to a crowdfunding page, captioned with *Please take a look*. Seb rolled his eyes. If Oliver was asking him for money to kick off his granola and weed brownies business, he had bigger balls than Seb would have given him credit for.

"What does he want?"

Seb shrugged and put the phone away again. "Doesn't matter. Come on, let's go find you a date."

———

In the morning, Seb was hungover. He hadn't had so much to drink that the night had gotten out of hand, but once he'd started to feel warm and loose, the soft abandon had been a relief.

Kenneth was in significantly rougher shape, moaning from the other double bed in their hotel room. "Did you learn to play the castanets overnight, or is that just my headache talking?"

"It's your headache."

Kenneth groaned and pulled the blankets up over his head.

Seb had dreamed of fire, but unlike the nights before, it hadn't carried away all the things he cared about. Instead, it danced over the pages, leaving curving lines in its wake, scarring without destroying. Changing what was there while the root of the work stayed the same.

On the night stand, his phone vibrated. It was Martin.

Did you see it?

See what? He didn't bother unlocking the screen. He was getting there, almost. If he could chase the thing that bubbled quietly in the back of his mind, if he had that to hold onto, maybe he'd be ready to face Martin. He'd have something to offer then.

"Can you make coffee?" Kenneth's voice was muffled and pitiful under his blanket.

Seb threw a spare pillow at him, but he got up and found the room's single-serve coffee maker and set it to brew.

He showered, still thinking about how the fire remade everything. Was it really any different than what he'd done for years? The fire had been more destructive, less intentional, but the end result was the same.

"Kenny," he said as he stepped out of the shower, "do you know anyone with cheap studio space for rent?"

"Planning your glorious return?" Kenneth's voice was muffled behind the bathroom door. He had the TV on; soft music played, and a woman was speaking, although Seb couldn't hear what.

"It's just an idea. We'd have to find some somewhere to work first, and they'd have to be willing to let me rent it for cheap, or maybe for free, at least until I can finish and sell some pieces." He opened the bathroom door and stepped out into the hotel room. Kenneth was propped up in his bed, a paper coffee cup on his night stand. He was watching something on his phone, his face creased in a frown.

"Are you listening to me?" Seb asked.

"Not really."

"I said we'd need to find me some cheap studio space. I'm

starting from scratch, so there wouldn't be a lot of money left for rent."

"Mmm." Kenneth paused the video. "I don't think that's going to be an issue."

"You know a place?" Seb rummaged through his suitcase for clean clothes.

"No. At least not in the price range you're talking about."

"That sounds like an issue then."

"Not really." Kenneth held up his phone. "Because I think you're kind of rich."

26

$\mathcal{P}$utting it all together took five days, and then another five days after Martin launched the campaign for Seb to come back. They were among the longest days of his life.

It had started as a much smaller idea.

"Seb needs to know he has a home in Seacroft," Martin said to Cassidy, pulse thumping under his skin.

"Of course he does!" Her conviction made it easier to explain.

"I want to make a video. You, Oliver, possibly Penny and Carol Anne. I want you to talk about Seb and how he's helped you."

"And you? We're going to film you too, right?" She said it like it was only logical, and not that Martin was more special to Seb than anyone else.

"Maybe." The idea of letting someone film him talking left him nauseous.

"Definitely." Cassidy's smile made his skin itch.

She broke the ice and had them record her first, with her drawings spread out behind her.

"Seb has been a great mentor to me. I always thought I was bad at school, like I just wasn't trying hard enough. But Seb showed me that it was because I was good at other things. I'm going to art school next fall, even though he thinks I don't need it." She grinned at the camera. "But I want him to know that it's my choice, and I couldn't have gotten there without him."

Penny was equally keen to help.

"Seb is such a fixture in this town. We're so lucky to have him here. Small towns like Seacroft have the potential to be hubs for creative communities, and artists like him put us on the map. Besides that, Seb is one of the most compassionate people I know, although he probably thinks he hides it well. He's so giving of his time, and his art. He donated a piece to a silent auction recently, and was integral to the success of the event."

Oliver sent a video.

"Seb is my little brother, but I've learned to look up to him over the years. He's always forged his own path and been a hundred percent committed to seeing the world his way. I admire him for the risks he takes. We don't see each other as much as I'd like to, but I hope that changes in the future."

The second part of Martin's idea had been to use some of the money raised at the blues night to help Seb get back on his feet.

When he asked, Carol Anne shook her head sadly. "Our budgets are all tightly controlled. We can't use it for anything other than what we'd already earmarked it for."

Martin had chewed his lip in annoyance. His idea had seemed so simple. "I don't suppose we could ask everyone to donate again?"

"Why not?"

So Martin figured out how to set up a crowdfunding campaign online, writing what he thought was a heartfelt but succinct plea to contribute to the cause.

Cassidy had read it with a raised eyebrow, though. "We should add the video to it."

"What? No!" Martin meant for it to be personal, something to share with Seb once they'd finished raising the money

"Everyone loves sad stories," she'd said. "But we still need to record you first."

Martin avoided that suggestion by recruiting other people. It had taken a few days because once the residents of Seacroft heard about what they wanted to do, everyone wanted to be involved. There were people who came and went in the bookstore, some who Martin recognized but didn't know by name, with simple stories of a wave and a smile every time Seb passed. They talked about seeing his pieces in galleries elsewhere and being proud to tell people that the artist lived in their hometown.

"You need to do one," Cassidy told Martin.

"I really don't think that's a good idea."

"Yes it is. Why don't you want to do it?"

Martin fought down every instinct that said this would be a disaster. For Seb, he'd try.

"The first time I met Seb, I thought he was a ghost. The second time, I nearly tore a piece of his artwork, and he kicked me out of his apartment." He smiled at the memory. "But he takes great care of the people close to him. He sees the beauty and potential in things others have cast aside or forgotten about." Martin bit his lip. "He saw me, when I felt like no one else did anymore. I hope he knows how much he's helped me. I hope we can help him too." His cheeks flamed at the thought of other people seeing this video, but he stared at the camera lens like it was Seb, standing at the back of the crowd in a darkened bookstore.

Cassidy gave him a grinning thumbs up as she stopped recording.

They all sent the campaign link out to everyone they knew, and then they waited. Martin sent the link to Seb too, hoping he would see the video at least and know how many people were waiting for him to come home.

It was disappointing when he didn't reply.

Donations were slow at first. They'd set a goal to raise ten thousand dollars, enough for new artist's supplies and the rent Seb would need to focus on his work. Oliver chipped in a few hundred to start, and he said some early anonymous donations came from their family. A number of townspeople made donations of varying sizes. By midday on the first day, they passed the two thousand dollar mark, but stalled out just below five on the second.

"We need more people to help," Cassidy said, staring at their tally. She kept hitting the refresh button on her browser, but the number didn't change.

The idea of *more people* was only slightly less terrifying than *public speaking* to Martin, but she was right.

So, despite the roiling in his stomach that told him he'd only get laughed at for his request, Martin called every community radio station and newspaper within an hour's drive of Seacroft.

No one laughed at him.

Town Rallies to Raise Funds After Local Artist's Studio Lost in Fire

The campaign appeared on one news site and then another. And donations from people Martin, Oliver, and Cassidy had never heard of started to come in.

On the third day, a complete stranger called Martin and said they were making a four thousand dollar donation and would also donate a piece of Seb's work they had purchased years earlier to the highest donation in the next twenty-four hours.

They hit twenty thousand dollars that day and doubled it when another collector made the same offer with another piece.

By the fifth day of their seven-day campaign, they had raised more than seventy thousand dollars, and the art collectors were still calling to find out how they could help. Cassidy said once that Seb had a following, and she hadn't been exaggerating.

But Seb still hadn't responded.

Martin sat in the diner. He was supposed to be reviewing an application essay for a friend of Cassidy's, except he'd been staring at his laptop screen for close to an hour and had failed to make any progress.

He clicked over to the crowdfunding page. Seventy-eight thousand, six hundred and seventy-two dollars. Every dollar of it for Seb, and he wasn't there to see it.

Martin glanced across the street as a truck rattled by, splashing through a puddle. The world outside was gray and burnt red from the last of the fall leaves on the trees. People rushed past, trying to stay dry under dark hoods and umbrellas.

And in the midst of it all was white. A bright flash that disappeared as another car slid by. Martin blinked, and the white-blond figure reemerged, standing perfectly still.

It was the ghost again, and Martin's heart leapt into his throat. He was afraid to move or to lose eye contact in case the apparition vanished. The man across the street stared at him, too far for Martin to make out the features he had been waiting to see for over a week. That wasn't good enough, so he groped blindly for his coat and barely pulled it on before heading to the door, calling over his shoulder to Penny to watch his laptop. He didn't know if she heard him, and frankly, if someone stole it, it wouldn't matter as long as the man outside was still there when Martin got to him.

It took two tries to cross the street; Martin was so enthralled that he nearly collided with a cyclist on his first attempt. He hurried over the pavement on his second, weaving as a car splashed through a puddle, but never taking his eyes away from the other man's face.

Seb stood, hands in the pockets of a dark coat. It had only been a week, but his face was harder than Martin remembered, the lips thinner. White-gold stubble coated his chin.

In another life, Martin would have hesitated, would have stopped on the edge of the curb to gauge Seb's reaction. In another life, he would have let Seb make the decision.

He couldn't take that chance now. If he let Seb decide and he chose to leave again, Martin would regret it.

He walked right into Seb's space and wrapped his arms around him, until he was sure the ghost wouldn't vanish, that Seb was real and back and here with him.

"You asshole," he gritted out as he buried his face in Seb's neck. Seb held him close.

"I'm sorry."

———

The first time I met Seb, I thought he was a ghost.

He saw me when I felt like no one else did anymore.

Martin's serious expression, the soft gray eyes and the crooked jaw, the private smile Seb had been lucky enough to be part of sometimes, had drawn him home.

Kenneth showed him the website, the crowdfunding page with the improbable sum of money at the top, but all Seb saw was the screenshot with Martin gazing at the camera. Seb and Kenneth watched the video, the familiar faces moving past. And then Martin. His gentle voice and serious eyes bounced nervously over the screen as he spoke. He looked tired and completely sincere.

"I'm sorry," Seb said on the street as he pressed closer, letting the world around them disappear for a few seconds. He reveled in Martin's solid warmth, in the ragged way his breath washed over Seb's skin.

"You came home," Martin said.

"I'm sorry I left." He shivered as a raindrop hit the back of his neck and slithered under his shirt. He wanted to be even nearer to Martin, feel the heat of their bodies together. They had been in bed, safe and possibly happy, when Seb's world flew apart. He wanted to be like that again.

"Did you get my texts? Cassidy—We—There's a lot of

money. So much more than we expected. You could go anywhere, do what you want to start over and—"

Seb stopped him with a kiss as the rain picked up around them. It streamed down, soaking them, and Seb didn't care.

"I didn't come back for the money," he said when they pulled apart.

"Penny. She'll want to see you. We should—"

"Why do you always sell yourself short?"

"I don't!" Martin laughed between kisses.

"You do. All the time. Did Cassidy have to tie you down before she made that video of you?"

"No!" Martin's pink cheeks said he was lying.

"I came back for you. I need—I saw you—"

"You always see me."

Seb warmed, despite the damp chill. He wanted to slip his hands under Martin's coat, feel the heat of him there, the solid realness of him. They were across the street and two doors down from the remains of his apartment. He'd been prepared for it when the cab dropped him off. The damage was better than he remembered, although still hard to look at it. But then he'd seen Martin, in the window of the diner, lit from a lamp that hung above his head. He looked warm and safe and . . .

"I'm ready to come home," Seb said, and he meant it. Martin tried to bring up the campaign again, and Seb shut it down with another kiss. He didn't want there to be confusion. He wasn't here for the money they'd raised, and while he was grateful to all the people who had participated, he was there for Martin.

Martin, who laughed softly against his lips. "Home. There's a small problem there."

"What's that?"

Martin untangled himself again, turning so they could both face the old bookstore.

"Well, you don't really have one. A home, I mean."

Seb squeezed him gently. "This is true."

"And . . . " Martin scratched at an eyebrow. "I'm not sure I'm going to have one for much longer, so—"

"What happened?"

An odd expression passed over Martin's face before he shuddered. "Straight people sex. You don't want to know."

Soon, the rain came down so hard that no amount of fuzzy feelings could keep them outside. They returned to the diner, because Martin had left his things inside. Leaving again took longer than Seb wanted because Penny had been watching them the whole time. She nearly tackled Seb as he entered the diner. She served slices of pie and dragged over other patrons to celebrate Seb's soggy return, but he was anxious to have Martin to himself.

For lack of any other option within a reasonable cab fare, they wound up at the nicer of the two motels near the beach. Its only real qualification to be nicer was being bought by a chain in the last few years and having a bigger sign. The room was clean though, and dry, and that was all they really needed.

Seb took Martin to the shower with him, arguing the hot water would do them both good. Martin's hair had begun to dry on the ride over and was sticking up at odd angles, and Seb smoothed it down.

The tiny space of the shower, behind the yellowing curtain which wouldn't quite hang flat against the side of the tub, was surreal. Seb nipped at Martin's chin, trying to make sense of the time since they'd been in a very similar position in the guest bath at his parent's house. Ten days? Was that all it had been?

Afterwards, warm and dry and sleepy, they lay, face to face, on one of the two double beds.

"Can we talk about the money now?" Martin said.

Seb pulled him close. "If you want." There would be time, but it seemed to be weighing on Martin's mind, so he let him speak.

"It's a lot. I haven't checked it this afternoon, but it's got a few days to go, and even if we don't get any more big art donations to spike the contributions, I bet it will be close to a hundred thousand dollars. You could do pretty well anything with that. Go anywhere you wanted."

"I could." Seb pressed a kiss to the top of Martin's hair.

"What do you think you'll do?" Martin ran a hand over Seb's chest, hesitation in the touch. Seb would be making up for the space he'd created between them for a while.

"I have an idea."

EPILOGUE

*T*he gallery glowed with strings of lights hung from the ceiling. The front window facing the street was decorated with daffodils and crocuses. Penny's staff passed around trays of snacks to the people gathered.

Martin smoothed the lapels of his new suit jacket as he came down the stairs from the apartment. Carol Anne stood at the bottom, grinning at him.

"You'll wrinkle them if you keep doing that," she said.

"I will not."

"Mom! Come on." Penny appeared and tugged at her mother's hand. "It's about to start."

Martin followed slowly after them, still trying to get the lie of the suit just right. Oliver helped him pick it out, and Seb's eyes had flashed with approval when he'd seen Martin slip the jacket on earlier, but nerves made it impossible for Martin to settle into it completely comfortably.

The gallery space was packed, full of people from town, and some who had come from farther away. Seb's family—Oliver, their sisters, their mother, and even their father—talked on one side of the room. Mrs. Green held court on the other side with a small crowd of her usual entourage.

After their investigation, the fire department ruled the cause of the bookshop fire to be accidental. They never officially confirmed the coffee maker started it all, but Mrs. Green said she still felt guilty about the fate of the bookstore and Seb's apartment. She had been nothing but accommodating when Seb had approached her about renting a storefront, along with the apartment upstairs.

"Looking very smart today, Dr. Lindsey," Kenneth purred. Martin promised Seb he would try to like the agent, but he wasn't sure Kenneth was working equally as hard to be on his best behavior.

"Thank you."

"And our Seb is quite the hit. I never thought this little town had much appreciation for fine art, but it appears I might be wrong, just this once."

Martin spotted Brian and Jess as they came through the gallery door. Brian waved. Martin could kiss his brother and his excellent timing as he excused himself and stepped away from Kenneth.

He was nearly across the room when a tangle of green eyes and curly hair collided with him.

"I did it!" Cassidy wrapped him in a tight hug.

"Did what?" he asked.

"I got in! Art school! My letters came today. Two of them! Can you believe it?"

Martin's eyes widened until his expression matched Cassidy's. He was about to shout his congratulations when a glass clinked, distracting them both. They turned to follow the sound.

Seb stood by the front window on a small raised platform put there for the occasion. His bowtie was back, as was his sly grin. His eyes flicked over the tops of everyone's heads, and he winked at Martin before his attention returned to the people around him.

"Thank you, everyone, for coming. We are so pleased that you've all come out to our first official exhibit, and the grand opening of the Phoenix Gallery!"

The crowd applauded. Someone whistled, and Martin turned just in time to see Brian lowering his fingers from his lips while Jess swatted at his shoulder with a smile.

"This first exhibit is very important to us. It's called Ashes to Ashes and follows the theme of rebirth, return, and rediscovering that which was lost. On that note, I would very much like to thank those of you gathered today who have lent works to this exhibit."

The donations had been a surprise. After the crowdfunding campaign closed, the updates were Kenneth's idea. People wanted to know what happened to their money, he said, so they sent out periodic notices, letting donors know about the progress renovating the Phoenix and getting it ready for its first opening. It shouldn't have been surprising when some of the people who offered up Seb's pieces that they owned as incentives to the campaign offered to lend others for the exhibit. Yet Seb had been speechless when Kenneth had called to tell him.

"As you look around, you'll find some carved pieces," Seb continued. "You'll also find works of poetry. If you ask Martin, he can tell you that he literally wrote the book on Werner Bergmann, whose poems are featured here today. Martin won't tell you a lot more than that, though, because he's not much of a talker." He smiled across the room again, and Cassidy sighed softly next to Martin.

"You guys are so adorable," she whispered. He flushed and stared down at his shoes.

"As some of you might know," Seb said. "I started my work in carved poetry. I would take old books and carve them into new words. My agent said the exhibits where I showed those early pieces were lacking because we only displayed the work, but never read them. I said that wasn't the point, but in keeping with the theme of this beautiful new space and rediscovering the things we've lost, I wanted to share something with you today. It's called One of Them Is Love, and it's by Werner Bergmann and Sebastian Stevenson."

Martin's head shot up. Over the last few months, he had helped Seb collect Bergmann's translated works. Seb had been tight-lipped about what he planned to do with the poems, but now he held a single piece of paper. The page itself had once been a plain sheet of white printer paper, but it was now punctuated by periodic black marks where words had been cut from whatever was printed on one side. The pattern reminded Martin of spiderwebs and lace, and his breath caught as he fumbled for Cassidy's hand.

"What is it?" she hissed, but Martin could only stare ahead as Seb lifted the page and cleared his throat.

"Three women standing at the crossroads.
They say they are Sadness, Loss and Grief.
But surely one of them is Love.
Surely one of them will open her arms
to me when I approach,
and wrap me up tight against her,
protecting me from her sisters
and the way that I have come.
Surely one of these women
will offer me comfort,
as far as I have traveled,
surely one will show me which is the next path.
The great tragedy of a journey
is I can only see to the next corner,
but at the same time, I must trust
that Love stands only two corners away.
And when I arrive on that second bend,
and find her twisted siblings waiting,
I can only choose to continue on,

in hopes that Love waits past two more corners still.
Or else I must join Sadness, Loss, and Grief,
and wait until the day Love finds me."

Martin's mouth hung open as he tried to hold on to the threads of what he'd just heard. He glanced around the room. Jess had her head resting softly on Brian's shoulder. Tim had one arm around Penny. The air felt heavy as people stirred and started to applaud, breaking the quiet spell of Seb's words.

Carol Anne handed Seb a glass, and he lifted it.

"Thank you everyone for finding us today, and to those of you who worked so hard to help us bring this together. And I'd like you all to raise a toast to Martin, who," Seb's smile quirked in the way that always made Martin's skin prickle "is my love, and without whom I would not have found this path. Cheers!"

Cheers and more applause filled the room. Cassidy giggled and hugged Martin, but she stepped back as Seb came to join them.

"That was . . ." Martin still couldn't process it all. He'd need to get Seb to read it to him again later.

"It was okay?" Seb asked, looking uncharacteristically shy. Martin launched himself at Seb and pulled him in for a hard kiss that could only begin to express what hearing Seb's words felt like.

"I love you too," he said. He had just enough time to see the white of Seb's grin before they were kissing again, despite the people milling in the gallery around them.

There was a cough, and Martin and Seb pulled apart to find Oliver standing close by, a bemused expression on his face.

"Seriously?" Seb grumbled. "Do you have an alert system for when there's a kiss that needs to be interrupted?"

Oliver grinned but didn't take the bait. "I don't know much about that kind of thing, but I thought your poem was . . ."

Seb clasped his brother's shoulder and smiled. Martin kept

his fingers linked through the ones on Seb's other hand, unwilling to let go just yet.

"Sebastian." Philip's voice rumbled low through their little group. Martin turned as Seb's father approached. There was some polite hand shaking, but none of it was overly familiar or all that affectionate.

"This is a very nice place you've made here," Philip said. "I can see the appeal, in a small town like this. Reminds me a bit of the gallery at Watersmith. We should talk about getting some of your work there. It's mostly reserved for students and alumni, but I think I could get them to make an exception."

Tension hung in the air as Seb's fingers curled around Martin's, but his smile was bland as he replied. "Thanks, Dad. I'm working on some new pieces, but Kenneth has me lined up for another show in the fall, so I'm not sure there's time for anything else right now."

Philip's expression was just as controlled as his son's as he turned to Martin. "And Dr. Lindsey, so good to see you! I was speaking to Angela the other day. That position I told you about didn't open up as quickly as I thought it would, but I believe there will be a place available with the history department in the near future. I could still mention your name, if you'd like."

By the time he was done speaking, his words were directed at Seb again. His eyes gleamed with a challenge, as if Philip were daring his son to stand in the way of the opportunity he was so generously offering.

The posturing was unnecessary, though. The truth was, Martin hadn't given the job offer much thought since that afternoon in Philip's office. Not with the fire and all the work to open the gallery. Not when the students he tutored through the fall and winter started receiving their college acceptances. Not when Cassidy spent the last week pacing in front of her mailbox and sending frantic texts when she still hadn't heard about any of her applications at the end of each day. And not when Seb lay awake the last two nights, talking in circles about all the things that might go wrong with their opening. Martin talked him down and promised he'd be there even if the whole thing was ruined by flash floods and celestial interventions.

It surprised him how little thought he'd given to Dr. Stevenson's offer, but Martin knew the reason why. He smiled and moved his hand to settle in the small of Seb's back. He was rewarded with a strong arm around his shoulders.

"Thank you, Dr. Stevenson," Martin said, "but I think you can see I'm very happy just where I am."

THANK YOU

Thank you so much for reading Top Shelf. There are more Seacroft stories coming, so please keep in touch!

In *Cold Pressed*, Oliver comes to Seacroft, where he meets Nick, a sexy single dad with a complicated personal history.

Follow me on Amazon to be notified of new releases, or come join my Facebook readers group (facebook.com/groups/allisonsalist). Or sign up for The A-List (allisontemplebooks.com/thealist), my monthly newsletter for new releases, giveaways, and recommendations.

The kindest thing a reader does for an author is read their book. The second kindest is to recommend it. Please take a minute to leave a review on Amazon or Goodreads, so other readers will know if this story is for them!

ABOUT THE AUTHOR

Whether I knew it then or not, I've been a writer since the second grade, when I wrote a short story about a girl and her horse. My grandmother typed it out for me and said she'd never seen so many quotation marks from a seven-year-old before. I took that as a challenge and have tried to break that record in all the stories I've taken on since then. It's good to have goals, right?

I live in Toronto with my very patient husband and the world's neediest cat. I try to split my time between writing, community theater stage management, and traveling anywhere that has good wine. Tragically, this leaves no time to clean the house.

The Pick Up

Kyle's life is going backwards. He wanted to build a bigger life for himself than Red Creek could give him, but a family crisis has forced him to return to his hometown with his six-year-old daughter. Now he's standing in the rain at his old elementary school, and his daughter's teacher, Mr. Hathaway, is lecturing him about punctuality.

Adam Hathaway is not looking for love. He's learned the hard way to keep his personal and professional life separate. But Kyle is struggling and needs a friend, and Adam wants to be that friend. He just needs to ignore his growing attraction to Kyle's goofy charm, because acting on it would mean breaking all the rules that protect his heart.

Putting down roots in this town again is not Kyle's plan. As soon as he can, he's taking his daughter and her princess costumes and moving on. The more time he spends with Adam, though, the more he thinks the quiet teacher might give him a reason to stay. Now he just has to convince Adam to take a chance on a bigger future than either of them could have planned.

Available at all online book retailers
(books2read.com/thepickup)